A Novel Mystery, Suspense, Romance Fiction

The
Gasping

Dana Rey

Dedication

TO ALL

Publishers Notice

Names, characters, places, and incidents written are either that of the author's imagination or used fictitiously. Any resemblance to actual persons, living or dead, or any events that occurred that one could suggest is the same or similar is entirely coincidental.

By payment of the required fees, or gifted by the author you have been granted the non-exclusive, non-transferable right to access and read this eBook.

Contents

Acknowledgements

Another author was involved in some character & scene developments, not all. The other author was not involved with the storyline that became the outcome, in any way.

The other author made the decision, not to have their name included on the book. (DA) is their initials and they gave Dana Rey all rights to the material written between the two.

One

Impatient, he continuously rang the bell, as he knocked at the door. Inside the house, James ran down the hall holding his pants by his belt attempting to do them up. When he got to the door, he unlocked it, hooked his belt into a hole and swung the door open, then tossed his telephone to his ear. He stood startled for a moment and surprisingly said, "Doug…my god, it's you. I thought what the hell is going on, is there some sort of an emergency?"

Doug looked strained, and justified himself in a serious tone, "Nope, there's no emergency. I thought you might be out back."

James wiped his forehead as he leaned up against the door, and shook his head in disbelief as he said, "I heard it just fine, couldn't you? It's set to extra loud.

Perhaps you should get your ears tested."

Doug had placed his hand on his hip leaving his palm facing outwards as he answered, "Yeah, I heard it just fine, but thought something might have happened to you. I tried the door, but it was locked," he answered in a drained state.

"I was in the bathroom. I had to hurry myself up when the bell wouldn't stop blowing my eardrums apart. I couldn't get up and run out just because you couldn't wait a mere five minutes." James informed him, annoyed as hell.

"Oh well. Shit happens," Doug commented with a heavy breath and highly annoyed.

James gave a mild chuckle. Doug looked even more stressed by his comment. James leaned into him as he embraced his shoulder with his hand, "Relax, or was that your attempt at it, while trying to be funny?" he asked.

Doug realized what he said, and gave a muffled laugh as his hands covered his mouth.

James could only laugh with his delayed reaction and walked out the door as he expressed, "I'm glad you came back for a visit. I've been on hold listening to ads, in between music blasting in my ear for over a half hour and its times like these that make me grateful to those mindful designers of cordless phones. This way we can be productive even sitting on our asses." "Funny James," Doug said shaking his head and slightly off a smarty type laugh.

"And how many times, have we've complained about waiting on hold….eh?"

Doug snickered with his reply, "So true." He noticed James wiping his hands across his mouth. His face scrunched, his arms rolled around as he thought to mention, "God James, I hope you washed your hands. You don't want those germs crawling inside your mouth. You might get sick."

James laughed as he scratched his face, walked out the door, and answered, "Of course…I did. Come with me." He padded his back leading him around to the side of his house. "Go take a look around the property, and I'll meet up with you when my call is done. You can enter through the gate. If the signals on these phones picked up out there, I'd show you around, but they don't. This gives you something to do, while I'm on hold. I see no reason to waste your time, while their wasting mine."

Listening Doug had his left hand on his hip, looked down the side of the house and slowly responded, "Alright…. there… James, I'll go take a boo. See you soon."

When Doug finished, he went back to the house and gave a couple of light knocks on the glass as he opened the screen door and walked into the house calling to him, but didn't get a response. He eased around the house sticking his head inside the living room and sitting area. There was no sign of James, so he continued down the hallway and peeked inside several rooms. He finally found James sitting in his office with his head tilted against the telephone, strolling through paperwork on his desk.

He held the doorframe with his hand, as he leaned inside and in a low whisper said, "Hey, James… I'm back." James looked up, "I'll be with you in a minute. Pour yourself a coffee and take a seat out on the patio." He covered the mouthpiece on the phone as he pointed to it, and whispered, "I'm still on the phone."

"Which way," he wondered. "Straight down the hall, you'll see the kitchen. The doors to the patio are off it," James mentioned switching the telephone over to his other ear.

Doug poured himself a coffee, walked out on the patio and noticed a slew of boats speeding across the water on the lake. He hadn't had the pleasure of seeing James home thoroughly and immediately the view engaged him.

He was gazing at the scenery when James walked out from the kitchen and noticed he had his feet pressed up against the glass, below the PVC hand railing. "Hey Doug, what do you think of the design and the view?" he asked.

Doug was startled with the sound of his voice. His body twitched leaving his feet to etch off the glass as they slid off making a squeaky sound with his running shoes. He adjusted his body to sit up and turned his head to respond, "It was nice, but I couldn't get the gate open on the back right side of your property, so I didn't get to see your entire property. I also couldn't figure out where the back entrance was to the house."

James flipped his head back and his voice went harsh, "There isn't an entrance where you were. I buzzed you into the smaller gate and left it unlocked for you to come back to the front. The gate you tried prevents anyone from gaining access to the house. I hadn't released the lock to that gate for you to go back there. Didn't you take notice when the Security Company was surrounding you and the house, something wasn't right?"

Doug gave a disgusted look as he answered, "You're shitting me right? I thought it was nosey neighbors checking out your property from some field back there. I had taken a rest waiting for you, and must have snoozed for a few minutes. I heard rustling and thought it was wildlife. Then the sounds got louder. I jumped up when I noticed a ton of men scattering around in dark clothing. As they did they were staring through the fences. They didn't hang around long. I stood up and looked at them with my hands on my hips, letting them know, I see you. Then I took my hand to my eyes and pointed it at them. They eventually left and to be honest, I'm too damn old to be startled like that, especially when, I wasn't expecting it."

"It wasn't neighbors it was the Security Company. They initially arrived at your first attempt to jimmy the lock. What made you try it again? You must have realized with the steel black fence over twenty feet high, and attached to the gate you messed with it, it was off limits. I had unlocked the gate for you to go back there, didn't that tell you something when I also mentioned I had to buzz you into the other gate?"

Doug fiddled in his nervousness and quickly commented, "I thought the lock was stuck. I also didn't hear you mention that you had to unlock the gate for me to go through. I can't understand why you didn't tell me not to go over to that side of the property. I'm positive I would have heard that?"

James placed his coffee down on the table, then sat and scratched his head as he thought to ask, "So, you mean to tell me that you couldn't figure out that part of the property is off limits just by looking at it?"

"No," Doug fumed out as an answer. James tossed his back up against the chair and his hands went to his head, "Well then, if anyone else is like you and they do by chance get through it, I'm happy to know they won't get too far. The security company would be right behind them, like they were you."

Anxious his head bobbed around leaving his chubby cheeks to jiggle as he said, "Oh… James….I didn't take notice of any cameras, but I didn't think to look either. I had no idea that touching the gate lock was going to cause such an upset. I feel terrible."

"I learnt the cameras aren't visible and the security system outback is on a separate monitoring system from the house. I don't know the actual specifications. Tonya and the kids hired them. Whatever it is they have going on gives them control over these additional added features they have installed."

Doug moved his body closer, "Come to think of it James, I did notice something in an odd shape sitting on top of your roof. It might be a camera."

James crossed his legs, "I couldn't tell you if it is. I've never looked up there. All I know is they decided when you touched the gate the first time to take a visit out here, and I wasn't aware they did. I was on the telephone when I noticed my lights dimmed up and down in the office, and a deep male's voice ask, "Who are you?" I thought someone answered my call. The music had finally stopped. I responded with my name, but he didn't respond to me. I repeated it several times too. I had no dial tone to indicate that my call was disconnected. Then the voice spoke again, but only to say, 'Who are you?" I gave my name again, and said, "Can you hear me?" I thought by this point, I'd hit the mute button going from ear to ear. I placed the phone on the desk, and hit all the buttons, while asking if they could hear me, but they didn't respond. I sat there feeling like an idiot saying, "Hello, hello, I can hear you, can you hear me?" They kept repeating, "What's your name?"

"You could have easily dropped the call. I know my chin must have disconnected my call on my new cell the other day. I must have hit a video button too, because when I pulled the phone away from my ear to find out where the light was coming from on the back, I looked to the screen on the phone, and there I was. I couldn't believe it, and shoved the cell back to my ear and immediately the call ended. I realized it had a red end button, so my chin must have been hitting that each time I brought the cell up to my ear and I was the one hanging up on everyone. Perhaps you hit the end button on your cordless."

"I heard a voice Doug, so the call couldn't have been disconnected." James sarcastically responded.

"I must have missed you saying the man was still talking on the phone," Doug laughed, "Perhaps your right, I should get my ears checked, it's been awhile since my last check up."

"Well either it's your ears, or your just not paying attention to what I was saying. I have to think here, and I'm not as sharp as I used to be. Okay where was I… Oh, yes…Suddenly, I heard, "What's your name. Identify yourself," I said, "Its James, can you hear me? Hello, hello," but he didn't respond say, "Hi James." I figured the prick was pissing me off when he spoke rapidly, "who are you, what's your name," like five or ten times in a row. I took it to be a recording by then."

Excited Doug sat straight up and had his I only speak with his hands going on, "These cell phones have all these apps that can access your camera, microphone, even our contacts and location. They can block your messages or redirect your calls and pretty much disable anything they want. They can screw with cordless phones and baby monitors too. They've been getting pictures of people in some strange situations, and blackmailing them. Don't you watch the news?"

"No, I haven't since way before Tonya's passed. I don't pay attention to technical shit, it's way too much for my head. For a while there, I thought I was fucking crazy, hearing voices. I imagined someone was spinning their fingers around their ear while calling me a kook, so I tried to settle myself down. Okay I thought, let's be rational here. I have no dial tone and no one is responding to me, so I figured it was the volume on the television set psyching me out and I had left it on. I had my television go on and off at times before, and the screen went black. It was the picture tube that went. I thought it was happening again. I picked up the remote, aimed it to the TV and seen small images in blocks forming across the screen. It wasn't lines with all those colors that spams or rolls across the screen, and a recording comes on stating, "this is a test of the emergency broadcast system.' It wasn't that. I wasn't able to turn the sound up or down and no station came in. I thought the battery was toast, or my picture tube was going again. I was still hearing the voice, "Who are you?" but now, he added, "Do you know who we are?" I was still saying hello, can you hear me while I held the phone to my ear and pointed the remote at the TV, but now those blocks on the TV started coming into focus. I looked closer, and saw me. I flew off my chair, landed on the ground, and crawled under my desk. The voice muffled and went rapid. I was ready to go mad, and for a while there, I thought I had, until they said, "James, is that you James? It's the Security Company identify yourself by providing us with your access code. I was screaming I don't know what it is, while spinning myself around under the desk. They forced me to enter a code in the security system, then gave me one number, and repeated it several times. I finally realized my identification number was my birthday and gave it to them."

Doug's had the look of disgust as he said, "You were watching TV right, and you think this is funny. It would have been something if it occurred. It would be pathetic to use your birthday. Never use it. Burglars figured out years ago our memories aren't that good, that's why we all use it. I made sure I switched my dates around, so it's still four, but not in the same order."

James stood up and raised his voice, "It's not a joke. They were here. I had to give personal identifiable information and locate my other codes. They asked who the short, old oriental man was on my property after I did. I let them know you were a friend. I had forgotten to hit another button prior to releasing the gate lock for you on my controls, so it was a double threat to them, they noted. I had been on hold for far so long it made my mind mush. I should have just hung up the call after ten minutes and said, the hell with these assholes. I'll have to remember to do that next time. They finally gave me access to my telephone line. I had lost my place on hold and had to call the number back, and wait in the call cue again, all because I hadn't learnt my lesson. Here I was switching my phones on the chargers, so the battery didn't die on me so I could sit and listened to rubbish to speak to a live person on the phone, and here they were speaking to me inside my house. I put some coffee on, poured a cup and came back into the office after the ordeal."

Doug interjected crossing his legs, sipping back coffee, "I'm sorry to hear James, it sounded frightening. But it's a good thing you have them."

"After all that, I'm sitting at my desk, I hear another voice, "James, do you want to come with us?" this time it's a woman. Immediately I pulled the phone away from my ear, and thought what the heck. I put the phone back and still hear the music blasting and some woman's voice, but it sounded distant. I thought oh, okay, it's one of those voices letting you know, they're still with you. It's like customers are kids not adults to them which just pisses me completely off. You know when they say, "Hey what's up do you want to chat." And you're thinking, not really, you've either over charged me, or had a process you neglected to fill me in on completely, so here I sit and wait like a fool. Anyways, while I'm sputtering all that into the phone, this woman was saying, "It's okay James were here." I thought oh shit she heard what I said. I put the phone back to my ear and held it tightly against it, and put my finger into my other ear. I heard the music playing. I screamed, "I'm on the fucking phone don't disconnect my call, if you're the security company. Then, I hear a males voice, "James, it's okay, you can talk. We're here, you're safe."

"Suddenly, about seven men rushed into my office. I dropped my cordless phone, and tried to jump up, but went back down. I was scared shitless.

The only thing I could do was scream at the top of my lungs. They stood there looking at me, so, then I said, "Who the hell are you people? What do you want? How did you get inside my home? I felt ambushed. I know if I had a gun in my hand. I would have just popped a few strings of bullets their way, but I wouldn't have stood a chance with them considering they were pointing guns at me."

"Oh my god James, did they take anything? You look okay for a man that just got robbed. Did you call the police? What a stupid question, I seen you on the telephone when I came in, of course you did. Sorry, I would have been back sooner, but I went back to unhitch my key from the lock. Like I said, it was stuck. I was only trying to work the lock free and credit cards don't work in those types of locks anymore. The grandkids had downloaded a flashlight and a zoom application on my cell phone. Thank god they did. I finally got my broken keys out. Had I known you were in danger, I would have rushed to you, and at least called the police, and gotten my key out later," Doug thoughtfully mentioned.

"No wonder the security company barged in on me like they did. They have complete access to my home when they feel it's warranted. They do this to make sure I'm not being held hostage, or being forced to say anything against my will, is what they told me. They don't knock, they come right in. I had completely forgotten they had the authority to do so. It was a long time ago when Tonya and the kids mentioned it. I had left the front door unlocked and open for you. They didn't have to break it down. It was the first time they've been here, and boy do they take it seriously. They checked the house out completely. When they left, a couple of them stayed in their vehicles outside, until you came back to the house. They had to make sure the lock wasn't damage and repair it if you broke it. Didn't you hear them say through the intercom system, "We're leaving now? I realized under the plastic on my desk, right beside my calendar, was where my codes were. Here I was pulling my filing cabinets a part, and had opened all the drawers on my desk.   They had scanned my fingerprint, and sent it to their system while I looked and finally said, don't worry about it."

Doug waved his hand up and down as he muttered, "Wow, that's pretty cool. It reminds me of my wives brother calling her the other day complaining that he had turned off his television with his remote and it came back on twice after he shut it down. He had no idea why it did. My wife mentioned, "We were watching the news and they mentioned that we must be careful with what we're doing online." He had mentioned, "He had been linking videos from his smartphone to his new smart television, using their Wi-Fi wireless connection. My wife told him, "You must have downloaded some sort of controlling virus then. It used to be the blue screen of death. God knows what it is now." Nevertheless, he didn't believe a word she said. He and his wife decided to blame their nephew they had visiting for psyching them out. He said, they can download remotes and use them from their cell phones to control what they use with remotes. People are so much in denial today…"

"I don't know Doug. I wasn't in denial, I was in fucking hell."

"Oh don't feel rotten, get over it. My wife and I upgraded from our flip phones, because they had the biscuit and we're still trying to figure out how to use them. We didn't realize it came with added features, where it made it complicated to make a simple telephone call. I'll have to read the manual when I get some time. The wife is into texting me now, because she's tired of me hanging up on her when she calls. With all this new technology, us old farts are supposed to be tech savvy, or our grandkids are supposed to take time out of their lives to teach us how to use them. Simple… isn't so simple anymore, that's for sure James," Doug laughed.

James had taken his fingers, rolled the skin around his cheeks with them while Doug was talking. Then, rolled his neck around and stopped when Doug finished to comment, "It all just an upset. I felt so confused when it all occurred and when I asked what they did to my TV this young man mentioned the security system runs underground, around the property, and cuts into the city services, in some way. It would have been simpler if the man stated we hooked up to the electrical panel."

Doug jumped into the conversation to add his theory, "No way James, how that hotshot explained it must be some sort of new technology, or they used wireless to live stream to their offices."

"I don't know, I didn't even realize they had these cameras installed in my home. Makes me feel sick to my stomach thinking there here, and I don't know where. He offered to show me, I said, get the fuck out of here. It blew my mind, is what it did. I think they do this to shock the shit out of people, because they certainly did that to me."

"It's just terrible James, sorry to hear. But, you must have read the paper or heard years ago when this new shit came out that women were complaining about having webcams, and men were calling them on their phones telling them, I know what you're wearing?" Doug thought to mention.

"What a day from hell it's been. No, I never heard that either, and what are you, the bad news reporter here? God… that had better not happen to me, or I'd certainly go mad. I never did speak with anyone on the telephone. When I called back, they left me in the call cue, and still had music playing after they closed their offices, for the day. I had no idea they did. It wasn't until I thought I was smart and called the number with my cell too. That way I figured, I'd have two lines in cue. My cell went straight into their voice mail system, which stated their offices were now closed. I thought perfect, my call is still in line on my house phone, and waited for another forty five minutes on hold, only to realize these pricks now play music, once you by passed their voice systems, and it doesn't matter if their offices are closed, they don't disconnect your call. "James stressed in a yelling.

Doug couldn't get over what he said, "Wow, Its high tech stuff, isn't it? Maybe your security company decided not to disconnect your call, when you screamed at them, not too?"

James dropped his head down into his hands and looked directly into his eyes as he said, "I didn't think of that, but logic tells us, they can't mess with someone else's phone system. They aren't cops, but it was a good thought there Doug," as he padded his shoulder and got up.

"People with money and million dollar homes, really do get the best of everything. I would have loved to have been here when they came in and seen all that shit happening to you. It sounds hilarious. If you had of known what was going on, it wouldn't have been the same. You'll laugh about it later on. It's never funny at the time. Look at it positively the company did an excellent job protecting you and your home."

"I imagine its high tech shit and considering you were the man they were after, they would have roughed you up, if I wasn't still in the house on hold, and I would have enjoyed watching them shock the shit out of you. Now that is seeing it from a positive point of view, my friend. On the other hand, if I wasn't held up by that call, I might have been roughed up too. They might not have realized who I was, and I wouldn't have known you screwed with the lock, you crazy goof. They kept security surrounding the property and the fences, just to make sure, I wasn't bullshitting them, and you weren't breaking in. Their visit today, cost me a pretty penny," James shared.

Doug covered his mouth with his hands, when he realized he had to pay and his face went pouty, as he thought to mention, "I'm sorry about the cost James. Come to think about it, it would have ruined my day too considering the walk around your property brightened up my day. What a bit of scenery can do for a person, is amazing. In all seriousness, your home is by far one of the nicest ones, I've seen. I didn't know it was sending signals out into space, when I tried to find a way in," he commented while taking a big drink and slamming his back into the chair.

"You're not supposed to know you're being watched when you do shit like that." James snarled wiping the sweat off from his forehead. "It's been... a screwy day. Let's talk about something more pleasant. So you enjoyed your walk around then?" James asked going in for more coffee. He had the back door open, poured some coffee in his cup. Doug walked up behind him as he refilled his as he spoke.

"I guess the best way to explain it is, I was immediately taken back when I walked to the back of the house. It had a quiet peaceful feel to it. I realized the designers utilized the flow of your property and incorporated the same materials throughout. The more I walked around, I realized it is by far one of the most mesmerizing properties that I've honestly ever seen. I don't think words can do it justice when each design had many elements of quality attached to it. I felt in another country back there. That came out wrong. I'm not saying that the front of your property isn't well designed."

"Thank you," James expressed. "Your welcome, James but, let's be honest here. You have the average large home with those big concrete slabs plopped on either side of the driveway. Everyone knows those are the big welcome to our home sign for wealthy people when we drive up. Then we're greeted to the long curved driveway and manicured lawns as we turn in. As we get closer to the house, we see barns that look like homes, and garages that look like fucking hotels. At first, we have to figure out if it's three or four houses sitting slightly off from the frontage of the main property. We always wonder if we're at the right address. We don't get out and knock at the door to ask. Nope, we're so fucked up, we don't feel like we belong so we continue to drive around that long curved driveway and end up heading straight to the exit, and it's too late by then. We don't want to humiliate ourselves, so we don't back up. Instead, it's like easy come and easy go. On our way out thou, we're teased even more by the view with the horses running freely behind the fences, which is an added touch," Doug rambled out. "Is that what you honestly thought?" James asked.

"What do you think? It's a peaceful run dropping off your mail James. Still today, I glance over at the horses when I leave. I always remember my first weeks coming up here. It was such a bitch for me, doubting myself constantly. I believed, I had the wrong house numbers, and those weren't houses like I thought they were. They were just barns, and garages that you had built, which are bigger than many city homes, still today."

"It's just a home Doug. You make it sound like we're out here not working for a living and bought it to tease assholes from the city who live in boxes and call those million dollar homes. You city folks love living in communities that have steam roller trains running down their streets, and all those trains are—is a lineup of parked cars packed together, because they didn't think to add parking for people that had homes on the same streets. Now you suckers, have to pay to park, or are begging to remove grass so you can park in front of your homes and it looks ridiculous to us country folks. It's a concrete jungle down where you live. I take the odd trip there to see a show, or sporting event and I'm having a good fucking day when I'm in and out of there," James complained.

Doug took it personally and dropped his hands on the glass patio table making a loud noise. It startled him as did their cups when they bounced up and back down. Immediately he wiped with his hand to see if it broke, as he expressed, "I totally agree with you James. I wish I had of thought of this lifestyle years ago. I just meant, you can't tell from the front of your property, it's even more outstanding in the back," Doug mentioned not wanting him to feel insulted.

"I understood what you meant. I played along. I thought it was funny how it rolled off your tongue. I can't tell you how many times, I've driven mail to their correct addresses. I realized it occurred more when you were on vacation," James laughed. "Oh … you had me worried for a minute. I'm sure there are days everyone fucks up, we are human after all," Doug commented quickly.

"I've tried to explain the details of my home, and it's not easy when someone who hasn't seen it can't visualize the details. I love looking into their faces when I try to explain it to them. They look way out there in wonderland somewhere. It's that blank dumb look I enjoy the most, because they think you're forcing them to think, and it's way too much for their head. It's like being a kid in school and being told to put your thinking cap on, because without it, you might not be able to think clearly. Most people don't remember it, but their minds are still programmed to think this bullshit fake look works. Rather than saying, "I don't know what you mean," they can't be bothered and out in space they go. They don't gap out deliberately. They might not have the knowledge on specifics to relate it to understanding. I know that occurred with me when the designers started talking circles around my head with the design elements and started talking specifics on the materials they were going to use," James rationalized and took a drink of his coffee.

Doug smiled, and nodded then took a drink and thought to mention, "I followed the flow of the yard and noticed the lake was close by. It seemed further away from the property then what it actually is from where I had been standing at the time. I didn't have as clear view with all the trees. So, when I came out here on the patio and seen the lake, right there, I couldn't believe it was so close."

"Yeah, I know what you mean. I thought that too when we first moved here. It's because the lake is closer at some parts and sits back in the distance at others all along the property line. It's nice down at the beach if you want to sit on the sand, and go swimming in the shallower parts of the water. Other parts are deeper, and you don't want to venture there, and think you can go in for a quick swim. There's no way back up on the land with the hills. That's why it's highly secured and heavily locked." James expressed then took a drink of his coffee and moved paperwork about in his hands.

Doug noticed he went back to holding the paperwork, and picked up the telephone, looked at it and put it back down, so he continued, "You wanted to know what I thought about the back of your home. Let me explain it the best I can. I couldn't get over the design layout. I know each stone was placed by hand individually and it's extraordinary. I thought when I first entered the back, the gardens and small waterfalls that offered lots of sitting was an added touch. I waited there for about twenty minutes and that's where I dozed for a minute or two and heard the rustling, and realized it was those men, on the outside of the fence. It freaked me out and I grabbed my heart when they left. They didn't say anything to me, and you didn't come out, so, I figured I'd get moving. I first walked over to the stone steps. I looked down and couldn't get over how the layout curved and how seamlessly the water flowed in-between the bushes and flowers, on both sides of the steps. I decided to take a walk down to see where it went. I ended up stopping on the steps when I looked across and seen a massive waterfall in the distance. I cannot explain how quickly my mind stopped rushing with thoughts when everything grabbed my attention. It was all so calming. The earthy tones in the stones really heighten the design. It wasn't intrusive at all. It was such a pleasurable experience, just getting to the steps and going down them. I watched how effortlessly the water flowed around everything on both sides of the steps and at the bottom, it blew my mind when it ended into a pool of crystal clear blue water. I sat down on the side of the pool, and seen on the right side was a fountain, so I made my wishes, and tossed my coins into the water. I noticed others did."

"It was Tanya's idea to have a small pool on each side of the steps. She wanted it shallow enough for little kids and the other side she believed would be for dogs, and the odd cat that came around. It all came to her when she wanted to ensure a consistency with the design. Then she thought it was important to have a sitting area where company could rest once they got to the bottom and that's how it came about. It was about a month after everything was finished, when company came. They went to look around with their children, while we cooked on the Barbeque. When we sat down to eat, the kids were talking amongst themselves about making wishes. Tanya looked at me, and we busted out laughing. Our company had a laugh too, because we had no idea anyone would have thought of doing something like that. As soon as everyone left, we went down to look. I took change out of my pocket and her and I tossed some coins in, made a few wishes and shared in a romantic kiss. It was funny to us at first, but it became an unexpected gift, with what they did. Neither of us thought of it as a wishing well," James expressed in pride in a shallow voice. It was almost as if he lived it then.

"It is now, and I loved it. After I gave, and did my wish, I walked over to the large waterfalls and immediately, I thought of dominoes while I followed the flow of the water. I wasn't expecting to see a pond that stilled in the water at the end. It was a smart move to have all the turns and twists, so the person looking for the first time wouldn't see what was at the end until they followed it completely around. As much as the stonework design and the waterfalls could have stood alone with so many other elements inside, it wasn't left, which surprised me. The idea to tier it, and join in the pond with more flowers, bushes, and waterfalls is spectacular craftsmanship. I continued walking along the path and seen several hand crafted birdbaths surrounded by the same stonework, which made it noteworthy. I couldn't believe inside they planted real trees, well grown, and the stonework arched around it throughout. It not only takes birds, but other wildlife away from the harsh weather conditions."

"I haven't been down there for a while. The ground keepers' deal with it," James mentioned. "The automatic feeder dispensers attached was a sweet idea. I decide to reload them. Whoever thought of employing the same stonework for something like that was incredibly creative. Everything caught me completely off guard and was a pleasant surprise. That is why I thought to take the time to explain how I felt, experiencing it. Thank you for inviting me into your home," Doug expressed in gratitude.

James stood up suddenly, brushed his hand under his nose, and then motioned his hand off to his side, as he said, "Come with me. I'd like for you to take a look at something, if you have the time."

Doug stood up, picked up his coffee, as James did. "I have the time," he volunteered with the look of wonder in his eyes.

"I'm glad you enjoyed the flow of the design. A portion of the patio extends over the lake on the other side of the property, which allows the water to flow, beneath us. Have you ever driven up onto a bridge and had the water freely flowing on both sides of you?" James asked inquisitively.

"Yes, I have. It's a nice drive especially when you hadn't expected to come across something like that. I can't even remember where I was when I did. Although, I recall it was sudden. I felt like I dropped out of the city and there it was, but for the life of me, I'm unable to place where I was when it occurred," he answered while caressing his chin with his fingers then bounced them off a few times. Then added, "I do know what you mean, but I can't pinpoint the location to give as a reference. That scenery does the mind good, if you enjoy that sort of thing and I sure do," Doug thoughtfully answered as they walked.

James had a moment of happiness, reliving his initial thoughts and placed his right hand out as he rolled it up in the air, to give the idea that he was the car driving over a bridge as he said, "I wanted that same feeling of driving over the lake on a long bridge with the water on either side." James described with a beaming smile then added, "Take a look around now and then look down. My designer achieved all I wanted and more."

Doug arched forward to look through the glass then suddenly placed both hands down firmly on the steel black railing as he lifted his body up brushing his shoes off the glass to help him up. Once up, he leaned his head over to look down, "It's a remarkable achievement. I guess with the steel gate, I didn't get the chance to venture over to that part to see how it looks below, but looking over the lake like this… is really impressive. Just like everything else on your property," Doug shared in amazement.

James looked at Doug leaning over the railing, "I used to get a kick out of Tanya when she leaned against the railing calling me in from the lake for dinner. She'd call my cell, I'd say, "on my way." I'd stay out on the lake just to see her come out. When she did, she'd be waving both hands in the air when she seen me. I pretended not to see her. She thought the only way I could see her was if she held a stick with a plain white pillowcase on it, and waved it around in the air. Once she did, I'd turn the boat around and drive towards the house. She'd wait until I came up to the house. I'd wave up to her, then drive into the boathouse, just below here, as she stood where we're standing now," James said pointing to the direction of the boathouse, "The entrance is right there Doug."

"Oh… okay," he responded quickly and sounded

out of breath. "Anyways, I'd waved up, and went under the patio and disappeared from her view. She couldn't get over it. I took her out on the boat a few times to let her experience it. Her only concern was, we didn't come out on the other side of the house. I had to explain to her, that the house wasn't over here," he conveyed with a laugh.

"The water must be pretty deep down there. On a hot day I can see someone having the urge to dive in from up here," Doug joked, but was out of breath.

James looked at Doug's body hanging half over the railing. "Doug what do you stand about five foot five? I realized you're just a few inches taller than that railing. Your eyes must have looked directly at the railing when you stood there. Sorry, I didn't think, or I would have brought a chair with us. I got excited, when I recalled Tanya and our kiss at the waterfalls the first time, and didn't take your height into consideration."

"Yeah, around that height, give or take an inch," he noted with a slick laugh, and continued, "All I could see was the railing and on my tiptoes it didn't give me the feeling I was looking for. I jumped up to see it with full openness. When you mentioned the boathouse, I looked way down that's why my hand slipped off the glass. I almost flew myself over. I'm getting older, but the body stills thinks it's as young as hell sometimes, and shortness runs in my family. It pisses me off at times like this, but other than that, I don't think about it," explained Doug. "

"Doug everyone has had the same urge to look straight down rather than enjoying the view looking out? We designed it with the glass so it was visible, even sitting down on a chair and looking out. You could have looked from every angle, if you stood back and it would have given you that open feeling," James assured him.

Doug came down, "I wanted to see everything I could see from up here. I noticed you didn't have anything around that I could stand on so I took it upon myself to get up. I wanted to see inside the boathouse, once you mentioned it, but like you said, it's hidden under the patio. If you think about it when you do go across a bridge with the water on both sides, you must admit, it feels more open when you're not looking through the glass in the vehicle window," he answered with a big grin and curled up nose.

"Oh…yes, for some reason it's so true. I used to do the same thing going over the bridge. I would roll down the window and Tanya would ask what I was doing while complaining the air was on. We thought about someone diving in from up here, that's why we made the railing just over five feet and keep the area clear, so there isn't anything here for someone to stand on. But… as you said, people will try to do just about anything to have an adventure, or to get some sort of a rush. We tried to take that urge away, but we can only try to stop an action, but cannot enforce it. If we could, we wouldn't have all the crazy shit we have going on in the world today. Come with me," James said nodding his head towards the direction he wanted him to go.

"Down below, when I'd drive the boat inside the boathouse. I'd dock the boat inside, and hit a button for the black fork steal gate to come down from overhead. When it does, it leaves the bottom of the gate resting in the water. The design works like a garage door. We designed it like that in an attempt to stop anyone from coming in from the lake. You know, thinking they can steal things from inside, or gain access to the house. If they do try, they'd have a shitload of hard work ahead of them. By the time, they got into the boat area the cops would be here, and they too wouldn't have realized they were on their way. When the season is over, I drive my boat further inside the boathouse, press a button for the lift and it takes the boat from the water and places the boat on its trailer. It all sits on a concrete pad inside. I hit another button the solid door comes down, and the alarm sets automatically for that one. I hit the other button for the black steel gate and it's closed for another season," James explained glancing at him to see if he had any questions.

They walked through the gate, James clicked the remote he had for his lock and they continued to walk along the concrete patio. Doug looked at his cell phone while he spoke, "I'd love to see it, and take the boat out on the lake, but I can't today. Perhaps, we can do it soon. It is getting late and the wife is texting about every three minutes wanting to know how long I'm going to be. When I walked around the property, I didn't think of all the planning involved. Although, I must say, it has a flow of simplicity and I felt the beauty of it. The design is very open with nothing closing you in wherever you go," Doug articulated.

While they walked James explained, "The open flow was part of our design expectations. I also wanted to enjoy my morning coffee, whether it's raining or snowing looking out to the openness of the lake. Therefore, they built this glass sunroom. It promotes that same sort of feeling and offers the mind those moments of peace it craves, and it is how

I start each day, rain, shine or snow. There really is nothing to set you into a form of peace, like what watching water does. When the water turns to ice, I can still look into the earth's beauty and feel it line with its openness. It is the greatest pleasure for me. Most people don't realize how fast the mind does clear, when you do it. There is such a stillness to it. I miss sharing it with Tanya," James mustered out as he choked back tears. They quickly filled his eyes. He took his glasses off to wipe.

Doug took notice of his tears and looked away, and decided to continue talking, "Oh that reminds me James, I haven't seen your new lady friend around lately. She came out for the mail a couple of times, when she was here. I also passed by her when she was leaving on the side road at different times," Doug mentioned knowing James does not divulge much.

James looked up from his paperwork, "Please… don't ask me about that woman. I want to relax. I think of her, and it ruins my day," he stated annoyed as he placed is glasses back on.

They walked back to where they started from and both sat, "I didn't realize it would upset you. I thought she was helping you out. Perhaps, you weren't well is the first thought that came to my mind. You don't look so good. I know a lot has happened to you today, but I have noticed the last little while you've been looking a bit different and I thought you were unwell. Have you been to the doctors? We are getting older, and should be seeing them regularly," Doug nervously probed.

James didn't respond or look up from the paperwork in his hand. Doug squirmed around in his chair waiting for him to talk, but he didn't.

"I've been on this mail route for fifteen years, and never realized your property was this large. Next year I retire and the wife wants to leave the hustle, and bustle along with the riffraff and move out of the city," Doug said to change the subject and lighten the mood.

James looked up at him dumbfounded, "You have been our mail carrier that long Doug and you've never been through our home, or on the grounds? I feel awful," apologized James.

Doug's got pissed off with himself as he tried not to say the wrong things to upset him and he did. His lips seamed together and air bubbled up between them. He moved the air around in a rolling motion and let out a loud blowing and popping sound as he spit out, "No need to feel bad, I've been inside the front interior portions of your home. I never had the time on route to take a walk around, or come back for dinner with the family when you asked. I must admit, Tanya and you did offer often. Today when I finished my route, I made a point to come back when you asked. Tanya and you never did miss a Christmas James. There was always a card, with a check inside with the message 'from our family to yours,'" shared Doug.

Doug got up and gave a big stretch, "It's way too comfortable sitting here. If I sit much longer, I'll be asleep for sure. We can go fishing on the weekend if you're up to it. The wife wants to go shopping and you know it's true, a happy wife, a happy life. I'll wait until tonight to tell her to start looking for a home in the country. She'll be thrilled. Thanks for inviting me James," acknowledged Doug.

James got up, "I'll walk you out. Her name was

Maria," said James. "Who? Your lady friend?" questioned Doug wanting to make sure James was answering his question from earlier.

"Yes...Doug. It's an upset to talk about her. I made a terrible mistake trusting her when I cashed in an investment that I had. The funds went into an account at her bank, after she talked me into some deal her family had going on with real estate. She told me, 'her cousin had contracts with properties from drug busts and sold them cheap. She wanted her and I to flip some for a profit.' We needed to have a joint account to do this, so I agreed."

James caught him off guard. Doug reacted by coming to a halt as they walked, "James my god, you haven't known her that long, have you? Why would you do something so stupid like that with a young woman you hardly knew," Doug asked in upset. His arms tossed around in the air as he displayed hurt for him.

James look went sour, and his tone went angry," No... I hadn't. We met.... after Tanya passed. Not that it's any of your business. But, now that I opened my big mouth, I just meant, I went to her bank with my check and it went into an account there. I've gotten nothing from Maria's bank and my statements from my bank arrived today with you. I was reading those on the patio. I'm going to take a visit to both banks after you leave. I need to find out what's going on. Something seems shady to me," James shared in a rushed tone.

'I'm sorry to hear this James. It's been a hard go for you since Tanya passed," sympathized Doug. "If there is anything I can help you with, please don't hesitate to give me a call," offered Doug.

"It wasn't even a week after we deposited the money at her bank, when Maria dragged me across town expecting me to invest in a condominium for her to live in. Do you believe she laughed about an added extra cost to furnish it? This wasn't a topic of conversation or any part of our initial arrangement. She was told any property would be solely in my name," James mentioned in a bewildered state.

"You have to be vigilant in these times James. People kill for entertainment, drugs, and money," suggested Doug.

"I feel shafted. Then about a week ago, I called Maria and told her I wanted my money and now. She cried and said call her lawyer. I called some dude who calls himself a lawyer, and he rolled me some long-winded story that my money was a gift to her, by me. Moreover, he suggested he had documents from her bank to prove this. The way the lawyer controlled the conversation, he refused to let me speak. It was a matter of fact with him. I called my lawyer but he was on vacation. I'll wait for his direction when he gets back. The same day I spoke to the two of them that night a knock came to the door. I opened it up, and a bat held by some man came swinging at me. Maria was with him. He smashed this table we had out front into pieces. I haven't heard from her since," confided James.

He offered some odd sounds out his mouth, and finally responded, "I wondered why the table was broken. You've had that as long as I've been delivering mail here. Was there something domestic going on with her and this guy?" he commented as they walked over to his car. "Yes, we had that table for years. It was a housewarming gift from my parents.' He gave a heavy sigh, and then added, "I don't know who the guy was that was with her."

"You don't have to deal with people like that James. Be safe, and call the police," suggested Doug.

"Yeah...huh......I will, if there is a next time. I'll have to set the alarm more often, especially after what occurred today. That was never a worry sitting home, or visiting the city. We often left our keys in our vehicles overnight, whether they were in the garage, or not. The enjoyment of country life was being away from the city trash. You meet a trashy person, and it comes to the country. How times have changed," sadly announced James as his lips sucked in then his nostrils flared. His head twisted shorts spurts back and forth, "It's all just a shame, really," he expressed in his disdain with it all.

Doug entered his car left the door open while he started the engine. He pushed the button for his power window to come down and then shut the door, "Think positive James. Things will work out for you at the bank. Call me later. See you soon. Bye James," Doug said as he drove away waving his arm out the window.

James drove to his bank, parked his car and waited to see his bank manager. His bank manager Mr. Slater called him into his office. James shared his confusion with the investment that he cashed in, "It disappeared can you tell me where the money went after I cashed it?" he asked.

He sat in a small cold office with his elbows resting on the dark- brown metal desk. His eyes fixated on his bank manager. He eased in closer to him while he was reading. His head went next to his,

"I waived my usual guarded and reasonable nature. I tried to be spontaneous for the first time in my life, for her. You've known my wife and I for over ten years. Tanya had just passed and my mind was foggy and still is," James confessed in worried whisper.

"You signed Mr. Johnston," Mr. Slater stated as he turned the paperwork around for James to see, "Right here. This is your signature. You signed three weeks ago. It was you who gave your money away to Maria. It was not the bank. I'll make you another copy for your records," confirmed Mr. Slater as he left.

James sat alone waiting for his copies, visibly shaken as his body twitched. He tried to think back to that day he signed. He recalled Maria standing over him in the same office where he now sits, 'Sign here,' she said as she pointed to the solid black line on the paper where Mr. Slater stated he signed.

After he signed, Maria was excited. They walked to a bar close by. James took a seat at a table and ordered a beer while he waited for her to fix her makeup. After she did, she walked over to the bar ordered two glasses of wine. His back was to her when she came up from behind him. She kissed him on the head then eased herself into a chair beside him, handing him a glass of wine. She took her glass to his. 'To us,' she said with a smile.

When they left, she cuddled both her arms around his left arm. Her head rested on his shoulder, as they walked to their cars. "I should have picked you up rather then you having to drive all the way down here to the city. Let me drive us in my car to my bank," Maria offered.

She drove James to her bank. He stood beside her inside her bank manager's office. His fingertips rested on the side of her waist. He was there a whole five minutes. A full smile emerged, as he placed his check down on the desk, "Please deposit this into that account, she has all the information you need. If you need anything from me, I'll be right next door. Please deal with her," he requested of Mrs. White her bank manager.

After he got his copies from his bank manager he drove over to Maria's bank. He kept circling around for a parking spot close by and couldn't find one. He finally gave up, and parked three blocks away and walked to her bank. He was told he had to wait to see Mrs. White the bank manager when she was free.

He sat down in a chair with people on both sides of him. Their arms brushed against each other's, on the armrest. He took his hands and folded them on his lap. It was nothing like the day with Maria. He didn't have to sit and wait. She had valet parking from the hotel next door, where she was staying. The sun was shining and it was early morning. Today, it's late in the afternoon, getting cloudy and he sits and waits.

Mrs. White finally came out of her office and asked each person what he or she needed to see her about. She came up to James, he quickly said, "I only have a quick question to ask." She took him in first.

His lips pierced together when she stated, "The money is no longer yours," he went into a frenzy unable to stand in one place and started stamping his feet and kicking them in the air a few inches above the ground ready to kick her desk or chair, but kept holding himself back. "Do you mind repeating what you said, because to me it sounded like you said my money isn't mine? How is this possible? Did you not put my check into a joint account with Maria? This was my agreement with her," he questioned in an angry and upset voice. "No, Mr. Johnston," answered Mrs. White.

"What do you mean nooo….? That's the only reason that I was even at this bank. Why do you think I gave my identification to her before I left? I also stated I would sign, if you required it," James said in horror. "Mr. Johnston you will have to speak with Maria. I've addressed your question and have other clients waiting," she enlightened him.

"I walked into your bank with a three hundred thousand dollar certified check. What the hell do you mean, it doesn't belong to me?" James expressed enraged. "This is a private matter between Maria and you. This has nothing to do with our bank, or me, Mr. Johnston. I've answered your question. Let me walk you out," she offered.

"Those clients can wait. You have not resolved my issue," he suggested. "We're done with this topic Mr. Johnston. If you have no other financial business that requires my attention, I do need you to leave. I have a lineup of customers waiting," she stressed as she opened the door to her office.

He stood up slapped his hand down on her desk. It let out a sharp noise for everyone to hear his displacement. "On that day, Maria and I stood in this office. I placed my check down on this very same desk. Did you only see the dollar signs spinning in your eyes and could not focus on much else. Perhaps, you and Maria had prearranged something and my voice went unheard. I put my check down right here, when you said, what sort of account would you like it to go into a joint? As soon as you said a joint account, I said put it in that one and dropped it down on your desk. You didn't hear me. You have no customer service skills, and I'm not paying for your mistake," he gabbled in haste.

"James… you didn't say this. You said deal with her, and walked out. Talk with Maria. I deal with our banking clients and at this time, you are not one of our clients. If you would like to open up an account, one of our client representatives will be happy to assist you today. You can request this, over there," she expressed as she stood at her office door pointing to where he was to go.

"I want my money along with an account statement on that money," demanded James.

"You're just upset today. Talk your issues out with Maria. You gave your money to her. It wasn't the bank, or me. Therefore, it's not an issue for the bank or me to resolve. I will walk you out," she informed him calmly.

"Where's my three hundred thousand?" James demanded. "You cannot be serious. You have that sort of money and don't understand you gave the check to Maria. Although you keep saying it's your money, it was deposited into her account. That means you severed ties to that money the moment you gave her control over it. Consequently, it didn't go into an account that held both your names. Considering this is the reality of the situation, I cannot share any information on her account with you," she explained.

"That wasn't my fault. It was yours. You didn't follow my instructions and this has complicated my life. It was your ignorance. You are the one to blame," yelled James pointing his finger in her face.

"James you cannot blame me. You cannot imply, I didn't listen or offer you suggestions. I asked you if you wanted a joint account that day to make sure I understood. It's not often that a person gives money like that away to non-relatives. I did not question your relationship with Maria. She volunteered you two were not related. All you had to do was say, put my check into a new joint account with both our names, before you left, rather than saying deal with her, and walk out. I thought it was odd that you left. That's why I remember it. You've taken up too much of my time. I must ask you to please leave," she offered as an explanation as she waited at her office door for him to exit.

Shocked, by what she stated, he ignored her pleas to leave. He sat down. She placed her hand on her hip, "I cannot believe how defiant and disrespectful you are for an adult," she said as he crossed his legs and placed his hands folded on his lap, "I'm not leaving," he informed her. She left her office. He screamed, "It's not right, I want my money removed from her account and a copy of all transactions."

She came back to her office, placed one foot in the doorway. Her left hand arched against the wall where she rolled each finger as she clicked her long fingernails in sequence against it. The more annoyed she got the faster she clicked, the louder it got, "James, it's not your account. If you don't leave on your own, I will have you escorted out of our bank," she firmly advised him.

James was ignorant to her request to leave, "I want my money. If you want me to leave, give me my money, or you're going to have to make me," he demanded with a confident firm look in his face, as if he was in control.

She waved her hand in the hallway two male police

officers entered her office, "Hi Mr. Johnston, can you please come with us?" The tall heavyset police officer asked. James refused to stand up to leave on his own. He gripped the two wooden armrests on his chair with his hands, "No, I shouldn't have to leave without my money," he complained. The chair went with him as they tried to lift him off.

The two officers stood on either side of him as they rolled back his fingers and removed his hands. "You know the money came from me. You told me, it was my account that day too. Who puts purple cushions on seats for clients? What an office you have there," James complained as he struggled to get free. They lifted him up by his arms, and carried him through the lobby of the bank taking him to the exit doors. She followed behind, as customers watched.

He let his legs drag behind his body, and spun his head behind to complain to her, "It was you that didn't hear me when you mentioned a joint account. I clearly stated put it in there, before I left for coffee. You are at fault for not listening to me. This isn't right," he complained.

"Stand up, or you're going down," the heavyset officer stated. James was quick to position his feet to stand, on the street.

Mrs. White stood at the bank door, "I never confirmed those details Mr. Johnston." "Go home." The smaller officer suggested.

He drove to the beer store then headed home, "Was it what they said, or didn't say with clarity which placed all the blame on me?" He uttered, as he drove the long country road home.

He was almost to his driveway, and signaled for his upcoming turn. Something was on his lawn, as he got closer he read, 'For Sale.' He turned right into his driveway, tossed the truck into park, opened the door, and walked towards the sign. "Sold" embezzled across.

The frontage of his property was no less than 50 acres away from anyone else's home on the same side. "It's all farm land, across the street," he stated as he scratched his head and glanced around the area to see, no one else was in sight.

He sat in his truck and called the number on the sign asking for the real estate agent named on the sign. The man said, "It's an answering service, sir. Please leave your name, number and a message.

"Just give me her cell number," requested James. "Sorry sir, all calls are directed to us to take messages. Sandra will return your call when she is free. What is your message, sir?" the man asked.

"Sandra Kline's name is on a real estate sign left on my property by mistake. I left my home no more than two hours ago, and have now just returned to find this 'Sold Sign' on my property. There never was a 'For Sale sign'. The sign is on the wrong address. Perhaps the sign company didn't understand how country property is numbered up here, and put it on my property by mistake," he explained.

James left his cell number along with his address for someone to call him back. He went home pulled a beer out from the case, opened the fridge door and tossed the case on a shelf. He went and sat on his couch gulped his beer back then stretched out on the couch and drifted off to sleep.

His cell rang. In a drowsy voice James answered, "Hello," as he rolled his body off the couch. "Is James available?" The voice asked. He paced around,

"Yes, this is James."

"I'm Sandra's assistant Don. The listing you called about Sandra sold. I was told you had some confusion with this property status on our website where it was listed for sale when you had seen pictures of the home. It does take some time for our IT department to update the website to reflect the status on our properties. If you look now, it display sold. If you like the area we can arrange at time for you to come into our office. We can show you other properties available for sale that aren't listed with us or on our website," suggested Don.

"No, I didn't go on the Internet to see pictures of my home," James tried to get out. Don cut him off. "Have you been to your bank to be pre-approved? The properties in that area are in the millions," firmly Don stated.

James interjected, "Stop, just stop! I am not looking for a home to buy and what you have stated is impossible. The address I provided in my message is my personal residence. This is where your sign currently sits. I left the property address with your message service. Why did you call this number? The people you hired to take messages confused the message I left."

"I was told to call you, because you asked about this property and for Sandra by name. I've already addressed the home address you provided has sold sir," Don confirmed his message details.

James sat on his couch twisted off the cap on his beer, "You're right, I did ask for the agent named on this sign to call me back. I also told the person a sign your company setup and left, is on my private residential property. Which you have stated is worth millions. I provided my home address details for you to take the sign down. Then I provided my name, and telephone number. This way you people can sort this out, and get back to me. The people who sold their home are missing their sign," clearly stated James.

"I see, sir, can you tell me more please," asked Don. "I never agreed for my home to be sold which is where this sign is located. All you have to do now is look up the seller's name, telephone number, and their address. This sign is to go there. My name is James Johnston, now go look up your seller's name, and you will find their name is different from my mine," suggested James.

"I see, sir. Please go on," Don requested. "In my message to your answering service, I provided my cell number. The people who sold their home will have a different telephone number. My home number is different from my cell, but that doesn't matter. Now, my home address is the one you expressed to me was sold," James let out with a sign of relief. "Yes, sir, I have that information, and confirmed to you the home is sold," Don agreed.

"Good, were on the same page. Look at your paperwork and read the details, I can wait." "Go on sir." Don expressed.

"You must see their details do not match mine, by now. Perhaps, the person who placed the sign wasn't familiar with how country property is numbered, and this caused the mix up," suggested James.

Don had the legal transactions in his computer, "I'm unable provide personal details with regard to this property Sir. I put the sign up myself, so I know for sure, it's not misplaced. If you come into the office with identification we can go over the legal documentation, if you're the seller," Don offered as an explanation.

James eased himself to the edge of the couch cushion, his frustration built and he got infuriated, "I'm the owner of the house address that I provided to you. Take the sign down. Can you not understand, I am not the seller? I cannot think of a better way to communicate this to you."

"Sir, the address you called about is one of our listing and was sold by Sandra. This means the sign is on the correct address. I placed the sign there myself. I cannot be clearer when I say, the property address you provided sir is sold. I cannot disclose any personal details on the sellers or buyers, over the telephone. We adhere to the Privacy Act. You can schedule an appointment with Sandra," communicated Don.

James paced around the house, grabbed himself another cold beer, stood in the kitchen, and yelled, "I don't have a fucking computer for me to go online to see pictures of my home, or to see another sold sign like the one on my god damn lawn. I do not want to see the sign anymore. Just take it down, or I will."

"We have no issues removing the sign, but the property is still sold sir," stressed Don.

"I've tried to explain to you. It is my home and where I have lived for over fifty years. I didn't' agree to sell it. Can you not get this through your thick fucking head?" James bellowed out.

"Sir, you must be confused, and I don't have to talk to anyone who curses at me. One more outburst, and I will most definitely hang up on you sir. I'm trying to protect your privacy. That is only if, you are the owner of the property," Don explained in a frazzled state.

James interjected, "How did you get inside my home to get pictures? Eh....huh...just tell me how? Just give me a straight answer. Can you do that Mr. prissy Don? And stop calling sir, god damn it. "I didn't take the pictures sir," replied Don.

"You listen to me. Get someone here to remove the sign now. Tell Sandra, to call me back. She has some explaining to do. Then I can tell her, you're a useless, punk, and a smart ass, and how does it feel to have this done to you," James yelled and then ended the call on his cell phone. Don heard a silence, "Hello, hello, are you still there?" There was nothing coming from the other end. He turned to the accountant," He hung up on me. At least with a phone, you can hear a click," Don whined.

"Let me sleep, so I can wake up from this nightmare and find out, it's all a rotten dream." James mumbled as he attempted to go back to sleep on his couch. Yet, his body fought the urge. His eyes flickered open and close while his body flipped from side to side. He was wrestles as his knees bent up. He tried to rest for a while in this position. Then one leg bent and the other was forced straight out. In his frustration, he stretched both legs out and adjusted his pillow, several times.

"I cannot get comfortable with all this shit floating around inside my head," he shouted through clenched teeth and sat up, "It's been over a week since I've seen Maria. She has something to do with this. She sold my home without me now, but how?" he slurred out in a drained state.

He called her cell, "I've gotten that damn message for a week. Her voice mail is full. How convenient for her now," he shrieked out in disappointment.

He embraced his bottle of beer and by the time he sat down on his couch, his beer was half-gone. He tried Maria's number again and still he wasn't able to leave a message. "I don't want this phone near me. Maria is never going to answer. Don't you get it, you've been had James, get it through your thick fucking skull," he wailed out smashing his hands against his head.

He opened up his pill bottle took two pills out and washed them down with the rest of his beer. He tossed his cell and pill bottles back into his coat pocket, and threw it on top of his coffee table in front of him. "I was used as a patsy. How did I let this happen? What can I do?" he muttered, as he gulped back beer.

"She's in with some form of professional thieves. Perhaps it's with the mob, bikers or some other shit. Keep the man with you while you rob him blind, and leave him high and dry. Everyone sees you together and thinks it is all on the up and up. I cannot believe this happened to me. Now our home, ripped away. How did they get inside? She swindled me at the bank, and wanted more money. She seen an opportunity to get millions, and took it. The greedy bitch. She didn't want me to Columbia to meet her family," he vented.

He picked up his house phone, "I'm too embarrassed to grovel to my family about my indiscretions. I cannot go to the police when they already sided with her at the bank. The real estate agent blew me off. It will be me that will be arrested. What a fool I was. What a damn fool," he shouted as he attempted to shut his mind out.

His facial pores perspired – sweat eased down his face as he glanced over his bank details. A few dropped on his paperwork, "No one listens. I've had to tolerate people and their ideas of the facts, but no one heard me," he criticized.

"I'm not going to allow a lifetime of hard work and respectability to be lost just because some deceitful bitch entered my life," he confirmed to himself.

He yanked open his filing cabinet, tossed the paperwork inside, and slammed it shut. "What can I do? There has to be some way out of this mess?" as he swigged down more beer.

"She had me looking towards a new life ahead with her. All so she could string me along and create chaos, until she left me with nothing," he yelped.

"Nothing makes sense with all I've done for you, Maria?" He shuddered as he attempted to block it from his mind, "No, I'm not going to live like this," he roared.

He went up the stairs to his bedroom. There at the side of the bed was an antique oak dresser. It was his favorite piece of furniture. He liked it better than his old worn-out chair in the living room. It had been in the family for generations with every scratch and dent, no matter how big or small held a special meaning for him. It was a small piece of family history that gave him comfort each time he touched it and was one of the few remaining items of any value to him that he still owns.

James tweaked open the top drawer inside there was a treasure trove of collectibles that James had saved over many years.

They were insignificant items to anyone other than

him. Just hand-made crafts his son made in grade school and paintings from his daughters. Strewn throughout, was a mishmash of old photographs, mainly of his loving wife. His hands wandered through the myriad of memories, "These small trinkets brought to me, are of a happier times. Now, I am ashamed, as I sullied the memory of my wife to indulge in my lustful urges. Tanya, how can you forgive me?" he expressed in deep regret.

"There is only one option left for me." He wiped away sweat and closed the drawer. "This is the last straw. I cannot take the avalanche of guilt overwhelming me inside," he spouted.

He opened the bottom drawer, "The squeaking sound it emitted reminded him of his childhood and the screech chalk made running down his school's blackboard." He often mentioned. Inside were a few folded shirts James never wore. He reached his hand around until he felt the bottom of the aged oak. He found what he was after. James pulled out a revolver. "It is a piece of beauty," he said in admiration.

He was fond of guns and was a regular at the shooting gallery. Until now, this was his only need for guns and he would cringe when shooters spoke about killing animals for sport, near him. James reached back into the drawer and pulled out a box of bullets. He removed one then tossed the box back into the drawer, and gently closed it. He incessantly rolled around the lone bullet between his index finger and thumb.

He eased the bullet into the chamber of the gun and sat in complete silence on the edge of the bed while he allowed his eyes to swivel around as he looked at the pictures of his family on the walls before him.

He opened up the center top drawer of his dresser, took out a picture of his wife, "All which is left is our memories my love. You were the forever in my life, always there beside me. We embraced and shared so many things and that included things, which were our firsts. We were each other's first date. We went together for our driver's license and we both passed. Then we shared in picking out each other's first cars. We were each other's first kiss. We saved ourselves for our Wedding Day. All I could do was hold your hand during our children's birth. I watched you hold back tears, until the lives of our children were released into the world to us. A part of each other once again, we shared.

"You held strong, when our life took a detour. It was the day we heard the word cancer and you alone it took on its battle. Helpless, as I watched the tears filled inside your eyes, and poured out of mine. Our children's mother lost her life. We shared in until deaths do us part. It was not a storybook marriage it was the life that was shared between us. It wasn't long afterwards when Maria entered my life and today sadly she has drawn my heart cold, when it was already hollow inside. It occurred the moment I lost you Tanya, my dear wife," he professed.

He placed the picture of Tanya face down inside the drawer. It took him a few moments for him to ease the drawer closed. "I will see you soon my darling," he assured her.

He held back tears, "Maria. Oh Maria why did you do this? You've taken away everything I worked my entire life for. You hold no value for human life, love or family."

James was slow when he brought the barrel of the gun towards his mouth. As he allowed it to enter, he felt the cold metal touch his tongue and screeched. He attempted to steady his hand to hold it in place. Yet the gun angled towards the roof of his mouth. He took it out, "It tastes like iron, but this is, the only way, there is no other way," he established.

He let the gun enter his mouth again with his finger held ever so slightly on the trigger. "Maria how could you betray me like this? " Pull the damn trigger," he demanded of himself, "Come on you can do it, what's wrong with you— you dumb bastard?" he mumbled as his lips closed down on the gun, each time he cursed at himself.

His facial muscles drew tighter and tighter together in his anguish. His hand more unsteady as his entire body trembled, so did his hand. As it did, it changed the placement of the gun, inside his mouth. The slant was going towards his cheeks, then his tongue. He grasped it with two hands, "to ensure a quick death, I want it straight," he ordered of himself.

He held it pointed in his mouth as best he could as his hands trembled, and then he let his left hand drop. At any moment, his life could be over.

Tears filled his eyes, a few rolled down his face. He tried not to notice, as he turned his hand, and then turned it some more. His tears boiled inside him and impaired his vision. As they did, his finger eased out, and rested on the outside of the trigger. "You damn son of a bitch, you pathetic asshole," He reprimanded himself as he wiped tears with the back of his hand. A mere second spun his attention and the gun evacuated his mouth.

This breakthrough moment, took him away from

his misery and self-loathing idiocy, which could have ended his life, to another desire. His tears became his protector and for this moment saved his life. His tears were slowly empowering his mind to break free from this deep state of hopelessness, and forced rage to erupt, and where anger took over and consumed his thoughts, which allowed his attempt at suicide to elapse.

He self-confessed, "Why, should I be the one to die?" He saved himself from the depths of despair, his endeavor at suicide this time, elapsed. Vengeance was now fueling his every action.

James dropped the gun to the carpet. His eyes followed and froze still on the gun. He finally allowed himself the time he needed to cry. He embraced his face with his hands, "I couldn't do it. All I had to do was pull the trigger and it would have been over, but I couldn't do it."

James temperament vacillated between anger and shame as he cursed the gun and himself. His anger empowered him when he came to an epiphany, "This is Tanya's home. I will not allow anyone to take it without a fight. She fought for her life, and the disease beat her. I will fight for her. This is something I can do. You will not beat me or her with this home, unless you're prepared to die as she faced her death, be ready to face me and your own demise," he voiced as he concluded the way to seek his revenge.

He came back from despair, "I will not allow you, Maria to take my life and get away with what you have done," he bellowed, as he wrapped his gun in a towel, shoved it into an old duffle bag he had beside the dresser. "I will find you Maria, but not to rekindle the flame. I'm determined to even the score." He settled with himself as he ran down the stairs, grabbed his coat, and took off out his front door.

"There is nothing to lose at this point," he exclaimed as he left his house and walked towards his truck. He stopped, and turned back around to stare at the home that he lived in his entire marriage, and where they raised their children, "It's ours, not hers or theirs to take, my love," he told Tanya.

Tears had aborted his eyes, "This may be the last time I see our home." It was as if, he was attending a funeral but there was no time for long goodbyes. James walked away, never to look back as he jumped into his pickup truck, and drove to the city to find her.

He parked his truck in a nearby city-parking garage, walked the streets with his gun in tow. James went in and out of buildings, "I must find Maria and even the score. Its vengeance, but to regain my pride, and honor the memory of my wife," he confirmed.

James headed to where Maria had worked, "This is where we met. I may get lucky and find her here." James lurked through the window with the hopes of seeing a glimpse of her, "She's not around." James was not surprised, "Why would she come back to waitress, when she has stolen all my money?"

He decided to walk around the area in the vain with the hopes of bumping into her. She was not at the gym, salon, the spa, and didn't live at the condo where he last met her. "It's a hopeless venture. I will assemble enough courage and walk back to the restaurant. I can do this, someone there knows her, and where she is," he persuaded himself.

James opened the door of the restaurant took four slow steps and stopped. His courage in question when he went backwards to exit, mimicking the steps he took to go in, "They may call the cops if I enter. Perhaps, she lied about me to people there. What to do? I am cold, lonely and my life is over, I'm being left with nothing," he rapidly spoke aloud.

James proceeded through the entrance of the restaurant with a slow pace caution. His steps were slower, and his body staggered as he walked. He held a blank stare in his glassy eyes. His head dangled down, his feet dragged and shuffled from side to side with each step he took. He acted more like a shy little school boy, rather than a man of his age.

As he walked, he lifted his head up then forced himself to look to the ground. His eyes peeked up and down while he walked. He unbuttoned his coat, slipped one arm out, then suddenly slammed his arm back in. He predicted, "By me sitting down, they may call the cops."

"My mind is clear," he said with a sigh. "I'm normal. This is a good sign. I'm okay. I'll embrace the warmth of my coat and keep it on," he agreed with himself. He took both hands as he overlapped each side of his coat in front of him and continued to walk. A huge sigh of relief came, "It took all the backbone I could master," he was pleased, "I'm able to sit," he said as he did.

He spoke everything aloud without realizing it. A table with senior patrons gawked and whispered amongst each other. The look on their faces seemed as though they felt liberated when the server spoke to him. They remained seated with their bodies turned as they tried to listen.

He looked foul in his heavy dirty gray coat. His hair was a long thin mixture of gray and white and sloppy. It had the look of not having being shaped for some time. His bangs hung in front of his face, and straggled below his nose. You couldn't tell if it was a comb over, or his bangs.

The back of his head displayed a greasy part, with black hair mixed in with the hue, and mushed together. His gray and white beard indicated he hadn't shaved for a few days. He stood close to six feet, and look to weigh over 220 pounds. He looked angry at the world and ready to pounce on anyone. People, who looked at him, got out of his way.

The server was a few tables away from the door setting the table with silverware, and menus when he passed by her. She heard him talking and turned around to see no one was with him. She followed behind. He sat down with his coat on. Yet the temperature of the room was warm. All the other patrons hung theirs on the hooks at the table.

In a worried voice she asked, "Sir, are you okay? Is there anything I can do for you? Would you like me to hang up your coat?"

James felt protected, "I'm fine. I want it on. I'd like a coffee and a glass of water, please." "I'll be right back with it, sir," she answered, then left.

The other customers turned their heads back and continued as though nothing happened.

James fumbled in his pocket for his medication. As he went to close the lid to the bottle it took a tumble to the floor, along with his medication. The server arrived back to the table with his order, placed the water closest to him, and placed the coffee off to the side, when she noticed a pill on the table. Her nose twitched up with the smell of alcohol that emanated from him."

From his seated position, he attempted to bend down in an effort to pick up the bottle, and the pills scattered within his reach.

The server endeavored to pick up medication scattered through the restaurant she could see. When she placed the pills back into the bottle, she realized what they were and thought he was in a moment of despair, "What is the medication for if you don't mind me asking?" "Sometimes I get quivers. " James replied to the odd query. After a long pause, James continued, "But they seem to be getting worse."

She looked down at a few of the pills she still had in her hand. "Sir, do you take several types of medication?" James body went stiff, "What... no, not at all. Just the one," James assured her.

The server leaned into him, "My name is Brandy. Sir, I know this is none of my business, but you seem agitated, and uncoordinated. I can smell booze on you. Not to mention several types of pills came out of your bottle. Not just one type. See... look... in my hand. I picked them up from the floor, after you spilled them."

"What are talking about?" smirked James. "Perhaps, your Doctor can help you. I'm not a doctor, almost finished my nursing course," she mentioned in pride.

"I came for a coffee?" James stated with a sense of bewilderment. "Sir, do you place your daily dosage of medication into the one bottle?" Brandy probed. James formed an emotionless look on his face, "Give me my pills, and mind your own business. No...god damn it, I don't. That is a noisy question to ask a customer when accidents happen. I just dropped my bottle, and what's with the calling me sir, is this a new thing for young people today?" angrily stated James.

She still had the bottle in her hand, looked at the name, and asked, "Is your name James?" "Yes it is. I see you can see read," James shot back sarcastically.

"James, you have several different types of medication inside this one bottle and they don't do that at the pharmacy," she whispered in a cocky tone, shaking her head in his face. "Well…. Why don't you explain to me how the hell it happened then, missy know it all," questioned James.

Brandy figured he was being coy with her, "I don't know sir, or should I say James, but the label on the bottle has the name Plineaplim. You do know this medication is a mental health care drug," she informed him. "Do you have other medication you?" she questioned.

"Miss, you must be mistaken. I don't have a mental health care issue," as James dug into his pocket and brought out another bottle of pills. Brandy was confused, "Sir, I asked you a moment ago if, you were on more medication, and you stated no. You've been drinking, and I'm sure you know it's a time to be cautious when drinking alcohol and taking any form of medication," she warned him.

James desired to protect his credibility, "For your information, I had a couple of beers a few hours ago and the medication is the same in both bottles," firmly stated James.

Brandy held the bottle in her hand, "The name is Plineaplim with the name Exapd included. She opened the bottle, emptied a few of the pills into her hand noticing the pills were different sizes.

She showed James the pills side by side. "See, sir, I mean James, they're different. And this bottle has two names on it. So it's not the same medication inside the bottles. People do place daily doses into one bottle or container for the day or week. There is a mixture of different pills in both these bottles. Not just two types of pills, but they are all the same color. I wondered if you could tell the difference? I'm sure if you didn't drink alcohol, and take pills together, you may have come to realize this," she expressed with one hand on her hip.

James went to edge himself off his seat, "How can you speak to me like this? I ordered coffee and water. You're not a doctor, so you shouldn't' be interfering in other's personal medical issues. The water is for my pill. I am not impressed with your accusations towards me either. I am a customer. You smell a beer odor, and it sounds like you have accused me of being a drunk and a pill popper. There are other patrons in this establishment. First, I will inform the owners and secondly young lady, what you've said is slanderous. What is it these days with people? They just say or do shit without consideration for other people or even the law. None of you would be as equipped to handle the same badgering you inflict on others. Yet, while people like you are running your mouths off, we're to sit back and take it?" James expressed, feeling more violated.

"Sir, I just want to see how well you could answer my questions. You may not have realized, but you did act odd when you came in." James felt confused, his face tensed, "What do you mean, I acted odd? And what are you now a cop, trying to see how well I can answer questions," he questioned unable to sit still. His eyes focused forwards and went down, when he recalled the bank manager stating his behavior was odd when he left the bank.

Brandy eased closer to James, "You were talking to yourself out-loud, where everyone could hear you. Don't you think it's odd? It could be the pills and alcohol and if mixed together. You may not realize what you're saying or doing." Brandy confirmed to him. "I didn't mix them together myself," answered James as he was becoming increasingly over heated and felt light headed. His body leaned to the outside of the bench, and his eyes rolled back. Brandy pushed him back behind the table.

Brandy was bold and yet firm, "Should I call the police?" "What do you mean call the police?" James answered with his head down as he flashed back the bank and the police. His emotional state was becoming more unstable, "Get away from me miss. Leave me alone please," he begged.

"You almost fell to the floor. Perhaps the police can help you sort out what occurred with the pills. You did tell me that you did not mix them together yourself. Don't you want to find out who did, or how it happened?" Brandy edged James on.

James was instilled in mental confusion," I don't know what you're saying," he moved his hair out of his face, "I have to see this for myself." His arm quivered as he lifted it up to fumble around in his jacket pocket.

Brandy waited patiently as he pulled out a case. He snapped it open, removed his glasses, and placed the case on the table. Brandy could see his body jiggled and sweat poured down his face. She felt a sense of urgency as she raised her free hand to her head, "Sir, I have other people to attend to." "Just give me a minute miss," he answered while he placed the glasses on his eyes.

"I'm concerned if you take these pills together. Have you taken the pills together?" Brandy asked with concern. "Yes.... I have that's why I got my glasses out to see what's got you all riled up," he answered.

"You can go to the hospital to find out what's going on. I can call you an ambulance. You were not walking straight when you entered and that doesn't happen with just one or two beers sir. It might be serious," Brandy said in an attempt to get him to leave and seek some medical attention.

James pulled her hand closer to look at the pills in with his glasses on. "See sir... go to the hospital. They're causing you the confusion. You can't walk straight. You almost fell off the bench. You have the shakes, and you're pouring sweat now too," she thought to mention.

"I can see they are different sizes, I hadn't noticed this before. They are all white. I thought they were the same. I'll see my doctor. I've been here before but I don't recall meeting you before. I do recall another woman, Maria. Do you know her?" he inquired to change the topic.

Her attitude changed when he said her name and her mouth dropped open, "Ah...Oh... Maria.... Umm.... yes, I met her one day. That was about a month ago. I haven't seen her since. Are you a friend of hers?" she thought to ask.

James hesitated to respond, took his glasses off, "Yes, sort of... I guess... I met her then. Wish I didn't."

He lifted his lone pill to his mouth, and paused to take it. "I'm putting the pills away until I speak with my doctor. I'd like to look at the menu and order something to eat. I haven't eaten all day that might be causing me some of the issues you expressed concern with," he acknowledged.

Brandy reached her hand out to him, "I can see your hands shake, so I closed the lids for you." He took the pills and placed them into his coat pocket.

"Let me know when you're ready to order," she said. "I'm ready to order now," he answered as he eyed the first page of the menu, "I'll have this," pointing with his right hand at a picture.

He ordered a ham sandwich and enjoyed each bite. Food was his savior for the time being.

The time had flown by and it was a twenty-four hour restaurant with the time now six in the morning. James had his head buried in his arms at the table as Brandy gave a little nudge on his shoulder, "Sir, you fell asleep and I didn't have the heart to wake you. I thought you'd enjoy a fresh coffee before I leave for the day?" He wiped his eyes, moved his hair around, as he expressed, "I'd love one. How long was asleep?" he questioned. "Around six or seven hours, but it's nothing to worry about. You did look cozy tucked away in this little booth. You must have needed the rest," she noted.

"Oh my," James exclaimed in embarrassment. "I'm so sorry. I had no idea, I fell asleep," he apologized.

Brandy did not want to upset him, and caressed his arm as she said, "Don't be sorry. There were no other customers here most of the night," she told him to make him feel less ashamed. "You work alone at night?" he asked.

Brandy smiled, "You sound better now, and yes, I

work alone at night. During the day, we have a cook, and extra servers, but I'm not so lucky on the night shift. I serve, do the cash, and prepare the sandwiches. We do not sell alcohol thank god, but, I'm sure... if we did, we'd have more business. It's a long night when there's no business," she shared with a friendly tone and smile.

"I have been here for lunch, and never realized it was open all night," James said.

James finished his coffee, "Thanks again Miss. I appreciate your kindness," he said as he was making his way to the cash.

As she was ringing his bill into the cash registered she slipped in, "Sir don't forget about your pills." "I won't and thank you Brandy, and call me James please." James reached into his pocket for some money to pay the bill and pulled out a twenty dollar bill, "Is this enough?"

She looked pleased, "Yes, sir, I mean James, it is. The coffee is bottomless. You pay only for the first cup." "Keep the change and thank you," said James as he left the restaurant with a much-needed rest, but he still did not know where Maria was.

Two

When Brandy arrived home she could not help but think of James and wanted to tell someone, but no one was there to tell, "Alone again," she chattered.

Brandy endures the long twelve-hour shifts with little pay, "its temporary," she'd tell herself while believing it would prepare her for shift work as a nurse, when she finished school.

Brandy loved people more than money and wanted a job, which helped others. Nursing was a great fit for her. Her job at the restaurant allowed her to meet and talk to people. It was something she loved.

Brandy was not a beautiful woman, but was far from unattractive. She was cute, in a plain looking way. Once she started University, she refused to fix herself up. Her long blondish- brown hair she pulls up in a ponytail on most days. Her wardrobe consists of dark slacks, and jeans. Even her tops are dark colors of blue, brown, and black. She cringed in stores when she looked at anything light in color of late. She used to love, white, peach, and even yellow. Not anymore, even her sweats are dark.

Her bright greenish blue eyes always look focused and clear. She holds an aura of nativity, and innocence's to her. She was getting a little thin lately she noticed. Even her sweats started feeling looser and looser, after every wash, to her it felt like. She was far from overweight, and could not afford any weight loss. It started to bother her at first when she noticed and soon she forgot. She was too busy with school, work, and now a new man.

Her parents are firm Catholic's when it comes to their beliefs with love, marriage, then sex, with children to follow. She still attends Church when she can. She was not into tattoos, piercing, or skimpy clothing. She had no statement to make with her body— she covered herself from head to toe in clothing, and layers of them, at times. She was not hiding behind them as people thought to ask.

Brandy did not know how to react a few days after meeting her new boyfriend when he questioned, "Why she wore dark colors and lots of them." She felt annoyed when he did. It was taking everything she had to keep a promise, she made, "What does the color of my clothes have to do with anything, or how many I wear," she snapped, and refused to comment further.

As she was digging through her drawers for a change of clothes for after her bath, she was thinking about her man's question. She knew why she had dark clothes. She was married to them until she finished her course. It was part of her motivation to do so.

Every day when she put on her dark clothes, it reminded her of her goals. Her reward would come when she finished school. She was going to travel for no less than four months, before she started her new career.

She loved to travel with summertime being her favorite season. The first drop of snow and her walking through it, her mind rushed to find a way out of it. Her packing started immediately. First, her shorts, skimpy tops, along with no less than three bikinis, and off she went to the airport to fly somewhere warm. She had a temptation when it came to balancing hot or cold weather and, warm always won. It became a tradition she made for herself. Before she started her nursing course, she would leave on a whim. It started with a quick trip to the travel agency, where she booked the quickest flight, to a warm climate, and stayed for months.

She knew she had this hate for winter, and off she'd go, despite any commitments she had at the time. Her body-craved travel, sunshine and it was a form of freedom she loved. The more she traveled the more brazen she was. She attended local churches wherever she traveled and met many new people. They usually knew where to get work and she held some amazing jobs, wherever she went. This permitted her to stay longer.

She believed dark and warm clothing would keep her grounded through the winter months. She had not spent a full winter at home in six years, before starting school. If it were still cold and snowing when she arrived home from her travels, she would lock herself in the comfort of her parents' home. She read job postings online, pretending to look for work. She had no desire to leave the comfort of the warmth. She never did until the snow melted, for the last time. She did not have a choice anymore. She was in her final stages of her educational career choice and with this came commitment. She had to stay home in the winter.

There was no way she was going to open up a drawer, in her apartment and find any summer clothes you'd wear on a vacation. She could not just pack a bag and go she would have to shop for some. There were days she tried. She had to ruffle through sweaters, winter coats, and boots to locate a small departmental area of summer clothes, in the stores she went.

It was all about winter. It was that time of year. While she browsed around looking for summer clothing, it gave her time to think, and reminded her of why she did not have any. She left her parent's home when she started school. Her clothes were there, along with her suitcases. She made a promise to her brother and knew it was a promise, hard to keep.

Brandy closed the drawer, "Where is my man?" She had a hot sexy man she loved thinking of as her forbidden lover. She felt a wonder of adornment towards him. She could not believe it when he said, "He found her interesting and was attracted to her at first glance."

For Brandy, he was handsome, healthy looking, tall, and treated her well. He seemed interested and attracted to her. It did not feel forced or fake. She had not been seeing him long, but Brandy was hoping it would blossom into a full-blown, long-lasting relationship, with marriage, kids, and a home together. She knew she would be the best mother ever, and was embraced with a form of happiness, and got giddy just talking about it with her friends.

She moved along with him quick. Everything was out of the ordinary with her from the moment they met. She didn't think of it as anything irrational, or impulsive. She rationalized, "How else am I supposed to find and seek love, if I let a moment of spontaneity slip between my fingers? I'd never known, what could have been, if I didn't go with the flow and give it a try," she justified with friends.

She hadn't introduced him to her parents, or her brother. He just did not come up in conversations. Meeting James made her think of Maria. "Why did he ask about her, of all people?" 'I wish I never did,' rang repeatedly inside Brandy's mind, "I'm kicking myself inside for not inquiring more at the time, as to why he felt the way he did," she expressed aloud.

Brandy was not a fan of Maria. She found her ignorant, when she laughed at her for continuing to work there. The only day Brandy met her, and she made her feel less than a woman.

She met John Paul in the middle of the night. She was sitting off in the corner studying, and had forgotten to lock the door to the restaurant, which she always does, when it was empty inside. She would wait to open the door when she felt it was a customer she wanted to let in. She would hook a note on the front door, back in five minutes. Then locked the door, sit down to study, and when she needed a break to clear her eyes and mind, she would clean.

When he pulled open the door and wandered in she heard the chimes at the door and looked up. "Hello, hello, is anyone here? Can I get a coffee? Are you still open?" Brandy jumped up from a booth in the back.

He wasn't bad to look she noticed as she walked towards him. Her eyes pinpointed parts of him, as she looked, and looked away. He was well dressed in a suit, and seemed to be polite. "Yes, we're open. What can I get for you?" "A coffee, an egg salad sandwich, and I'll take some chili," he ordered.

It took a moment, for Brandy to prepare his meal. When she finished, she sat close to the door. Just in case she had the urge to run out or call the cops, if he tried anything.

While she sat there, she wrote on paper, 'I detest this shift, and how it makes me feel worried, much more in the darkness of the night, as one man sits steps away from me. I will seek pleasure in my life, when this job is no longer part of my daily life. If the owners knew, I only let uniforms inside, during the dreary hours, past midnight.'

This man ate, paid, and left. It was around three thirty in the morning before, he did. While he was there, he was reading material he had removed from his briefcase. Brandy was too far from him to see what it was, he was reading.

The next night Brandy had remembered to lock the door and he was knocking on it. The open 24 hour sign was always on outside. The dark shades made it difficult to see inside the windows at night, unless you got up close enough to peek in between them. She could see out better than people could see inside. She walked over to the door opened it up, "Sorry was in the bathroom. Are you eating in or is it takeout?" she asked. "I'm eating in?" he answered, as she took the back in five-minute sign down.

He spoke to Brandy as she prepared is meal, "You work here at night alone? It's scary isn't it?" "Yes, it is. I lock the doors and, look out to see if it is a person I want to let in. It just happened last night when you entered a patron left late, I didn't think to check the door. After ten most customers that come in are only here to use the bathroom and order a coffee, because they feel bad, I think. I learnt past midnight, it's the odd cop or city workers. Rarely do they order food and if they do it's takeout. This shift will be cut down or out soon. It's been weeks waiting for the boss to make his mind up. It should be any day now."

John Paul came in the next night. After he ate he walked up to her and asked to sit with her, and she agreed. They talked until her shift was over.

She shared personal information with him about her family and school, "I'm surprised to hear you have a rich brother, who lets you work here alone," he commented. She assured him, "We aren't close. He lives his life and is busy." She showed him pictures of her family on her cell. John Paul and she took pictures together on their cells.

She complained, "The woman in this picture is Maria. She laughed at me for working here when she was too proud to be a server herself. By the end of next month, I've finished my nursing course and I'm sooo, sooo.... looking forward to my new career," she shared with a bright smile and a sparkle in her green eyes.

John Paul was always dressed in suits, which she thought was odd past midnight and wanted to know what work he did. When she asked John Paul laughed, "When it's Business, its Business, nothing but strain, stress and headaches and suits come with the job."

She attempted to unwind after her emotional night, "I'm yearning for a warm embrace. I feel unsettled," she muttered and brushed it off, "It's just James."

When Brandy came home from work the last couple of mornings, she found her man in her bed. She handed him a key a week ago Saturday, and said, "Feel free to come and go as you like," she was hoping he would take it. He had not known her long and had to question her intentions, "Are you sure, just come and go? I'm not moving in with you, I have my own place," he shared. "Come and go, as you like. This will give us more time to get to know each other," she expressed calmly her purpose. He took it.

She was exhilarated when she'd come home from work open up her bedroom door, and gapped inside. She caught a glimpse of him naked in the bed. She'd run her bath, put on her tea and quietly go back in her room to look for clothes for after her bath while trying not to wake him.

She presumed he had some early appointments and left early. She dropped her tea bags inside her coffee percolator went into the bathroom, turned on the water for her bath.

"My life is so boring and too routine," she uttered. This was her morning ritual and all Brandy did for now. It wasn't an exciting life since school began.

"At least I had some sexual excitement to break up the monotony of my routine, but it's vanished, since he took the key," she said when she came to realize it.

Brandy heard a key fumble to open the door. It was her man. It must be him. She briskly walked to the door, peeked into the peephole, it was him. The excitement ran down her body as she moved in happiness, she stumbled to unlock the door. She had to jump out of the way, when he got the door unlocked and opened it first.

Brandy believed she was falling in love for the first time in her life. "Hi sweetheart," she exclaimed as her man entered the door. As soon as the door closed, her lips locked onto his, which prevented him from speaking. She held his neck with the palm of her right hand, which trapped him between her and the door. He attempted to ease his body out of her path, but the force she had on him held him there. It wasn't until she let go and said, "I missed you John Paul," was he able to move.

"What are you doing? I'm not in the mood. I have to get something," he expressed. Brandy stood in his path. He attempted to move around her and she moved where he went. Frustrated, he said, "Move, please," the tone of his voice went to a high pitch screech.

Her body stumbled with it, "What's wrong?" she questioned. "I already told you why I'm here. Why are you blocking my way?" he asked abruptly.

She hesitated to move. Her nostrils flared open while lines formed around her eyes and her cheek muscles tangled together, "I've never seen you like this before. You've been calm and communicative since we've been dating. Your voice just raised and you seem upset for no reason at all. If you have issues with work or your family, you cannot take it out on me," she specified.

"Brandy.... You can't be serious, date, when did we date? We met, talked and drank. Oh, yes.... Let's us not forget we had sex,.....what sex...oh....let's think here, a whole two times. Then you tossed a key in my face. Why did you bother? We haven't spoken in days, as he peered in her bedroom holding the frame of the door.

Brandy followed him around. "A couple of days I pass out here. Then you wanted me to have a key for what purpose? Is it convenience for you?" he said in a whisper as he grazed her shoulder going by. She lost her balance. He glimpsed in the bathroom, walked to the kitchen, "Oh, I see you made some tea," when he noticed no one else was there, he let out a heavy gasp.

John Paul was at her apartment earlier. As he slept, the sound of a key entered her lock. He heard a man cough and reached for his clothes that he had placed on top of her brown silk laundry basket. It was about four feet from her bed. He couldn't reach them by the time he heard the door close and glanced at the alarm clock. It was just after four in the morning, another cough this time closer to her room. He knew she didn't want her family to know about them.

The room was dark when he rolled off the bed and scrambled into her closet. The door was on his side of the bed and open. He eased the door partial closed behind him. The man opened up her bedroom door, turned on the light then left the bedroom. John Paul heard the fridge close soon after he did. However, he didn't hear Brandy's voice.

He sat on the floor in one position, holding her clothes in front of his face and body. At first, he thought it was her brother. He realized it wasn't when the man came back into the room and rummaged through her drawers and the stuff on her dresser.

He couldn't understand why she didn't tell him about another man. The man stayed for about forty-five minutes and left. But for John Paul, it was a long forty-five minutes crunched inside her small closet.

When the man left, John Paul was disappointed that Brandy didn't tell him her ex still had her key. He made himself a tea and waited about an hour before he left and went home. In his confusion, he had forgotten his briefcase. Once at home, he couldn't sleep. He figured he'd sneak by, and catch them together when her shift was over.

He gave himself heck, for not confronting the man at the time, and felt like a coward for hiding when he realized it wasn't her brother, but feared what the man might do, and wasn't going to jump out nude to find out.

Brandy was at a loss for words as she watched John Paul pour himself a cup of tea and didn't bother to ask if she wanted one. When he was done, he walked himself into her bedroom, fluffed her pillow and rested his upper body against it. Brandy watched from the door. He took a long drink of his tea, and as he pulled it away from his lips he asked, "What is it now Brandy?" He stated in haste. She walked up to him, gave him a kiss on his forehead, ran her hands through his hair, "Enjoy your tea, we can talk after my bath," and walked herself towards the door to exit.

His mouth opened, words didn't form a sentence as he struggled with what he wanted to say, "Bran… huh…. Brandy, can I talk to you, it's important?" She turned around, as soon as he said Bran, "Not right now, we can talk after my bath and cuddle. I'd enjoy it," she told him.

He heard the bathroom door close. A few minutes later, he heard it open up again. He heard the drawer close in the kitchen and the movement of a spoon in a cup. He drank his tea as he walked into the kitchen.

Wrapped in a towel she poured a cup of tea to take into the bath. He stood beside her, and refilled his. He reached for the milk, and slightly touched her bum as she walked away. The towel wasn't long enough to cover it. She ignored him.

Brandy went into the bathroom, slipped herself into the tub, and ran more water. She started to complain to herself, "He raised his voice, pushed me, and seemed to be checking out the place. I need some rest. I'm exhausted." and with that she closed her eyes and tried to relax her worried mind.

Back to the bedroom John Paul tried to work on some paperwork, and grumbled, "What is her problem?" He tossed his paperwork back into his briefcase. "Women are a headache." His mind raced with anger and pure disappointment. "She could have just told me something about this dude," he mumbled.

"We can't talk now," John Paul said loud enough in hopes Brandy could hear him.

John Paul walked into the bathroom, Brandy looked at him dumbfounded, "What are you doing in here? Go," she indicated. "Here—it's this you want?" he went to take off his shirt, "Go, it's too small in here for two to bathe," she expressed shyly.

He bent to his knees on the floor, brushed her hair off her face, and eased his fingertips up her legs, as his lips embraced hers. She held his head in her hands as they kissed. He eased his hand along Brandy's inner thigh to ease her into the mood.

She jerked herself back, and pulled away from kissing him. "Enjoy this, relax," he assured her. "This is what you want," he whispered in her ear, and went to kiss her again. She turned her face away, which left him speechless. She pulled at his hand to remove it from her inner thigh. His strength was too powerful. She yelled, "Get away from there." She got herself up in the tub to a standing position. His hand slipped away, "What are you doing?" she gulped.

He was not in the mood to decipher her irrational behavior, "What are you doing? I thought you wanted sex?" His broken voice said. He was cut off from speaking. "Just leave. Get out of here right now," she ordered pointing her hand towards the door.

"We met a couple of weeks ago and you asked me to take a key. I have to ask, do you always do this with men? Do you have sex only when you drink? We haven't had any without it. You told me not to come by your work, and to stay here and rest. Is this like a roommate thing we have going on? What is it really to you? Why did you bother to give me a key?" he questioned in confusion while waving his hands around.

Brandy had returned herself to a seated position. "What is it that you want? Please leave me to bathe in private," Brandy begged. He surged his lips onto hers and pulled her naked body up by her underarms. They kissed for a few moments, she didn't detest.

He stopped and went to remove his shirt again. She yelled, "Stop, stop... please, don't." He stopped. "You don't want to make love. Why did you grab my neck, and kiss me at the door? Then you walked out to the kitchen almost naked? I thought you were hinting you wanted sex and didn't come straight out and say it," ran out his mouth as he stood there feeling rejected. He went to walk out and stopped himself.

Brandy quickly responded, "No…. No…that's not it. Not right now. Have a little respect. You cannot walk into my private space like this," she told him.

John Paul's face pulled together as an anger emerged in him, "It must be nice to have a man run through your apartment any hour of the night, who is he?" he asked.

Brandy was confused. "Why are you talking about yourself like this?" she questioned in confusion and exhaustion.

"Come on Brandy just tell me. It's okay. I will forgive you. It's better to talk about things now," he said as kissed her on her cheek.

"Get out of here," she ordered. He walked out of the bathroom and left the door open, "I guess you just can't make up your mind if you want sex or you just don't know what man you want sex with?" he complained as he walked. Brandy yelled, "You're a drunk. Just get out of here," she yelled in disgust.

He rushed back into the bathroom, "Are you telling me to leave. I never touched you inappropriate. Here is how you kissed me at door. She was standing. He stepped into the bath, grabbed her by the neck, and pressed her up against the wall of the shower, "You want a kiss? How does this feel? I thought you wanted sex. I did the same thing to you did. How does it feel?" Brandy was beside herself, "I didn't think of sex. I was happy to see you, that's all," she expressed nervously.

"If you knew what I was feeling inside when you did what you did, you'd understand me, and have cared about me. I came in here and kissed you, and tried to relax you. For what it's worth, I wanted to make love with you. It didn't matter where, but to at least get you started. Does it take you to drink to have sex with me Brandy? Think about it, that's the only time we have had sex. You are not into the same morals as you say your parents are with the concept saving yourself until marriage. Now look, my slacks are all wet," he expressed as he pulled at his wet slacks.

"Stop it. The only thing coming out of your mouth is sex, sex, sex. Just leave me alone," she fumed as she grabbed a towel and wrapped it around herself. "I cannot bathe in peace," she expressed in hurt.

"Stop complaining. When you kissed me was it just a chokehold for a kiss? Who does that? You're acting like some fidget chick. I can't make sense out of you. We had sex twice, and you pulled out a key. We never spoke about it before hand. You never talk unless you're drinking. You don't say good morning when you get home. I'm awake, you know. This happens when people sleep at strange places. We wake up with every little sound until we get comfortable. The sound of keys going in a door in the middle of the night really sends us into a state of confusion," he vented.

Brandy screamed, "You have the nerve to say that I only have sex when I'm drinking, when you're the one who provided it, and drank with me. It wasn't me buying coolers or vodka, it was you. Perhaps you have sex with so many women you can't keep us straight," she fumed out in her confusion as she attempted to make sense out of him.

"Perhaps, you should direct that question to

yourself when you are the one who handed me a key and neglected to tell me who else may have one. You could have mentioned look out at night— I have my old lover, coming in when he feels like it. You think I didn't need to know this. I'm not drinking now, but I see now, you cannot make love to me without it," he divulged as he walked back out of the bathroom.

Brandy placed herself back into the tub and proceeded to wash her face. She stopped washing and yelled, "You handled me aggressively. Leave, just leave."

John Paul flew back into the bathroom, "Ask Maria, I'm sure she'd have no issues making love with me, and can pleasure me in ways, you never have. Might I add, she is a beautiful woman," he said then walked out of the bathroom.

Brandy was in disarray, "Maria, eh….that's what this is all about. If that's what she loves, you two…..can do it together. If you don't get out now, I'm calling the cops, and leave my key asshole," she stood back up grabbed her towel, and placed it around her, "I'm totally exhausted," she said exasperated.

John Paul stormed back into the bathroom, and screamed at the top of his lungs, "You have a big mouth in here. Try calling the cops from this." He slammed her cordless telephone. It smashed into pieces, "You're being selfish… You wanted sex when you kissed me at the door and kissed me back in here. By the way, I left when you got home to give you back your privacy, because all you did was walked in and out of the room the mornings I was here. I was awake and figured you wanted me to leave. It took me a while to realize this. It wasn't even a relationship to you. Now I know, you never cared about me at all."

Brandy hollered, "What does that have to do with anything? You smashed my phone over a few words and a kiss. You're just one of those assholes that drinks, fucks and abuses women when you don't get your way. And those assholes go off topic and never talk straight or deal with fuck all, just like you."

He walked back into the bathroom, "Is this so? Now you're labelling me. This nursing course has really gone to your fucking head, so much so, now you're psychoanalyzing me. First, I'm not communicating, but I used to. Now, I'm in your way. Of course we cannot miss, I'm a topic switcher. Let's add a drinker and an abuser. Thanks for the love." He lifted up the toilet seat to take a pee. "Get out of here you annoying bag of shit. I don't want to see you going to the bathroom. So you can get yourself off," she said enraged while covering her eyes.

"What did you say? You've never had a boyfriend this is normal shit. Everyone goes to the bathroom. What I have seen you naked and you've seen me, but I cannot piss or shit, around you. You cannot touch my manhood, or go down on me. I bet I cannot brush my teeth in front of you either. By the way, if I were in the mood, as it was earlier in the kitchen. You would have seen it firm and long, but you sent it into hiding. I would have jumped inside a shell with everything you said," he said with a smile to lighten the mood.

"You're an abuser, smashing my telephone, just get out of here," she whimpered. John Paul bent down to pick up the pieces of her cordless phone he smashed. "I'm sorry Brandy. I don't know what came over me. I was horny, and I'm confused but this is no excuse. I can't make sense of you," he attempted to apologize. She shouted, pointing her hand towards the door, "You're abusive, get out of here. Leave right fucking now."

John Paul stopped picking up parts of the phone. He was disappointed with himself, "I'm not an abuser. You've never touched me, and I have you. By the way, why don't you dress up and act like a lady who has more to offer than a job? While you're at it, leave the good girl shit alone when it comes to sex and maybe you'll learn something. I care for you deeply. I truly do. If you took the time to talk, you would have learnt this. I'm a nice guy. I'm honest, and I love openly. You cannot say that about yourself. You haven't even told me about the man who wonders your apartment day or night," he ended up bellowing out...

Brandy stood silent while he got out all his aggression out. "Sorry, if I upset you. I didn't mean to hurt you. Perhaps it doesn't feel right now but I did ask you to talk. You could have considered I do have to go to work. Five minutes is all it would have taken, but you couldn't even give me the time of day. Communicating and making love, has never been so complicated for me. I cannot make sense out of you at all," he attested.

It was too much for Brandy, "I had sex with two men in my life. This is all new and I had no expectations when I gave you the key, but respect is to be there. This is something you don't have, "Just leave, and leave my key," she demanded emotionless, and firm.

John Paul left the bathroom, went into the bedroom. Brandy heard him say, "I'm getting the fuck out of here." She heard the wheeling of a suitcase, which sounded like it rolled towards the door. She didn't know his briefcase had wheels. He slammed the door close. As soon as he did she ran out of the bathroom, looked around to make sure he did leave, and locked the door.

He still had her key, she believed. She had to get her locks changed. She took her cell out of her purse. While she sat on her couch in a towel, she searched the internet for a locksmith to come right away.

Tears graced her cheeks. She fumbled to get dressed, "I thought he was the love of my life," as she wiped and sobbed. She noticed a fifty-dollar bill on her nightstand under the pieces of her broken phone. It made her cry more. She hadn't noticed her key was in the mix.

She was slow to get dressed and when she did, she poured herself a tea, "I wasn't alone when he was here with me and now again, I'm alone," she said aloud.

She waited over an hour until the locksmith. He installed an extra dead bolt and rekeyed the locks. As he was about to leave, "Please, don't give the keys to anyone a man or a woman," she requested. "I'm not the only locksmith in town. I don't know other companies' policies, but my office won't. I do know you have to have permission from the building to change the locks, but since you said, you felt for your safety, I changed them for you. Make sure you give them a key. They'll have issues, if they cannot enter," he explained to her.

She waited about an hour and a half, after the locksmith left, and left. At first, she waited for an elevator and then changed her mind, and ran down the stairs to exit. The stairs took her out to main floor lobby. She looked onto the street to see if John Paul was around and noticed he wasn't.

Three

James was disturbed by the pills, "My doctor must have given me medication, and I forgot?" He sat with his head tilted, his face in the palm of his right hand, outside a pub, at a patio table while he drank his beer.

Then it came to him, "Maria, she was the only one in my home since Tanya passed. She drugged me— to steal from me. She's done a great job," he grumbled.

"Married at twenty, James was with his wife Tanya until the day she passed of cancer. His wife and he were always hard pressed for time in a day. We had our kids in sports and dance classes as youngsters. We both had careers. Together with our kids we picked out Colleges."

The waiter interrupted, "Would you like another beer?" the male server asked. He seen James cell phone propped up on the table and listened while he spoke into it. He thought to ask, "Are you someone important or famous or something?"

"I'm fine, I don't need another. I'm just making a memoir," he answered.

James forgot where he left off, and had to rewind to find his spot and started recording again.

"When our kids were done with school they found careers and life mates. Today, they have children of their own. Life was wonderful to experience in this way before it ended for Tanya. We didn't have to deal with trash, until I brought trash into my life and home," he confirmed.

He took a drink and started again, "I wanted to ensure my thoughts were recorded, in case something else occurs before I find Maria. She took three hundred thousand from me, and now sold my home and I don't know how any of this occurred. I've been out of the loop and not with the times and was new at being single when we met. I didn't think people were so low life. I didn't protect me. It was my fault. I've lost everything. All I have now is my life," he stated in his recording.

James went into the local city library and found a secluded computer near the back. He was now, suspicious wherever he went. He looked over his shoulder with any loud voice or sound. He popped his head inside parked vehicles to see who was inside. Slow moving vehicles that went by him, he gawked at.

James wanted to make sure he was safe, "No need to attract unwanted attention," he told himself. He took his glasses out from his case, when he sat in front of the computer.

James was never much for computers. He was over forty years old before he even turned a computer on. He knew enough on the computer to use the search engine, and opened up the browser. Once it was on the screen, he typed with his right index finger, reading the word -E-X-A-P-D he got from the prescription bottle. James hit enter on the computer.

Many sites displayed in a list. He took his mouse clicked the top one. He pressed the back arrow, going back to the list. He looked for one with non-technical language in an explanation he could understand. James read with horror the results: "Exapd is for, treatment of, acute manic episodes and a maintenance treatment in bipolar disorder."

James hurried to type the letters to the second drug name, P-i-n-e-a-p-l-i-m

The web search provided no hits. In his nervousness, James typed the wrong letters. His heart was beginning to race. His breathing became heavier as sweat streamed down his face. He re-typed the letters. This time he got the correct spelling.

Plineaplim is an anti-psychotic medicine. "Oh My God! Why am I on anti-psychotic medication?" James shouted but caught himself and looked around to see, if anyone had noticed him screech. An aged woman threw him a sour facial expression. A few teenagers snickered. James scanned the rest of the contents to find out some of the side effects. "Drowsiness… weakness… tremors… dizziness, and confusion."

James reread, Tremors was a side effect. "I told Brandy I had some tremors. Yet, at no time did my doctor mention any bipolar disorders to me. Or had he?" as he covered his mouth, "Am I crazy?" he slurred.

James held each one of the pills in his hand as he spoke to himself, "I don't know what these are. I can't research them." He left the library, and walked up the main street. "I have to do something," he surmised.

He called his lawyer and it went to voice mail. He left a message, "Its James Johnston. I'm leaving a message, if anything happens to me, get my cell phone and see my video. I met this woman named Maria. She intentionally gave me, anti-psychotic medication in an effort to end my life. She's a damn bitch. She somehow sold my house and stole my money," he screamed and hung up. James knew he was in earshot of several by passers and did not care.

James walked around the downtown core of the city. He was confused, baffled, and furious. He let himself walk into people, as he pushed them aside. He walked across the street on red lights, and J walked standing in the center lane with traffic bypassing him in both directions.

James had walked himself to his physician's office. "My God!" he grumbled. "A visit to Doctor Flannery is a good omen."

He walked into the building, approached the office door, and took a few deep breathes in. The security guard saw him wallowing in nervousness. James licked his lips, swallowed a few times, and opened the door to his doctor's office. He walked towards the office secretary. She was engaged on the phone and smiled to him.

He stood to his side to give her privacy and seen the room was full of patients. "Good day James, how are you today? Do you require an appointment?" The secretary asked. James spun around to face her, "Hi Katie, how are you?"

In a happy spirit, Katie probed, "Good James, what do you need today?" James leaned into her, "I must see the doctor today Katie. I'm experiencing some issues with my medication." "I'm sorry James. I have a full day as you can see by the amount of patients here. You know to call, and leave me the details. Dr. Flannery confirms his availability and places you accordingly. He doesn't see walk INS. It's not a clinic James. Please leave your number, and go home. I will call you when the doctor decides, where he'll fit you in," she explained. "That will not work for me. Just squeeze me in today. I'll take a seat and wait," established James.

"I have no available appointments today," Katie answered as she displayed her open palm towards the waiting room for James to see.

James looked around the waiting room, and knew he was about to cause himself undue embarrassment. He aimed his finger at Katie, prepared to raise his voice, as he cleared his throat, "I realize you hold an office full of patients Katie, but how many times have I burdened you with an unannounced request that I must see him now? Don't respond, I'll answer that question for you. Never… not once…not ever. That's right, not before today. I'm here telling you right now, I have an emergency, which requires the attention of the doctor today. He is the only person who can deal with my emergency."

"I'm sorry to hear James, but it can't be accommodated today. However, let me look through my appointment book and find you the first available appointment, since you don't want to let the doctor schedule you on his time. Oh, it's not looking good for you. The first available date is two months away. I can put you on the cancellation list," stressed Katie. "It's unacceptable, I'm not leaving this office until I speak with him today," James cried out.

Katie was a sweet secretary, but like most gatekeepers, her word is the last. It came from the Doctor himself to secure a systematic flow with his patients for his office. "The physician has informed me to tell his patients, if they have an emergency they are to go to the Hospital. Would you like for me to call you an ambulance James?" Katie queried.

James had sweat streaming down his face. A blotch of red patches started to form. He looked like a burner going from low to high...

"Katie, let me speak to the doctor now please. I have been a patient here for the last ten years. I have never once made a request of such sorts. I'm not some drug infested street person. I'm just an old man who demands to speak with his doc today. I'm not in need of an ambulance either Katie. If I was, I would have walked or driven myself to the hospital, if that was where I needed to go. I'm here, and it's his direct attention and answers, I need. Could you please let Doctor Flannery know that I'm here and I'm waiting, for my appointment? Thank you Katie," James vented out with confidence.

James went with such intensity in his feeling and emotions and his health looked to be failing. Katie didn't know how to answer. She looked towards him, and changed her tone, "Either I call the police or let you see the doctor. Do you think you have an appointment today with the doctor James?" "Yes, an appointment today," he acknowledged.

She looked around the office and noticed all the patients seemed entertained while she was in a state of confusion and James looked to be losing his mind. She resolved to bring the issue into another room. She stood up, slanted towards James, "Please follow me," she requested.

She walked James over to an empty examination room and directed James, "Sit in here and wait for the doctor. I'll get your file and ask the doctor to see you as soon as he is free," Katie reassured James. "Now James, you said you were having a problem. What is your current problem? I will need to let the doctor know," she asked.

Like a child gone into a state of submission, "I'm having a problem with my medication," James answered. His calm and passive voice was a quick change from the rage he displayed moments earlier.

She stood at the door, "Okay James, please place all your medication on the desk in front of you so the doctor can see what it is you are taking. I will bring your file in a moment," she reassured him. "I'm sorry for my outburst Katie. It is important," he apologized. "It's okay James. The doctor will see you soon," Katie answered with a soft smile and light nod.

Katie left the examination room and went to another room where the doctor was attending to another patient. She tapped at the door, and waved the doctor out to the hall. Katie expressed, "James Johnston is having a loss of memory. He had been a patient of yours for almost twenty years, and didn't recall this or the office process. He was acting irrational and confused. He doesn't look well. He may need to be assessed at the hospital Dr. Flannery."

James could not sit still. He paced back and forth in the small room, waiting for his doctor to appear. An examination table set off in the back against a wall. He went to sit back down on the steel straight back black chair, and changed his mind. Instead, he walked to the sink, turned on the water and cupped his hands tossing water on his face. He tore down a brown heavy paper towel from the dispenser. Pat dried his face and flipped the paper into the trash.

"I hope I didn't scare Katie by making a scene. What if Katie called the police it will put me in an uncompromising situation. I wonder what Katie would do," he whispered.

He peeked out from the room to examine the reception desk. Katie was talking to an elderly woman. The waiting room filled with a myriad of bored patients some were flipping through magazines. A few business types were on their cell phones, patiently waiting for their turn with the doc. He looked through the glass windows to see the security guard in the hall just outside the office.

He seemed half-asleep. His gray hair and visibly decrepit body showing through his wrinkled uniform, the old man was surely beyond his expiration date. This normalcy put James at ease. "If Katie had called the police, surely there would have been more commotion," he muttered as he eased his body into the chair and tried to relax until his physician arrived.

"Hello James," said Doctor Flannery with his arm outstretched extending his hand to James. "Doctor thanks for seeing me last minute. Thank you, thank you," James replied as he continued to shake the doctor's hand.

"Loosen up there James, you'll pull my arm from the socket," the doctor joked. "Sorry," James said while still shaking his hand. "What is so urgent? You displayed confusion and your head looked like it was ready to pop off Katie noted. It is all red, and you're sweating in a ventilated room," the Doctor said concerned.

James had shortness of breath as he spoke, "Doctor, could you check these pills you prescribed for me." James asked as he removed the pill bottles from his pocket and placed them on top of the doctor's work desk. "There appears to be different pills inside," James continued. "And what exactly are they supposed to do for me? Do I have a mental illness, and you didn't tell me?" James speech was rushed as he asked.

The doctor appeared puzzled. He looked at each bottle and read the label with interest. Doctor Flannery emptied a few tablets from one bottle in his left hand. With the index finger of his right hand, he separated each one in his palm. Then he poured them back into the bottle and repeated the same steps with the next bottle.

As James sat, he wiped off perspiration. Unaware of the response he was about to receive. "James, I didn't prescribe this medicine for you. Your first name is on the bottle, but it's not your last name. Its close, but not the same and I'm not the doctor who ordered it. Where did you get them, and can you tell me why there are at least four different types of pills in each bottle? One looks like a painkiller, which I would have never prescribed to you or any of my patients. You have a few of those, right here. I took them out," he asked waiting for James to tell him what he knows.

James became frantic, "I don't know doctor. This is why I'm here. I read online two are for mental health issues. The others," he took a breath... "I just don't know." Dr. Flannery eased his face towards James, looked into his eyes, "These drugs on the label aren't ones that I prescribed for you. Where did you get these?" the doctor questioned. James accused the doctor, "From you doctor, don't you remember?"

Dr. Flannery analyzed the bottles for

imperfections, "Drug stores don't dispense a mixture of different pills and place them inside bottles. And like I said, it's not your name on either of the bottles. It indicates the date these were dispensed was about a month ago and the amount of pills inside each was sixty," explained the doctor. "Are you sure doctor?" James pleaded.

"Where did you get these James?" The doctor demanded to know. "I got them from you doctor, don't you remember? I was here a few weeks ago," James confirmed.

The doctor got annoyed, and firmly stated, "James, I don't give pills out to my patients in pill bottles, and I didn't prescribe these pills for you. Like I said, it's not your name on the bottle label."

"I didn't say you gave them to me here doctor, I said, you wrote me a prescription. Why didn't you tell me I had mental health issues?" James questioned in confusion. "Hold on James, I have to read your file," the doctor noted.

Doctor Flannery looked through James medical chart. He flipped back and forth his page files. "James, according to my records, you haven't seen me in about a month. You have to stop taking these pills? I did not prescribe those for you. I prescribed a mild pain pill and thirty pills, not sixty. That is not what's inside these bottles. In addition, I wrote one prescription, with no repeats," the doctor confirmed to James.

James clothes were now drenched in sweat. He could not believe what he what he heard. He was now beginning to doubt his own sanity. Yet, he knows what he sees, "Are you telling me I'm crazy? I see the bottles and researched the pills at the library," he educated him.

"Here James, see for yourself." The doctor said as he pointed to James appointments on his chart. James leaned in to follow the doctor along.

"I prescribed you a mild pain pill after you slipped on some ice and hurt your back. That was about eight months ago, see here. Do you remember?" he mentioned.

"Go on, doctor." James urged. "Then you were prescribed a mild sedative, two weeks after the death of your wife. It's written here. That's over three months ago and you mentioned suicidal thoughts at the time on those. We took you off them. A few of those pills are inside these bottles." Doctor Flannery said looking in his eyes. "Are you remembering?" questioned the doctor.

James chest rose up and down heavily as he listened, "I don't recall a lot from that time," James admitted.

Doctor Flannery remembered James confusion, "Yes, you were experiencing a tough time. Then I referred you for psychiatric help to guide you over the loss of your wife. It is written here. You went to see him. Here is his report. He prescribed you medication to calm your nerves down and it was thirty pills with no mention of this medication on his report. Do you remember this? He is this same building, on the fourth floor," he asked to confirm James awareness.

James got more annoyed and overwhelmed, "Just get to the point. I cannot remember everything," James fumed in annoyance.

Doctor Flannery jumped back when James raised his voice. He adjusted his body to remain calm towards him, "James, I understand, you're overwhelmed, just calm down and listen. The psychiatrist indicated you didn't go back to see him after your third visit. I think a few pills he prescribed you are also mixed up in this mess of pills you have here. Here's his report," Dr. Flannery said, as he highlighted the comments in yellow marker and added, "His name is on the bottle as the prescribing doctor. How can that be if you never went back to see him?" he questioned in complete confusion.

"I forgot, I seen him," James interjected. "It's okay James. Then, you came back here, we spoke about you joining a gym, and we agreed, no medication, because with the thirty pills you were feeling much better. Do you remember this James?" Doctor Flannery asked. "I don't know, but I did join a gym," James quietly replied when he remembered.

"You told me you did join a gym, in this visit, and stated you were feeling a little more relaxed and just wanted to check in with me and chat. I wrote that here," Doctor Flannery commented as he marked it with highlighted marker. "Then you hurt your back at the gym, about a month ago, see here. I ordered a mild pain pill. These painkillers in my hand are stronger, and nothing I ordered. It's the same date on the pill bottles you have there. Have you been ingesting all pills in these bottles without looking at them?" he asked in an authoritative voice.

James listened patiently and answered, "Yes, of course I took the pills in the bottle, two, three and sometimes, four a day, and got a repeat when they called me to pick it up." "James, this could be why your moods are all over the place and why you're sweating profusely. It could be the pills. I need you to go to the Hospital for some blood work and to get you evaluated. You can rest for a few days at the hospital as we clear out all the medication. I have to figure out what else is going on with you. I need to listen to your heart and check your blood pressure and I'll take these pills from you and call for an ambulance." He picked up the telephone, "Katie, call an ambulance."

James wasn't capable of fully understanding what the doctor was saying to him. "Are you sure doctor?" he rambled as the doctor took his blood pressure.

"The only thing I can think of is they asked your name at the drug store and gave you the person named on these bottles medicine by mistake and didn't bother to recheck when you went for a refill. Perhaps, two males with similar names came at the same time. Nevertheless, where did this painkiller come from? Why did you put your other pills in the bottle? And why did you tell me that you took all the medication the Psychiatrist prescribed, when you clearly did not finish them? Perhaps, mixing these together caused confusion and you do look like hell. You have never looked this bad. You're not taking care of yourself James," the doctor expressed with concern.

James was incapable of sitting still, "Yes, I was, and I did." Dr. Flannery picked up the pill bottles, "James this medication didn't belong to you. Did anyone call you to inquire if you had the wrong prescription? And who do you know that takes strong pain killers like this?" he questioned in his own confusion.

James went into a state of despair, thinking the doctor had all the answers for him. "No! That isn't so, it's your files. They must be mixed up. Look at it again. Maria couldn't have had friends at the drug store to screw me up there too. She was the only one with pain killers, in my home," James shared in his confusion.

Dr. Flannery tried to calm, "It's okay James, let me just sit you back down. That's it. I need you to tell me about Maria?" " She is sucking me dry. Look at your file again," James ordered. "My files are fine. You shouldn't be ingesting medication that isn't intended for you," the doctor expressed decisively.

James was not in an agreeable state, "I cannot believe this — my name is on it you said?" "No James, that's not what I said," Doctor Flannery answered.

James shook his head in disbelief, grabbed the pill bottles from the table, and stuffed them back in his pocket. "I have to go doctor," James said, as he opened the door and ran out of the office. "Wait James, I called for an ambulance. You have to go to the hospital," the doctor bellowed out as he followed him out of the room.

In his haste, James tripped over a walker stationed beside an elderly woman that was sitting in his path. He picked himself up while still in running mode, failing to reposition the walker back to its original state "Don't take any more pills," the doctor yelled from the front door of the building when James ran down the street.

Doctor Flannery, called James daughter and left a message stating, "It was urgent and had to do with her father."

James was still running, "He was trying to commit me," James muttered as he ran.

He had no idea where he was going, but

instinctively headed to a small quaint park. James spent many afternoons there. It was a quiet, peaceful park with a small pond in the center. Trees were abundant with everything from huge oak to white birch. Squirrels scurried everywhere between the bushes and the other wildlife, which included the odd raccoon and skunk.

It was very close to the downtown core, but once in the park you could not see or hear the bustling city that surrounded it. It was an oasis dropped in the middle of a concrete jungle. James went there frequently with his wife throughout their marriage. They enjoyed having picnic lunches and feeding the myriad of ducks and birds that congregated around them as they sipped wine and ate French bread together. This is where James knew he was in love with his wife. It was also the last place they were together outside of the Hospital, before she was too sick to leave her bed and, cancer took her life.

As James entered the park, he slowed his pace to a fast walk. He could feel his body beginning to relax as fond old memories engulfed him. He soon spotted a park bench that was not far from the grass that he once enjoyed many picnics with the mother of his children. He was exhausted. He sat on the bench to regain his breath and composure. "I'm too old to be running like that. Why did he make me run?" he expressed. "I need to gather my thoughts. My life is in shambles," he convinced himself.

James reflected on his life as his body recovered from his run. His heart was beating less rapidly now. Even though James was an athlete in high school and ran many marathon races, these last few minutes made him realize, "I'm getting old," he mumbled out.

James did bring Maria to this park when he was with her. She did not protest going, but he could tell this place did not hold the same magic for her, as it did for him. He sat and tried to remember the times he was here with Maria, "In hindsight, I wonder if she was just pretending to enjoy my company while she arranged this conspiracy of hers and why would a woman go to all that trouble? Could she have been that deceitful? Why did she pick me? I had money, but am far from rich?" James was so tired. He could hardly keep his eyes open. "When did I sleep last? His exhaustion began to overcome his reasoning.

Then he spotted her. He could not believe it. Why was she here now? It was Maria. She was at the other end of the pond. James could recognize her even from that distance. Maria had a certain stance and always wore large, distinctive sunglasses when she was out. "She must be meeting someone else." Despite still being, exhausted James picked himself up and began to run towards her. He was unsure what he would do when he reached her but he knew he had to confront her. Maria did not see James coming until it was too late to run. James could see her face full of fear and surprise.

"James!" Maria gasped. James grabbed Maria with both hands by her blouse. "Why have you done this to me?" James yelled. "Please, James, you're hurting me," Maria pleaded. James ignored her and continued to hold and shake her while asking, "Why Maria, Why?"

"James, I have done nothing to you. What do you mean?" "Where's my money?" James uttered. He shook her more violently in the hopes of coercing the information out of her. "James, I love you. Why are you doing this?" she pleaded convincingly. James was not taking the bait. "Don't give me that shit Maria," he blurted back "I want to know why you did this to me?" "Please James, let me go, you're hurting me. I will explain. Please my love," she requested.

James was not buying any of it. In fact, it made him even angrier. With one hand on her blouse, James grabbed Maria's petite neck, with his other hand.

"You bitch. You are not going to bullshit me anymore," James shouted as his hand squeezed her neck even harder.

"James, James," Maria coughed and sputtered as he continued to squeeze. "You deserve this Maria. I loved you and you did this to me," he screamed. Maria's face was turning red with lack of oxygen and she could barely speak. She gasped for air while at the same time she began flaying her arms in the hopes of knocking his hands free. She was too small to overpower James. As she was beginning to lose consciousness, Maria made one final attempt to get free. She mustered enough strength to raise a hand and with all the force left in her, she swatted down with her long nails across the right side of James' face. "Ahhhhhh," James squawked as he let Maria go.

This was Maria's chance. She started running away from James as he screamed out in pain. James could feel the blood trickle down his cheeks, he placed his hand on his face, took it away and seen the blood. James pursued her like a vigilante. Maria kicked off her high heels to give herself added speed, but it wasn't enough. She could feel James gaining on her. His hand grabbed the back of her hair. As he did, she flew in the air and landed on the grass with a thud.

Maria kicked and punched lying on her back, but James was too powerful. Again, he grabbed her neck, but this time with both hands. James would occasionally let go with one hand, but only to repeatedly punch Maria in the face. Bloodied and lacking oxygen, Maria knew she was going to die, unless something happened.

James punched her repeatedly. James knew she was now dead, but he kept punching her. "How do you like it," James screamed and cried at the same time.

"Hey, what's wrong with you?" James could feel someone grabbing him from behind.

"Let me go, leave me alone." James was now crying uncontrollably over the lifeless body. His face buried in her bloodied chest, apologizing to her. "I'm sorry Maria. What have I done?"

"Hey mister, wake up. Are you okay?" James could feel himself shaken.

James found himself sitting on a park bench with a strange man overlooking him. "Are you okay mister?" the man asked again.

"Huh…. Yeah…. I'm okay…." sputtered James. "You must have been having a nightmare. You were screaming. Are you sure you're okay?" "Yeah… yeah…. Huh… I'm fine… thanks, but please leave…" James said as he waved the man away. The man left.

James was covered in sweat, and tears flowed from his eyes and rolled down his face. However, there was no blood, and no Maria. He was dreaming. James was now even more exhausted, than before.

Four

As he embraced the serenity of the view looking out to the night's sky, through the stain glass windows, a peaceful calm, embraced him. His hands eased across her body systematically as he rubbed cream into her skin. A soothing feeling displayed in his body as it swayed with the movements of his hands, as he sought to entice a contentment within her, as he felt in himself.

The silence between them lingered for close to an hour before he thought to break the stillness, he felt. He removed his hands from her body and she slowly opened her eyes. He bent down and whispered in her ear, "How long have you lived in this Condominium Maria?"

As she laid there naked a towel covered her behind. Maria desired to continue the satisfaction he was pleasuring her with, "JP, just tend to your massage and leave the personal questions alone." JP was the short form Maria used for John Paul, depending on her mood. Maria stressed her need for privacy, as she added a long drawn out 'pleeeeeease' at the end of her sentence.

"Come on Maria, you act like this is a game and you know damn well why I am here. You like it just as much as I do," John Paul stated with confidence.

"I'm feeling a need to be pampered today. Can you hold and caress me, cuddle— you know what that is? I'm still not well," Maria, voiced her needs sympathetically. She had a natural seductive look to her always, to him. She reached her hand out, mustered his sweater in the palm of her hand and pulled him closer to her. "I need you today more than anything else in the world," she asked of him.

He adored her, and knew she was in a state of vulnerability. Although she expressed her desires, his ability to consider her needs lapsed when he pleasingly pointed to his manhood and declared, "I know you Maria, you want this," he bragged knowingly. His lips formed a kiss, and his breathing eased out a heavier pace, as he spoke.

He pulled his free hand up to his head, ran his fingers through his wavy blonde hair, his soft blue eyes gave a wink. His tongue eased between his pressed lips and slightly dangled in and out of his mouth. "Aren't you going to finish my massage?" Maria knew it was over, but wanted more and asked.

He held up the corner of his sweater, his tanned waves of muscles were in her view. He inhaled as she glided her fingertips across his stomach. He jerked with the chills, as he did, his abdominals sucked in, and his slacks slid down slightly. She caught a glimpse of his cut pelvic muscles, and slid her hand around and down inside. It was desirable for Maria. She seized the moment, she felt. With every tender touch along her body, he had her already promoted a relaxing arousal in her.

He removed his hand from his hair, pulled himself away from her – her hand fell down. His hands went towards his waist. Gradually his sweater lifted up and over his head. John Paul was so confident, so into it, he clenched his manhood in his hand from the outside of his slacks and ran his hand up and down presenting an erect penis in full desire. "This Maria is for you," John Paul proudly exclaimed.

John Paul reached out embraced her hand in his, and eased it back towards manhood, as he guided her hand with his, he expressed his desires, "Do you want this Maria"? "Oh, yes, so much I do," declared Maria. "Maria, this is for you, can you see how much I want you"? "Can you feel how much I yearn for you? I need for you to tell me what you need me to do for you today?" he expressed.

Maria's head twisted to look out to the city. A delicate light from the flaming candles gave a peaceful and romantic aura, adding to the mood, while, the sound from the soft music that played relaxed her even more. Her lightish brown hair shined. John Paul held back his immediate desires of seduction to bring her to the same state he was in. As she remained on the table, he ran both hands through her scalp and hair. Her eyes closed as he did. Maria moved after a few minutes, so he stopped. She twisted her body up and moved herself into a seated position, and had exposed her open legs. JP was able to take in a quick view, before she closed them. She propped herself back with her right arm. JP stood before her. He had a clear view of her naked, uncovered breasts, inviting to him. JP, gently came in from each side of her arms, and tenderly massaged her breasts together.

Her eyes closed as he lowered his body taking his mouth to her nipples. She watched in excitement. Her hands embraced his head. His fingers moved around, in an effort to heighten her desire.

As JP, stimulated her breast, Maria slipped herself off the table, and placed her backside in front of him, as she did, she lifted her left arm up clutching his head, bringing his head down towards the side of her face. Her back before his chest, as she enjoyed the embrace he had on her, as his arms wrapped around her, holding her firm. She felt completely comfortable in his arms, "I love it when you hold me like this," she shared.

He sprawled her upper body towards the table. She grinded her bottom up and down against his, meticulously, as he leaned against her.

Maria was lost in the moment, and spun herself around unbuttoned and unzipped his pants, and eased his slacks down and off. Standing there in his black dress socks on his feet, he lifted one foot up at a time as she pulled each one off. She embraced his desire with her hands, carefully stimulating him as they kissed. She led him to the bedroom, by his arm. She brought him into her as they went down on the bed. He eased on his side, beside her, separated her legs and placed his fingers inside. As they kissed, she caressed his manhood, with her hands. He waited until he felt her wetness increase and her tighten. "Maria, you're getting there." he express as he kissed her and placed her legs, for better access.

He lifted one leg up, as he eased his body on top of hers. He permitted his manhood to enter her at a slow pace where he slid it up as far as he could reach and brought it back down just before he'd exiting her and gently went up and down a few times before he increased the speed of his thrusting and suddenly removed it. When he did, he stared into Maria's big brown eyes. Maria's head tipped back onto the pillow. She wanted him now, her body requested him to enter her again as she grabbed at his ass, her body moved towards him, in an attempt to pull him in closer to her. He kept his distance.

She looked towards John Paul's penis and seen it was long, thick, circumcised, and he was hard. The movement inside her was now gone. She needed to seek her yearnings. It was too much for her to tolerate. She wanted it now. "Put your cock back in me, John Paul," she pleaded.

His left hand, held him up as he allowed her to see his desire, "You're not ready yet," he exclaimed. This turned into a game of wits. He knew he must enter her again to release his own desire. John Paul caressed the shaft of his penis with his right hand a few times. He knew he would cum, if he did not pull out and needed to keep himself hard, but did not want to get off just yet.

He rolled over took the head of his penis, and rubbed it against her clit. He entered Maria after much pleading, moaning, and gasping, from her. John Paul was confident; he had positioned himself well, in this lustful war of wits. Maria felt John Paul inside her. She had gotten what she wanted.

This was not about love. It was not even about sex. It was about the state of sexual building. Letting it creep up then edging it to heights of intensity and stopping before letting it go. They were with each other. John Paul's legs pounded off Maria's legs, as he pumped harder and harder in an effort to drive the height of her sexual peek. It was at this moment that Maria began to gasp for air. She lost total mind and body control, when she felt the depth of her sexual hungers. The only thing that would subdue Maria, in this state of separation, would be the release of her orgasm.

John Paul could hear her heave and sigh with every thrust of his manhood. He knew this meant Maria loved every second of their lovemaking. She even called it 'Her Gasping.' The gasps of joy grew louder the harder each time John Paul graced her inside. He knew it would not subside, until he came inside her. A loud shriek heard. They both came. The gasping was over.

Five

At a small café, Brandy sat in a corner by herself, sipping coffee, still visibly shaken long after she left her apartment. She had no desire to work that evening, but had to honor a commitment she made, "Josie, it's too late to get anyone to fill in for me. I've called everyone to fill in and no one is available. I'll do my shift, but I wanted you to know, it will be my last one. I quit after tonight. I've waited for you to tell me when you were cutting down the shift, or letting me go, and you've strung me along for almost a month now," she expressed to her boss.

Josie, was not being a reasonable employer, "Don't you think you're being selfish, Brandy, when we kept the shift going for you?" Josie told her in disappointment. "You're a very unappreciative young lady," Josie added.

"You should be happy that I've decided to leave then Josie," sharply stated Brandy. "Brandy, please take the week off, after your shift tomorrow. I will work the next five days for you. Perhaps, you're just exhausted. But right now, I can't do anything we're out of town for a wedding tomorrow," quietly informed Josie.

"No, thanks Josie, I'm done. I'll leave the key on your desk when I leave, and you can mail me my pay," decisively stated Brandy as she hung up.

With each, lift of her coffee her hands trembled. As she reflected on her morning, "Would he do this to her again or was it just an anomaly?" she wondered.

Well, she sat in stress and worry, other patrons noticed she was in an agitated state, and could not help but stare. Her hands constantly moved. She would cover up her face with both hands then her fingers ran across her eyelids while she closed them tightly shut. She would pick up her coffee and place it back down without taking a drink, and repeated the same pattern. Yet, she had not taken notice, with what she was doing.

"Miss, are you okay?" asked a concerned older woman as she stood at Brandy's table. Brandy was in a state of removal from where she was, and did not hear her. When Brandy removed her hands from her face, the old woman touched her arm lightly.

"Miss, are you okay?" the older woman repeated. She was in her late sixties, short and petite, and professional looking. Brandy was shocked to see a woman with big dark brown eyes, long wavy gray hair, which sported a shimmer of black through the front, like a skunk, and she was staring into her face. Stunned by the woman, Brandy's hands embraced the table and she flew against the back of her seat.

"Excuse me," Brandy fumed, "Is there something

I can do for you?" she asked. The old woman moved herself away from Brandy's face, "Miss, I'm sorry to bother you. I noticed, you seemed upset," the older woman stated with a concerned stare. "I'm fine, just tired. Thanks for your concern," Brandy quietly answered, not sure how to respond to this strange woman.

"I did not mean to pry, dear," the old woman said even though she was in fact prying. "I'm just concerned. Perhaps, I can get you something to eat. That usually helps," the woman suggested.

"No…I mean….thanks, I have my own money." Brandy busted out. "It's been a long day. What time is it?" Brandy asked to change the subject. "It is four-forty eight pm," the woman answered as she looked at her simple but elegant silver watch. "Where has the day gone?" Brandy snared. "I have to be at work at six," she expressed.

"Oh my," huffed the old woman. "I'll leave you alone, sorry to have bothered you," she said apologetically.

"You didn't bother me," Brandy said with a smile. "I think the lack of sleep is getting to me. Working and going to school, with exams can really take a toll on a person," Brandy offered as an explanation. "Yes, dear they can. I do hope you take better care of yourself, rest is so important," the old woman compassionately mentioned.

With that statement, the woman proceeded to turn around and walked to the front of the café to exit the establishment.

Brandy decided the old woman might have been right about not eating. She was rather hungry. She glanced at the menu and noticed there was not much to choose from. All it had was a few sandwiches, soups, and wraps. There was no seat service. Brandy made her way up to the counter to order.

Brandy stood in line waiting for service. A woman tapped Brandy on the back of her shoulder. As she turned around she looked down and then up. She stood face to face with a taller woman standing behind her, holding a black purse in front of her chest. Her dark peach long fingernails were hard to miss, along with her dark even toned arms, and soft silky skin. She looked up. It was Maria.

"Brandy how you are?" Maria asked. "I'm fine, how are you?" Brandy replied with the customary greeting. She was surprised to see Maria and tried to avoid eye contact. "Fabulous Brandy, I'm just fabulous, but you don't look so hot," said Maria with a wink.

"I see you haven't been back at the restaurant working. Are you working elsewhere?" Brandy asked, trying to snoop, but not wanting it to look like she was.

"Oh no," Maria said as she shook her head, and waved her right hand in the air, "I never worked there. I just popped by. Did you ever see me serve anyone?" she added with a chuckle. "I was speaking to the owners. Nevertheless, I'm moving back home, just wrapping things up here, before I go. Do you have a few moments to talk before you run off to work Brandy?" wondered Maria as she asked.

"Oh sure," Brandy agreed. "I'm getting something to eat, before I start my shift. I have a table over in the corner." Brandy pointed in the direction of her table. "Wonderful," answered Maria with a smile. Her peach low cut top, made it impossible not to see her cleavage pop. While her short black skirt, and laced up black heeled sandals, showed off her long dark tone legs. She was sexy, and it was undeniable.

Brandy ordered a chicken wrap, with soup, from the café associate. Maria ordered the same. They walked together carrying their trays to Brandy's corner table and sat across from each other. Maria commented on how peaceful it was where they were sitting. Her long natural brown hair shined with the sunshine coming in from the window and gave it highlighted effect. Her sexy haircut graced the front of her face and blended into the back. "Your hair is really healthy looking." Brandy commented." "It's all natural, thanks," returned Maria as she knocked her hair off her shoulders, getting ready to take a bite of her wrap.

As they ate their meal, they exchanged pleasantries. After a while, Brandy got tired of playing nice with Maria. "You're going home, you mentioned. Are you going alone or is John Paul going with you?"

Maria went into an interrogating tone, "What the hell are you talking about, John Paul, coming with me? Why do you ask?" Brandy regretted she even brought up the subject. Yet, fumed at Maria, "Did you know we were living together?" she stated in pride.

Maria laughed, and spluttered out, "You... and John Paul, no... I didn't. I do know a man named John Paul, but the man I know does not live with a woman. You're obviously having man troubles and you look like shit."

"Come on Maria, what's your relationship with John Paul? I've seen you twice and you've not had one decent thing to say me. I'm getting used to your ignorance," Brandy commented in hurt, but still expected an answer, and goggled in her face waiting for a reply.

Maria played with her long fingernails, "I really don't know him? Why don't you tell me everything? I'd love to hear it. First, I must say, you look like shit girl. Your hair is pulled out everywhere, like you were in a catfight, with some crazy bitch. Your clothes are wrinkled, sweat is pouring down under your armpits, and you have a shit load of coffee stains all down the front of your white blouse. You must be going home to shower and change before you go to work tonight," Maria flew right to the point, unable to hold back her ignorance when she noticed, she couldn't let it go.

Brandy hadn't noticed and looked down to see long thick stains, on her white blouse and lifted up her underarm and took a look. By now, she was ashamed. "John Paul and I were talking before you came around the restaurant," Brandy bellowed out in embarrassment. "Well, that's your business and I've already told you that I never worked there. We met one day, at the restaurant. So, now you're jealous thinking I ran up and took your little boyfriend away from you? Is that what you're getting at?" Maria said acting like a superior being to Brandy and she had all the answers.

Brandy shifted around in her seat, "Whatever Maria. Are you ashamed you almost had to waitress to earn a paycheck, but high maintenance Maria just couldn't bring herself to do such a thing? So what, did you convince yourself, you never went there to try?" Brandy angrily stated back to her.

Maria was infuriated with Brandy's antics, and

innuendos. She was picking up her purse and dropped it back down, "Whatever shit it is you want to say to me Brandy, get it off your chest."

Brandy growled, "Well, it would have been nice to know you and John Paul were fuck buddies, and friends, before he had a spasm of animalistic behavior towards me. Notwithstanding, the fact, he had no issues yelling, at least you love making love to him. "

"What do you mean he told you we fuck? In those words?" sarcastically laughed Maria. "Yeah, that's all the man knows, he can fuck. Good luck with him." Brandy gave it no thought, when she raised her voice.

"Don't go all ballistic on me when we're both adult women here. And we both can decide who we fuck, Isn't that right? I introduced myself to you, and I'm supposed to tell you whom I'm fucking. You are some seriously deranged chick. You don't know what discreet is, do you?" Maria added shaking her head. Took her purse, and went to get up.

Brandy's temper got the better of her, "Yeah, I do, but I'm not an idiot either." Maria giggled, "Then why are you rambling to a stranger, about your sexual issues and who you live with, while accusing me of fucking him? As I stated, I don't know the man, you're talking about. I bet you mention my name and he tossed it back into your face and figured saying I fucked him, would piss you right the fuck off. It has obviously worked hasn't it? Perhaps he was talking about someone else named Maria, for heaven sakes. Did you even think about that? No… no... no... let's just ram a woman you met once and slam her with my poor relationship issues today," Maria stated then probed, "How do you know it was me he was talking about?"

Brandy was too self-absorbed in her own pain, "Nice mind game Maria." Brandy couldn't stop herself, she put her hands on the table, looked into Maria's eyes as she stood up, "Let's just say, had I known he was a pig, and was fucking you, I never would have fucked him….. Or…given him a key to come and go at my place, so freely. As far as discreet goes, talk to him, he tells his fucks, Maria is beautiful too."

Maria prodding, "Honey, dear, do you really need the details then. I bet all he ever did was fingered you and you thought it was his dick. You're so fucking naïve and stupid. You don't give anyone a chance to talk."

"I heard all I need to hear from you Maria, and him. You two deserve each other… I hope I don't see you or him again." Brandy stated as she waved good-bye, "Bye bitch," Brandy added walking to the exit.

"Just remember you have a gold mine sitting between your legs, honey. You look like you could use the extra money." Maria hollered to Brandy.

Brandy yelled back, "Yeah, I see you're using your cunt with older men too. James… poor thing. What are you sucking him out of, or were you just sucking his dick, for money? Don't even answer. I don't want to know… I guess discreet, missed his concept of understanding too," snapped Brandy, as she exited the café with her hand still up in the air.

Brandy needed someone she could confide in and trust. She needed her brother Dave. He always gave Brandy great advice. He was a few years younger, and lived not too far from the restaurant. It would be luck, if she'd able to get a hold of him at this time in the day. Dave had many friends, men and women alike, and was a social butterfly.

Brandy worried his flamboyancy would get him in trouble with gay-bashers, but Dave always shrugged Brandy off as a nervous Nelly.

Brandy called Dave from her cell at work. She could hear it ringing at the other end. "Please answer Dave. I need you," Brandy said in a whisper, "Come on pick up." "Hello?" came a high-pitched voice at the other end.

"Dave, Dave, it's me, Brandy." "I know my sister's voice, and your number comes up." Dave laughed." Why do you always say your name?" he questioned.

"I don't know Dave, just habit I guess. Can you stop by the restaurant tonight? I need to talk to you?" she requested. "Well sis, tonight's shooter night at Sticky's Bar. I always get lucky on shooter night you know," he laughed as he said it.

"Please, just for a bit Dave, I need to see you. You can go to the bar later," she tried to persuade him. "By then all the big dicks will be taken sweetheart," Dave joked. "Why do you always talk so crude Dave," Brandy said embarrassed. "Oh come on. You know me, when couldn't you take a joke sis? "Dave snapped back in an upset tone. "Dave, let's not go over this again, please," she pleaded.

"Is something wrong sis," Dave was now sensing there was a problem, "Brandy you never call last minute for anything," he questioned her.

Brandy grabbled, "No..., maybe....I don't know....I just need your ear." "Well okay sis. I will meet you about tenish, or soon thereafter. I can always get a big dick anytime with these great looks," Dave gestured to lighten the mood. Brandy gave a mild chuckle. "Thanks Dave. See you later." "Bye sweetie. See you soon," Dave said, and ended the call.

The restaurant was exceptionally slow this early part of the evening. As soon as a straggled customer left, Brandy locked the doors, poured a coffee, and sat in a booth and fell asleep and had not realized it. She heard sirens from fire trucks and woke up. It took her a moment before she read the time on her cell. It was just after two am. "Oh my god Dave, I forgot. Shit!" Brandy shouted as she remembered he was to come by…

Six

Dave sat on the couch in his two-bedroom Condo sipping white wine from an oversized wine glass. The living room was laboriously furnished, and the décor calm and peaceful. Dave had superbly placed one of kind paintings on the walls from a local artist, and he was not alone.

"More wine Conrad?" Dave asked his guest. "I better not Davey, wine makes me silly," Conrad answered. Dave took the wine from the table and proceeded to fill Conrad's glass to the rim. "Oh Davey, you're going to get me drunk," Conrad giggled.

"That is the idea," Dave laughed as he poured. Conrad chugged down a heaping amount of wine. Pointed his finger at Dave, "Well, if I get too drunk it will be your fault." Conrad said. "You don't worry about that Conrad baby....I'll take care of you. Just don't drink to the point that you feel like you're going to be sick, okay," Dave said as he laughed, and moved in landing a wet kiss on Conrad.

"There is more where that came from, so drink up," Dave suggested. "Mmmmmmmmmmmm," Conrad moaned as he grasped Dave's head and continued. Dave ran his right hand through Conrad's short ginger brown hair, as testosterone began to fill the room. Conrad's lips pulled at Dave's bottom lip. Their tongues moved in and out, as he did. Conrad held Dave's petite neck in his hands while their heads slightly moved around as they kissed. Dave's hand eased down Conrad's arm and stopped on his bicep. His arms were too wide for Dave's hand to wrap around, so he squeezed his muscle. As he did, his lips skidded away from Conrad. They both took a deep breath, "You're so sexy and your arms are so big," Dave expressed, as he took a long drink of his wine. He put down his glass and his lips came together and rolled, as his tongue eased out and quickly went in. Conrad was very patient with Dave.

Dave leaned over to sift through cd's on the coffee table. "Let me change the music Conrad" said Dave. "Is that Diana's new CD? I could make love to her all night." Conrad slipped in suggestively. "It sure is," Dave, answered as he slipped the CD into the player and turned the volume up just enough to hear the sexy vocals of Diana emanate from the speakers. "Oh, thank you Davey. If I were a woman I would be her," Conrad suggested as his hands went up both sides of his face and ran through his hair as he sat and moved slowly to the grove of the beat.

"But if you were a woman, you wouldn't be here,"

Dave said as he laughed and seated himself back down beside Conrad. Dave sipped some wine, placed his glass down and on his way up he caressed Conrad's inner thigh, and placed his lips on top of his. Dave continued upwards along Conrad ABS slightly easing his hand across them. He dropped his pinky finger on the head of his penis and moved it around in a circular movement. As he expected, it was fully erect.

Conrad was surprised, "Don't be afraid to touch it. How many months has it been, and that's the first touch it's received."

Conrad attempted to embrace Dave's hand with his on top of his manhood. Dave pulled away. There was a knock at the door and the bell rang. "Damn!" shouted Dave. "Don't answer it Davey." demanded Conrad as he embraced his arms.

"Let me just look through the peephole, it's probably just a wrong unit knock. Don't move," Dave said as he gave a quick peck on Conrad's cheek, and escaped his clutches to head towards the door. Dave squinted into the peephole—it was his sister Brandy.

"Give me a Sec sis, "Dave answered as he fumbled to unlock the door. The door opened a crack as Dave forgot to release the safety catch. "Sorry sis." Dave re-closed the door and unfastened the latch. Rather than inviting, Brandy in, Dave went outside to the hall, stood beside her, and closed the door behind him.

"What's up Brandy?" Dave said in a hurried voice. "Can I come in?" Brandy asked with a puzzled look on her face. "I have someone inside. He's gorgeous, and rock hard," Dave said with a smirk. "Already," Brandy said in disbelief. "Didn't you come to see me at the restaurant?" she asked inquisitively.

"I forgot. Sorry sis, you didn't say it was anything pressing," he smirked with his answer. "I really need to talk Dave." Breaking down in tears, Brandy leaned her body towards Dave, and placed her head on his shoulder, while wrapping her arms around him.

"But I am... with someone and..." Brandy interrupted Dave in mid speech, "I had a man living with me, and he told me he was sleeping with a girl I met at work. I had to change the locks Dave. He was a pig... a real pig... or into something, I don't get. I need to come in." "Of course sweetie," Dave said hastily when he realized they were still in the hallway.

As they came inside, Conrad was standing there with a mystified look on his face. "This is my sister Conrad. Brandy this is Conrad," Dave expressed.

Each nodded uncomfortably. "Sorry Con, but you will have to go, family problems. I'm not sure Brandy wants to share what's upsetting her, with strangers. You know what I mean," Dave expressed nervously.

"But Davey... I'm not a stranger, we've been dating for months now and we're ready to take our relationship to the next level. I'll know everything by the morning, we're that serious, tell her," specified Conrad, not wanting to leave and feeling the effects from the booze.

"Con, I will explain later. I will call you tomorrow. Please go." Conrad shook his head in defiance. "No, I'm not going, I've been drinking, and you said you'd take care of me. Puff... with your concern. I'm going to the guest room, and that's where I'm sleeping," Conrad complained upset. He pulled his suit jacket off the coat rack, bent down to pick up his overnight bag, and pushed in between Dave and Brandy. He gave a disgusted grin at Brandy, as he breezed by, slamming the bedroom door closed behind him.

"I'm sorry to ruin your evening Dave," Brandy voiced, as she sobbed uncontrollably. "Hey sis, don't worry about him. He will go to sleep, and you are more important. Now, come in and tell me what's got you running the streets this late coming here, when you're supposed to be at work." Dave said as he put his arm around Brandy and led her to the couch where he had embraced Conrad just minutes earlier.

"Can I get you something sis?" Dave asked. Brandy answered in a low whisper, "No thanks," "Let me, at least make you a tea," suggested Dave

Dave walked to the kitchen to prepare tea for the two of them. In the living room, Brandy sat in disbelief noticing the wine glasses. Dave glanced in the room several times, while preparing the tea. Brandy was mumbling aloud and had intermitted tears drifting down her cheeks, she wiped with her fingertips, before grabbing a tissue, from his box on his table.

She was not herself. The Brandy he knew who was full of energy, worked out, and looked healthy all the time. Now, she has lost weight and she looks dirty. Her cheekbones had sunken in, and the usual natural glow in her face was gone. Her face was pale. Her hair looked ratty, dry and unkempt, tied up in a ponytail, with patches of hair pulled out. This left an appearance, of a homeless woman or someone on drugs. What happened to his sister? He worried.

He walked into the living room and placed the two cups of tea on the table. Brandy reached for her cup took a sip and gave a loud gasp, as the tea touched her tongue.

"That's hot," Brandy yelp as she placed the tea back on the table. "I'm sorry sis." Dave instantly replied. "I'm not drunk, I need some milk," Brandy stated with a pinch of arrogance.

Dave picked up the wine glasses, and wine Conrad and he had. "I thought you drank your tea black sis, sorry," Dave apologized. He went to retrieve some milk in the kitchen. "I don't want to upset you more," he told her.

In the refrigerator, Dave had milk and cream neatly placed beside each other. Dave poured a small portion of milk in a creamer cup and returned to his sister. Dave sat to the right of Brandy, the same place he sat moments earlier with Conrad. He giggled. 'For a brief second all he could think of was Conrad. He erased the thought and turned his mind back to Brandy.' "What are you grinning about?" asked a bewildered Brandy. "And what is this music playing?" she questioned.

Dave blushed as he realized Brandy had caught him. "Sorry sis, I'll turn it off. It was a night of romance you interrupted. "Have you slept with Conrad yet?" Brandy inquired. "No…" quietly whispered Dave, "Not yet, and shush, he is in the other room and has ears like a hawk," Dave added.

"It's serious you love him, don't you?" Brandy probed. "I think so… Come on sis, when have you ever known me to be so out there with my feelings like this?" Dave said in fact. "You fall in love every week don't you?" Brandy said with a small laugh. "Do you think I am a man whore?" Dave responded with disgust. "I want the same things you want in a relationship, the closeness, comfort, feelings of being loved, respected, and at peace with trust. It's never a thought or a worry." " I know you have a big heart Davey. And mom and dad always say, love works what it can out, and always come from there first. But it's not always easy," Brandy said apologetically.

Dave brought back the subject to Brandy "I'm taking over the conversation and you came here with a problem and all we're discussing is my love life. Sorry sis. Enough about me," Dave urged, "Let's talk about, what's going on with you?"

"You're going to think the worst of me. I met a man at work. This might sound cliché, tall, dark and handsome, it's not specific, but it's fitting. My mind screamed my type, as he stood in a two-piece black suit at the door of the restaurant and asked, "Is this place open?" when I said, "Yes," he went towards the counter, unknotted his silky gray tie, and let drape down the front of his mauve dress shirt. As I waited for him to order, he undid his top button. I'm surprised I didn't trip over a table, pretending to get my hair out of my eyes to get behind the counter. It had to be obvious my mouth had dropped to the floor," Brandy shared.

"Brandy, that's nice, but what does this have to do with him cheating on you?" Dave questioned.

"All the man wears is designer suits, highest of quality and has impeccable taste. His nails are so well manicured, I couldn't' see a nail unshaped, or dirty. The style of his hair is model picture perfect. Even his shoes shined. He switches them up so much, I never realized, there were that many styles to choose from, for men. I never did ask his height, but he looks to reach six feet. And Dave, the smell of him is unbelievable, irresistible, really," Brandy sighed as she talked. She was still in awe with him.

"Were you in love with him, his style, good looks, or grace?" Dave questioned. "I need you to understand why I noticed him. He presents himself every day like this, Dave. We sat talking at my work, drinking vodka and coolers. He picked up for us. I shared information about me, and, our family. I let my mouth go on its own and it rambled and sorry, but I actually told him that you had money. I caught myself, and said we didn't talk much. I didn't realize it at the time, but he didn't speak about his family or himself. I don't even know his last name, or where he lives or works. That's how private he is," she shared.

Dave waited for her to stop talking and reached out to hand her drink, "Here's your tea, sweetie," he said as he did.

Brandy took a couple of fast sips and continued on, "It was the first time, in a long time. I sat down and spoke to a man, on a personal level. I didn't question why, or where's it was going. I guess the alcohol eased a mood, in me. I can't be certain what I was thinking. And maybe it wasn't right in your eyes, but we became friends. It was about a week after we met when we thought it would be romantic to book a room at the inn next door, and we had sex. He walked me back to work around four in the morning. Please Dave, don't give me that look of disgust. It was the first time we were intimate," she shared and started to cry heavily again. She immediately covered her eyes, feeling as though she was going to be judged and not understood.

Dave jumped up swayed his arms around in the air, "You did what? Were you drunk, or in fantasyland, with this man? Why? Why?...why... Brandy, do you run out and do crazy stuff like this without thinking it through? You're impulsive. When it especially comes to sex you don't run out and do whatever the heck you feel like doing," Dave expressed with concern and in shock as he shouted.

Brandy was ashamed. She kept her hands covering her face. Dave sat took a drink of his tea with his legs crossed and said nothing. Branding took a drink of her tea, placed it back down, "Okay, let me finish. I complained to him about a girl I met at work. John Paul is what he stated his name was. When I told him to leave, he said he was sleeping with her. It was odd when she showed up at a place, I've never been before. We only met once at my work and here she is standing behind me while I stood in line to order my food. I couldn't believe it. It just freaked me out. I figured he was bragging and went out and got her and sent her into the restaurant to display look at us. She was dressed like a fucking movie star for fuck sakes. We sat down to eat and I complimented her beautiful hair, and she humiliated me. She pointed out every fucking flaw of mine right to the coffee stains all over my shirt and told me, I look like hell," Brandy bawled through it.

Dave had noticed too, his eyes rolled as he tossed his hair around, as she spoke. When she finished blowing her nose, he attempted to console his sister, "It's better to know he is a cheater now, rather than getting your heart broken later on. But in days you bed this man. I want to slap you for that," he added in disgrace.

"I'm in shambles Dave. Please let me finish, please. I gave him a key to my place to come and go, as he liked. He stopped coming by the restaurant the second I did. And I know...before you say anything… I was stupid," she acknowledged of herself.

Dave rubbed her shoulder, "Brandy it's not only stupid, it was careless. Sorry, I had to get that in. Go on."

Brandy sobbed, "We haven't had sex since he took my key and he was sleeping when I arrived home a couple of mornings. And when I came out of the bath, he was gone. Yet yesterday, he complained, I never say good morning to him. Yet look at how easy it was for him leave without saying anything to me. He went on some pity party saying, it's not easy for him to sleep at strange places, so he heard me when I came home."

"That happens for many people Brandy," Dave added.

"Then he said he left to give me my privacy and continued on his rage that I let a man come and go in my place, anytime day or night. I assumed he was talking about himself. I've given no one else a key, but you."

"Privacy, what sort of privacy, his or yours? To boot, he is telling you, he can come and go whenever he likes. Furthermore, I've never used your key," snapped Dave.

"Dave, yesterday he wasn't at my place when I arrived home. I ran my bath, went into the kitchen and heard a key in the lock. I was genuinely excited to see him, and ran to the door. My hand embraced his neck when he entered and we kissed. After we kissed, he spoke in an authoritative voice, and moved me out of his way. It was a light tap. But, it wasn't the strength, it was the idea, he believed it was acceptable to push by me," whined Brandy.

"Why would he do that?" Dave questioned in concern and worry. "Perhaps, he felt I violated him. After the kiss, he stated he had to get something, but I didn't pay much mind," she confessed.

"He sounded in a hurry, that's all. Think about when you and I came back into the apartment, Conrad brushed by us, because he was pissed off. We understood and let it go." Dave suggested.

"No, it wasn't like that. He peeked in every room in my little apartment, and deliberately graced my body leaving me to lose my balance. If he was in a rush, he would have gotten what he wanted and left. Why didn't he leave, rather than barge into my bathroom to get me in the mood, for sex," complained Brandy.

"It's not uncommon to want a quickie, and that's all it was to him. Don't take this in the wrong way. Perhaps, you aren't ready for a live in type relationship," suggested Dave. "He hadn't done this before. I freaked out... and yelled no... no the moment he touched me in the tub. He did stop but he could have waited to cuddle after my bath," Brandy expressed, in between blowing her nose.

"Brandy, he may have wanted to indulge in a little intimacy. Perhaps, it's as simple as that," expressed Dave.

Brandy rolled her eyes, and sputtered out, "He left a briefcase. It wasn't a big deal. He could have clearly said, I need to get my briefcase. So, I brought it on. Is that what you're suggesting?"

"Brandy does he works through the day?" Dave asked. "Yeah, that's what he told me," she sadly answered. "Okay, perhaps he figured if he hurried you up in the tub, he could have sex, and cuddle long enough for you to fall asleep. He took a few moments, before he left, and went into the bathroom to see you and seemed to talk about what he was thinking," Dave suggested.

"He didn't ask, and he became aggressive in the bathroom. I told him he was acting like an abuser and I was crying," whined Brandy.

Dave looked confused, "Wait, you were in tears and he continued?" Brandy was lost in her own despair. Her hands waved around in the air, "I felt violated. The moment he came into the bath. I should have locked the door," suggested Brandy.

Dave felt uncomfortable with what his sister was confiding in him, "Brandy, you had sex quick with him. Perhaps he figured you were more sexual and aggressive. Obviously he enjoys experiences shared," Dave answered in strain.

Brandy carried on, "I was devastated and threaten to call the police. He smashed my house phone. Then he shifted the blame to me, saying, I have never touched his private parts. He followed with him making love to the girl from my work. To top that off, he rubbed it into my face that she was beautiful and said I don't fix myself up. I told him to leave and changed the locks. He clearly finds her much more beautiful than me," she cried.

"Sis, what are you nuts? You cannot even confirm you have his real name. He clearly expressed his desires were for the other woman, not you, sunshine. That's not what you need," added Dave in disappointment for his sister.

"No, I don't know where he works, and I didn't think to get his last name. What am I supposed to do, ask for identification?" she stammered.

Dave was disappointed in his sister, "You look like someone spun on drugs. You've lost weight, your hair is ratty. We have to get you cleaned up. You look like a... I don't even want to say it...." Dave vented in distaste.

"The second man I've slept with and look at me. I thought he cared and believed he was a genuine loving and honest person, and it didn't hurt that he is gorgeous," Brandy snuffled.

Dave sadly interjected, "Well, you were out of it the moment you missed seeing past his good looks. The man provided you booze, the second he met you. That got you into bed. He knew you were naïve and easily led. " "I trusted him. This made me naïve, and forced me to be at fault," Brandy asked while she wept blowing her nose into a handful of soggy tissues.

"Honey, you can report him to the police and we should go to the Hospital to see if you were dropped any sort of drugs. You look sick," Dave stressed.

Brandy was shocked to hear what he suggested, "Please Dave, no, don't make me go. I will not know what to say. We didn't live together. He still has his own place, and I have no clue where it is. What do I say? I met a man, had sex, and gave him a key to my place. By the way, I didn't get a last name, and had no sense to ask for his address either. I sound like a whore. Thanks Dave I feel worse coming here," she anxiously stated.

Dave got more annoyed, "You don't want to do anything to help yourself sis." Brandy was already displeased with herself, "I didn't come here for you to rub more salt into my wound. I came for a tender ear and some love." Dave got angry and stood up, looked in her face, "Why didn't you think of all those things before tonight just boggles my mind? Damn you Brandy, something isn't right with you," he affirmed to her.

Brandy felt worse about coming to see him. She stood up, walked towards the door saying, "I can leave Dave. You've obviously been drinking, and I cannot take anymore belittling."

Dave was feeling a little high from the wine, "Sit down. Yes, maybe I had some wine and I'm cutting to the chase trying to figure out what the hell is going on with you. Perhaps my mouth isn't a little more tactful. But what did you expect from me, not to slap you back with what you already knew was wrong?" Brandy cried harder, "I need you to listen, not chastise me for my own stupidity. I'm doing that myself," she yelled.

"You don't have to say or do anything, you don't want to do sis. Perhaps, now you can get back your life and can let this creep go. Let's call a cab and get some blood work done at the hospital," Dave urged.

"Sorry I ruined your date Dave, but in the morning not now please. It was even odder that this old man came to the restaurant dropped his medication, he looked like a drunk and asked about Maria. It's the same woman John Paul stated he was fucking, and rubbed in my face, she is beautiful. And now you tell me, I look like shit, that's all I've been hearing," she yelled through her tears.

"Oh Brandy you're just exhausted. Calm down, it will seem better when you get some rest," Dave said as he sat her back down on the couch.

"Yeah… well… this old man, had drugs, and a ton of them, in two pill bottles. I told him to go see a doctor. When I ran into this woman, she was laughing at me, for spilling my guts to her and suggested, I didn't know what discreet meant," Brandy whined.

"Oh, don't worry sis. It's stressing you out. Let's get you some sleep. We can talk more in the morning. Perhaps, it will make more sense then," Dave said as he wrapped his arms around her, and squeezed her tight.

"Now, you go take my bed and I'll take the couch," he offered. "The couch will be fine for me," Brandy suggested. "Never you mind. Now get in the bedroom. We will finish this talk tomorrow. " Dave said as he padded her bottom, taking her to the bedroom. Brandy felt relieved to be at her brothers' place, "You're always, here for me Dave," she said as she kissed his cheek, and he shut the door.

Seven

James stood in front of the ATM machine and stared at the big money machine in a trance-like state, deep in thought. "Go ahead. Try it damn you," James whispered to himself, as he placed his card in the machine and waited for the customary greeting from the big hunk of metal. At one time, there would have been thousands of dollars in ready available cash for the taking. However, like everything else, Maria had access. He was sure his account would be empty. James began punching his password with one finger 8-2-6-9-2. It spelled the letters of his wife Tanya. He never had the heart to change the password after she died. He then punched in the amount five hundred. The machine sputtered and clanked trying to decipher the information punched in.

"Please machine, please," James, pleaded, holding the sides of the machine, as if, he was talking to an actual person.

Money started to spit out, twenty dollars bills were waiting for him to grab, when he looked down. "It worked. I don't believe it," James shouted finding it hard to contain his excitement.

James grabbed the money and stuffed it into his pockets. The machine's screen displayed, "Do you want another transaction?" He opted to try for another five hundred, and then another, until it stopped allowing him access. He was able to get fifteen hundred. A balance receipt chugged out at the end. He still had over five hundred and fifty thousand dollars in this account. "Maria did not get it all yet," he said in excitement.

Whatever the reason, James now had some money. Yet, the excitement faded fast, when reality crept back in. He had to make sure, it wasn't a mistake.

He waited in line to find out he had to speak to the Bank manager. He waited for over an hour to see him. Mr. Slater put a limit on transactions on his accounts. Stopped any checks written out to cash with the details James provided and gave James, a thousand dollars in cash.

Mr. Slater got up to escort James out and said, "Now James, I cannot guarantee with the information you provided all checks you signed will be stopped. As I suggested setting up new accounts and transferring all your money into the same type of accounts, was securer way to go."

James at first was relieved, and then changed his mind, after he persuaded himself to think the way Mr.

Slater expressed with securer. No one but him could access it, unless he shared his details with someone else. It all resonated true in his head, "I think you were right at first. Let's make new accounts, with all new numbers, but everything will be the same as my accounts now. I should have said okay, let's make new accounts. But, I didn't trust you when you couldn't help me out with the last big chunk she took," he added as an insult.

Mr. Slater bit his tongue and agreed. He transferred his money to his new accounts. He told James, "The other investments held the names of his children, which they could not touch without them present, or unless James had legal documentation which permitted him legal access without them," but he didn't go into what those were. For James account, he received a new bankcard. Mr. Slater then told James, "His new checks were automatically ordered, and would arrive, by mail."

James freaked out, "I don't have a home she sold it. Why do you think I pushed for new accounts? She is a professional thief who can swiftly swindle in and out of everything. She would have figured out a way around my accounts somehow. If we left everything the same, no matter what we did. So what you did at first was a waste of time," he complained.

"We can change your address, when you know your new one. I'll cancel the order for your checks in the system now. Your accounts and family investments are still under your current address, which will need to be updated, when you know your new address," Mr. Slater informed him.

James had to set up a pin on his new card to access the banking machine. Mr. Slater took him to a machine and wanted to make sure it worked. James picked the same pin.

James bitched to Mr. Slater as they walked, "The investment I cashed in and you did the certified check for was deposited into an account at that woman's bank. Her branch manager knew the money was mine, and didn't bother to make a new account with both our names. I now realize how easy it was for her to do this. How can people sleep at night, doing this shit? I bet they're friends," he surmised as he complained.

"Sorry to hear James, but you can call a lawyer, or the police, we've already been over that part of your concern. You signed yourself here. I've done all I could today. Have a nice day," replied Mr. Slater as he walked away.

James sat at a restaurant drinking a coffee and called his lawyer. His secretary patched James through to his lawyer. He bellowed out, "I came home found my home sold. This young lady I met has robbed me blind." He gave him the details of the investment he cashed in, her name, cell number and her lawyers name."

The lawyer tried to calm James down, "James, please think, what do you recall. I need the Real Estate Agents name and number that's on the sign." James pulled out his wallet when he remembered, "I think it's the same lady that came to my house asking me to sell and I told her no. She must have left her card and the thief went into my wallet and left it inside," James vented.

"So you had a real estate agent visit you James, before the 'for sale sign', and sold sign went up?" Mr. Fattastantas questioned. "Yes, but I told her no, I wasn't interested. Her name is Sandra. It's the same lady," James confirmed. His lawyer urged James, "Go home and I'll call you after I find out more."

James lawyer was his wife's lawyer for almost thirty years. Tanya, James wife had inherited money from her family after they passed. Their lawyer Mr. Fattastantas, near his retirement, in his seventies was still going. It was just luck, he hadn't retired yet. Mr. Fattastantas, dealt with Tanya's will after her passing.

James hadn't spoken to him since his wife's death, at the funeral. Mr. Fattastantas had removed Tanya's name from the title of the house after she passed and placed the adult children's names on title with James. James was overwhelmed with Tanya's death and didn't recall anything the lawyer had mentioned to him then.

Mr. Fattantantas provided James and his children with the necessary legal documentation. James adult children did not want James overwhelmed with minor details, and had the lawyer talk to them.

Yet, when James called, he didn't mention his children had signed to sell the home. Mr. Fattastantas continued to press James, for the possibility. What James left in voice mails to him, and now on the phone James, was all over the place. Mr. Fattastantas contemplated James children took power of attorney of James.

The lawyer called James several times throughout the day, asking him questions and kept him updated. "I've got all the necessary legal forms James. And I have compared the two signatures with signatures I have on file for you. It looks like your signature, but its messy," Mr. Fattastantas expressed. "How, I didn't see or sign anything." James pleaded with ignorance.

"James you had no authority to sell a home without all parties to the ownership signing, which included your own adult children, which this agreement lacks," Mr. Fattastantas said to pressure James to admit he sold it without his children knowing. All James said repeatedly, "I didn't sign or know about it, where would I live?"

Mr. Fattastantas telephoned James children, but had no luck reaching any of them. He left messages, indicating, "Something wasn't right, all of you knew that you were on the title of your father's home. Why aren't your signature's parts of this sale agreement for your dad's home? Your father apparently doesn't know anything about this sale?" was the message he left." He had to ask them personally, if they took power of attorney over James.

He had to leave for the day and still hadn't heard back from any one of them. He made up an emergency motion and submitted it into court to stop the sale of the home. Considering, it wasn't a legal binding sale with all parties, to the ownership. He had the right to proceed. He handled all home sales for James children and had no knowledge, on this one. It just felt off to him.

James was too tired and couldn't bring himself to the idea of going back home yet. He didn't feel he had a home anymore. He rented himself a hotel room, headed to the bar, ate, and had some drinks before retiring to the empty room. He tried to drift off to sleep, but couldn't. He took a shower, had a shave and went down to get a haircut. He came back up and tried to sleep again. He tossed and turned in worry venting aloud, "Maria is costing me, even more money and inconveniencing me, with a new address.

She has no idea how much this is killing me."

James woke up at noon, went down for breakfast at the hotel and drank coffee, while he read the newspaper. He checked his voice mail. His lawyer confirmed a hold was on the sale. James called the office. His lawyer hadn't arrived back from court. James decided to go up to the room and had a nap. All he complained about before drifting off, "Now, I have to pay even more money, for everything the lawyer needs to do, because of deceitful Maria."

He woke, after five in the afternoon and figured he'd make a visit to the Real Estate Agent that he now devalued just as much as Maria. He walked into her office, asking for her by name. The secretary checked, "She's here. Your name sir, so I can tell her who is waiting," she asked. James didn't want to be kicked out if he gave his full name and answered, "Jim."

Sandra came out and did not recognize James. He was the only person waiting. She walked over to him, "Are you Jim?" "Yes, I am," James replied. "I'm Sandra," she confirmed.

"What can I do for you?" she asked. "You owe me an explanation. How did you secure a sale on my home?" he vented out. She looked to him confused, "I don't understand. I don't know who you are. It must have been another Agent that you were dealing with?" she calmly and professionally suggested.

James went into a tangent, flinging her card around her face, "Here, doesn't this card belong to you? Do you want to sell your home? Mind you, I do not need your permission. I'm an Agent, and that's my name. It's Sandra Kline to you."

Sandra looked at him confused as she stepped

backwards to talk to him, "Oh yes, it's my card. I hand them out with my flyers. I don't understand why you're here, sir," she questioned.

"My name is James Johnston. Does it sound familiar to you?" The moment he said his first name, she realized where she had seen him before. Her face formed a' V', with wrinkles in between her eyes on the upper bridge of her nose and when her nose scrunched together, her upper lip raised up, and she backed away from him.

Sandra was assured she knew everything she needed to know, "Yes, well James, I'm here dealing with all the legal issues with your home, with my broker. A ton of legal documents came. The purchasers can sue you, if you back out of the deal now. The purchasers bought in good faith. The law will protect the buyers, not you," she said in a confident state.

James leaned into this petite, Asian woman and yelled, "I already called my Lawyer before coming here and I'm well aware that the sale was already stopped by a judge. How beneficial for you to leave this small yet, very important detail out. Whom the fuck do you think is paying him to do this? Let me ask you are you the seller's agent, or the buyer's agents?" James vented.

"I'm not going to justify that question with an answer, Mr. Johnston," smirked Sandra.

"When you came to my home, a young woman invited you in. You stood at my front door in my home, and asked her to get the owner of the house. That is what she expressed, when she woke me up from my couch. Where you were standing you could clearly see a man on his couch, sleeping. She woke me up asking, "Do you want to sell your home?" I was sick. My head couldn't lift from the pillow. You spoke from the door. Do you want to sell your home? I never got up. I kept repeating no… no… leave… me alone, please… I recall this faintly only now, because it felt like it was a dream at the time to me. I was suffering in massive sweats and when I went down sick, I couldn't get up. We have never spoken face to face. You left a flyer at my home and I recalled seeing your picture on it as well as on the real estate sign. Do you recall Maria, at my home? She is a dark haired young lady?" James questioned.

"Yes, I do recall Maria." Sandra answered proudly.

"When you entered my home, was I not sick in massive pain, passing in and out, in my home, on my couch?" James asked. "Yes, I believe you were on the couch, but I cannot say for sure if you were sick," Sandra answered.

"We've never sat down, and talked about me selling my home. I've never spoken to you. Something isn't right here," James added.

Sandra knew right away James was right, "Excuse me James, I don't plan on talking to you, about this matter."

James snapped, "Yes, that's because you know I'm right. I told you when you walked into my home. I was not interested in selling or moving. I stated, no, several times when Maria asked me and you pushed and pushed from the doorway, asking the same fucking question. Now I realized it was you," James expressed.

"James come with me into my office. We can speak privately on this matter. Agents and other clients will be frequenting this area," expressed Sandra.

James followed Sandra to her small office. He gazed into the windows of other offices as they walked. He seen couples sitting down talking with either a man or a woman, and figured it was clients with their agent.

Sandra stopped to get her and James something to drink. "Would you like a coffee or a bottle of water?" she asked. "I don't want anything," James snapped.

They walked into her small office, she offered James a seat, and then sat at herself behind her desk.

"I have never seen your face besides today, when you walked into the small waiting room out there. You didn't know me either. This is the first time we've spoken. You've never given me one of your business cards. Maria must have placed your card in my wallet, because that's where I found it. The question I have is, how the hell did you sell my home without me knowing about it?" James asked calmly believing she was going to share the answer.

"What are you trying to get at, James?" Sandra inquired.

James noticed she was sitting there with her fingers entwined together on top of her desk. Like she wasn't going to answer anything he wanted answers to, "What did you two women do, worked your magic listed my private home without my consent? Got your friend or family to buy it, and sold it for less than market value? That way you could steal my equity. Moreover, stated, this is all its worth, to support your lowlife bullshit? What for? Well, of course, it's most advantageous as an outcome for you, or someone else you know? Isn't it," James accused her.

"Oh my James, we have rules to follow. That didn't occur to you," Sandra replied.

"I heard this sort of shit occurred with friends and their families. Once agents were in the industry long enough, they mastered this con. I'm old, and been around the block. No one complains when it's good for him or her. Sadly, my friends had no money to fight back, and couldn't' prove shit, without a lawyer," James sputtered out.

"Oh my, Mr. Johnston, you do have some sort of active imagination there, don't you," ignorantly commented Sandra.

"You agents can play it out to look straight up. The many games real estate agents play, some, not all play. Price it low and tell the client this will bring in multiple offers. Excuse when it doesn't the market is down. Yet, similar homes sold for a profit in the same area but you neglected to disclose this to clients. You're in it to position it on the low end of the scale to bring it down from its true market value. So when you sell it, you have established a lower form of equity for the client, and easy pocket change for yourself. That equity is not yours, and wasn't earned by you. All you worry about is what your take is going to be when the commission comes rolling in. The profit margin isn't much different for you when it's a few thousand bucks, when you list the home, but the home owner takes the loss. Now what do you say Sandra, what do you know," James asked.

She just sat and listened, and tried to follow along with what he was saying, "I have no idea what you're trying to imply once again Mr. Johnston," commented Sandra.

James looked to his paper, "It's not always to get multiple offers, and to drive up the price when you list it low. You simple-minded assholes use it to steal equity from sellers any way you can. What did you say the inside of my house is fifthly and you took pictures to display how dirty it was, to lower its value in the market? You better realized I spent well over a million on my grounds alone," James expressed.

"We had one client looking for a house out your way. There was no statistical data in your immediate area with similar homes that sold. Real estate has risen through the years, but the last home that sold in your area was over twenty years ago. You cannot expect to get anywhere near the price for your home as what city prices go for, even with the land James," suggested Sandra.

"I didn't list my home for sale and I sure as hell wasn't looking for a price. Do you know what custom built is? You couldn't sweat hard or long enough for me to explain it to you. You have no fucking idea how much it costs to build a home, or to add to one. Out of curiosity, did you see all my property before you priced it? Or did you look from the front door, figured its low end, and priced it low? I have over 100 acres, and this is waterfront property. I built another home, at the back of my property and it's rented out," James yelled out.

"I didn't know you had two homes on your land, nor did I realize it was that large, and waterfront too," nervously answered Sandra.

"Why does this information matter? It proves you didn't speak to me about my home, you dumb bitch. You are a scammer who swindles people out of millions, while helping yourself and your friends. You do this to suck equity from homes and transfer it to you or someone you know. If the title goes to them they can sell instantly for a profit. This con is used on the city streets and was always used in smaller cities. You spin sales as a new agent by taking on first time homebuyers. If they don't have the money for city property, you ease them out of town. This helps you get commission as a new agent. New agents usually deal with first time homebuyers. The only clients you have when you start, are friends and family other than first time homebuyers. After you've been in the industry long enough you milk homeowners about forty thousand of the true market value this is how brazen some agents are at the start. It can build up to fifty or seventy thousand easily. That is not disclosed and hard to prove. When you're the agent who can play with pricing values, and roll them around, who can one complain too?" huffed James.

"James, please leave… please," begged Sandra.

"I heard cons like you looking to add listings to your resume, will even suggest to clients lets list your home higher then true value, hoping to either rise the neighborhood up in value. Another way to place the property higher is to steal equity by easily preventing showings, and not accepting offers. You agents use higher prices to get clients to sign with you, so you can secure the listing. Then you use the excuse it was your client trying to seek a higher price for their home when no offers come in and you never showed it. Months go by, and the listing expires, and not a single offer came in, or if it did, it was exceptionally low and no one seen the other offers, because no one answered the call to accept the real offers. You were either too busy, or had to go out of town. Why do you do this? The number one reason is using the clients' equity to help out your family or friends to secure decent equity for nothing. What for? So, you can flip it and make a profit the moment the deal closes. You can re-flip the property for the true value in equity the client missed during the initial sale which is the listing you took advantage of," James shared.

"Okay, Mr. Johnston your home is sold and the matter is currently going through the legal process in court. I have nothing more to discuss with you, please leave," Sandra requested. She was tired of sitting listening to him rambling on and stood up.

He ignored her request to leave, "You shouldn't play with money which belongs to someone else," James fumed out. "Okay, James I think you need to stop now," ordered Sandra.

"Commission is so slight for the agent, when listing it doesn't make a difference what it sells for to agents. Don't hate the player hate the game is the saying, isn't it. Clients divulge too much. Agents can worsen a situation and it's hard to trace. Especially if a homeowner doesn't know such a fraud existed. I never thought this shit could be real or get pass the system today and it still does," James vented.

Sandra was annoyed with James and his allegations, and started to squirm in her chair, "A family bought the home. Another Agent had a family looking for a home in your area. That was the only reason, I was up in the country handing brochures. In those, I attached my business card. People work through the day, leaving me to place my package in the homeowner's mailboxes. My material might have something like this. If you were looking to sell, we have buyers looking in this area. If you would like a free evaluation on your home, please contact... When I went to your home, Maria answered, and invited me in. What transpired became the sale of your home. Someone, on your end, accepted the offer, and faxed it back. It went off to the Lawyer, for closing. That's as far as my knowledge goes." Sandra disclosed.

"What lawyer, I've had the same legal firm for many years. Why would I change lawyers for you?" James questioned.

"We recommended one, on the telephone when your friend or assistant Maria, faxed it back." Sandra confirmed.

James was fuming with rage and disappointment. His body poured out sweat, his hair he continued to toss away from his face, and it had been cut, but he got used to this habit, and didn't realize what he was doing. "I don't have a business, or an assistant. I didn't agree to any legal transactions with regards to my home. If you communicated with her, it's not me. If you took her word for things, it's your legal issue and not mine. The only conversation you had with me was when you tried to push me to list. Your rational was, just to see what I would get for it. You were highly pushy. Had no respect, that I was unwell when you were in my home. At what point, wasn't it clear to you, I wasn't well? I didn't get up to speak to you that should have been enough for you to understand. When, I said, please, leave, no, I'm not interested and no, no, no, again... ... no... clearly... The word no, means, no. I didn't stand up or go to the door, or show any interest in selling my home. Due to the fact, it's was not something at any time, I wanted, considered or thought about doing In addition, I was deathly sick on my couch, in my home," James shouted.

"What are you trying to say, I falsified a sale on your home and had my friends or family purchase it? That didn't occur to you Mr. Johnston." Sandra assured him.

"You have to know if it had of went to close, Maria has no financial interest in my home. And at no time, did she have any sort of legal signing authority on my behalf. To make matters worse. I had no such knowledge of these activities, until after it sold. That is fraud. The owner of the house has to first, be aware, agree and sign, and that is me. This isn't a forced sale from a bank, Missy. And my lawyer has informed me, on some of those plays too," informed James.

Sandra wasn't sure how to deal with James," You signed to list. Here is the paperwork. Do you remember on the couch you agreed to list for thirty days? I left the documents at the door, in hand with Maria. She asked me to wait in my car, she came out, and everything was signed. Here is the Purchase Agreement with your signature. Are you saying you never saw these, nor signed them?"

"I don't recall signing anything that day and in my condition. What were you desperate for commission that you didn't think to talk to me in a state of wellbeing? You should have known better. Two moments to confirm with the owner, which is me. Did you ever come to my home? Or call my two telephone numbers, to speak with me, after seeing me so ill, on my couch? This is the first and only time you and I have stood face to face, and communicated. This means, we have never spoken regarding my home, where I agreed to sell it. Isn't this correct? You cannot deny this," James firmly stated.

"Yes, James, this is the first time, I've had any formal communication with you, regarding your home," Sandra agreed.

"When a person tells you to leave and expresses they have no interest to sell and says, no, clearly no means, I resist your repeated requests to sell my home. Was that not enough for you to forgo force by coercion, or persuasion? You know this is true. I had no interest, in selling my home. I never would have ever agreed to sell it at any time. The service of selling or buying homes was the service you were offering. You never did call, after being told no, and I yelled, I'm not well. That was me, screaming out in pain. I was also on medication, prescribed by my doctor. A person cannot drive while on this medication. That condition also means a person isn't in any state to agree to any legal transactions. That was me a state of duress," James informed her.

"Would you like to leave now, James?" Sandra asked.

"I am not finished yet. I would have called you, if you had put a for sale sign on my property. That would have been as far as you two women got, when it came to swindling me out of my home. I have lived in this home, since the day I got married. It was a wedding gift from my wives family. We raised our kids in that home, and it will remain, in the family line. My wife had this stated, in her will," James shared.

Perhaps, you're upset now, because you realized how much this home means to you Mr. Johnston." Sandra suggested.

"Don't try to switch this around on me. There

never was a for sale sign. I left my home for a couple of hours, and when I returned, a sign stating for sale and sold sat at the entrance of my property, facing the side road. When I left my home and drove down my long peaceful driveway to the side road, no sign was there. I would have noticed it...I left for a messily two hours. This sign blew my fucking mind and the decent man that I am. I took my time and called the number on the sign, believing it was placed on my property by mistake. For which I was told, the sign wasn't misplaced and my home sold by an agent named Sandra." James voiced riled up.

"I can explain the sign James." Sandra tried to explain, but was cut off by James.

"Sit down and listen to me. You were persistence in my home, now it's my turn. You need to understand what you've put me through. When I called the number on the sign, Don called me back. I tried to express my concern with the sign. An asshole would have ripped down the sign, which I didn't do. I believed the sign was misplaced. Don played with legalities, and treated me like trash. I hate the game and the players, and that's you and him too," James sputtered.

"If you don't leave my office James, I will have no choice but to call the police," threatened Sandra.

"Don was evasive, and told me I'd need to display identification to prove I am who the fuck I am." Without the fuck, but please tell me, what fucking identification right now, was shown to you? You took those legal documents out and showed them to me? Aren't those private documents that state who the seller is, and who purchased the home? I showed you nothing. What fucking privacy act did Don ramble on about that you people actually follow. He was spinning protocols, neither of you respect or follow, and you even admitted to me, that you have never spoken to me regarding my home," James bellowed out enraged.

Sandra felt she was being interrogated, "James I had no idea you weren't aware or in full agreement of the sale. I surely didn't believe for one minute anyone would have signed on your behalf, or I never would have taken the listing. Let alone, involved a purchaser to go through this mess. Apparently, your children are to sign your Lawyer noted. This sale was quick, two days James. It all occurred in two days. I ordered the sign and the sale cleared when the sign arrived. I had them put sold on it, at the same time," pleaded Sandra.

"The sale was contaminated Sandra. As a professional Agent who deals in personal properties which are investments to their owners. The equity belongs to them and me. Your commission is small potatoes, with sales transactions of this magnitude. Isn't it also standard for an agent not to leave any possible commission on the table? You would have offered to assist me with another home purchase, which you never did. Why, because you were hiding something," firmly James stated.

Sandra couldn't believe James was still rambling on, got up and went to her office door, "Stop it James, you're digging for issues where no issues were, or are on my end," she raised her voice as she stated it.

"Where would I live, if I really did agree? You never called me back, after Don, spun his bullshit," added James.

Sandra was beside herself. "James, I most certainly did call your home after Don spoke with you. I left several messages. You hadn't returned my calls. It's not something anyone would think to consider, someone falsified your signature as you have suggested occurred to you. What benefit would this woman have to gain from something so evil?" she questioned in innocence.

James now believes he knows the answer, "I bet the money is scheduled to go into an account at her Bank, without my name right? Are you part of some fraud that takes money from devastated and disoriented victims, after losing their spouse? Isn't this what your scam is?"

"It's not like that…. James," was all Sandra got out. "Don't tell me that you didn't play me," he yelled.

Sandra was disgusted and yelled, "Get out of here James," she said pointing her finger for him to exit her office. "I don't have to tolerate you and your allegations. You're a drunk, and a pill popper. When I came into your home, I could not help but take notice of all the pills, and booze in your living room. Don't make accusations of me, or involve me in your deranged love triangle, or suggest criminal activity occurred, by me or my assistant," she told him.

"No one has power of attorney over me. So figure out your next lie, or play considering I do not do drugs, and my doctor can prove this. I was already there. As I told you, I was sick, and who the hell are you to complain to me about what I can do or did, inside my own home. I can have a drink or two in the privacy of my home. I'm a fucking adult man here. I do not drink often or excessively. That woman Maria does not have any sort of power to sign any legal documents on my behalf. Perhaps, she falsified a signature that she got you to believe, was mine. Nevertheless, as a professional, you knew to talk to the owner of the home and that person is standing before you. Do you know what this has done to my life?" he cried.

Sandra just wanted out of the confusion," I wish, I never met you. Please leave and don't include me in some scam that you and whomever that woman is to you, made up to ruin my reputation as a Real Estate Agent. You seem to know all the swindles maybe you should teach a course on real estate rip offs. I've been doing this for six months and spoke to my broker, the moment your Lawyer called. He is dealing with the legal portions of this transaction, not me," she pleaded in pain.

James shouted, "You better be prepared to be sued." "Go please, just go," begged Sandra.

James interjected, "What do you women do, read the obituaries. Show up at the funerals check our family and us out. Then you follow us home that gives you our address. Follow us again, when we leave home. Pretend to bump into us and chitchat, at a common establishment. You pretend to be compassionate and understanding towards our loss. This gets us to trust you. We divulge personal information and this shows we were in a state of vulnerability from our loss. You already knew we were suffering. It was undeniable. It spins us in a way, I cannot even begin to explain, and you'd never understand, unless you loved, and loved with everything you had. You wouldn't understand how that feels, your heart is selfish. It's not like one of those rides, we hop on and someone else puts the brakes on that we went on it because, we had a choice, and when we got off that ride, we were happy and still in a state of disbelief. Happy we took the time to experience the ride and at peace, we're safe. Those rides are at amazement parks. On the ride you two women took me on, it had no brakes. It spun me upset down, around, and around. I didn't know I was being spun on some ride. That's an unfair advantage" expressed James.

"James, there was no ride. If that's how you felt, I'm sorry," expressed Sandra.

"You keep us busy and take us away from family, friends, and resources. You play the victim, and get hurt. We caused it in our state of confusion and loss. You, threaten to sue us... Therefore, we invite you to our home, while suffering in pain ourselves to help you. At the time, we felt worse for you, than ourselves that's when you grab any available cash we somehow divulged to you we had. Your friends are, lawyers, real estate agents, and bankers, and god knows who else," James bellowed out.

"Calm down… your wrong James. It's nothing like that. I only came to your home that day, I've never met Maria before this," Sandra tried to speak over him and firmed her vocal tone.

"It's easy for you, after we're drunk and stoned, on whatever drug you spun us with. It's the morning after, we cannot say we were stoned, as legal documents cannot be signed under intoxication, or drugs and be classified as legal, now can they. I was sick, just plain fucking sick. Therefore, you took pictures I bet, of that one moment in time, I was. I looked bad and, it was just the one time. I'm the real victim here, but I cannot prove this to a judge, with all your evidence. I would not have known about your pictures, until disclosure came around. That's when you've plotted the humiliation on me to get me to settle some legal claim that would be more beneficial to you all. He wasn't drunk when he signed, your honorable judge. It was the night before when he drank. Just ask him. And that would be a truth that I would have had to admit too," cried James.

"James go please, go. I have no idea what you're rambling on about," announced Sandra.

"No, don't you interrupt me again... Sandra. I caught the play. "There is no play, James," she dribbled out before her voice was overtaken by his need to talk even louder over her to be heard.

"Oh come on whatever you dropped me with, I didn't remember that day or you. I see you keep yourself well maintained. I bet your outfit cost no less than five hundred. Your car is a Porsche, or better. Your purse is top of the line. Your home is by the lake. Perhaps a new Condo in the city, right on the lake for late night stays. Let's not forget to include, several properties you own, you do rent out."

"James, I do own a couple of homes, and my interest in real estate came from my family. I do drive a BMW, and I have not been an agent in real estate long. I already told you this. I have a family and my own money. I didn't need to steal yours, or anyone else's to get what I have," she expressed.

"If you had money, and enough, you wouldn't be working here. What are you doing trying to remove a snag to jump over the next hurdle in your game? Moreover, that hurdle is me. You won't get this sale with me alive and fighting you bitches back. You call yourselves diva's, 'Women n Business n Power', I betcha," sputtered James.

"Sit down James. Let me get you a drink of water. Your face is red, with blotches all over it. Your heart is pounding out your shirt. You're not helping your health here," Sandra pleaded at a loss with what to say or do for him.

"If you see an obstacle in your plan, you change topics, flash a little more skin... Do shorter skirts and go braless in public. Our focus is you bitching about all these men looking at poor little ole you. It's all about you. One more card, dropped. By then, you have been to the land office. Checked any of our property titles to make sure you have clear cash. To top it off now you know how much we paid. The cash split from the sale, is the difference if any mortgage is owed. You may state you paid to make the property presentable, or was in such disrepair, it had to be priced this low, or this high if the suckers dead. Either way, I owe you that extra bit of money, you never spent. Yet who is to say you didn't?" shouted James.

"James stop, please, go, I cannot watch you're going to have a heart attack, if you don't settle down," Sandra tried again to interject.

"You know the date of closing, not me. By that time, I am fucked up inside a hospital wall. What with a heart attack, now, because crazy, a drunk and a pill popper, did not work for you, yet. I see you have clear pocket change and used a lawyer that I don't even have a name or have a number for. I bet all the men you diva's Bitches in Business n Power swindled had no mortgages were near retirement. I imagine some were fucking ugly they were happy to have someone beside them. It wasn't too bad for you women, you looked well kept. Those suckers really did smile and often. That sucker is just one more asshole off the list of men, who somehow abused women in some way and was the asshole with cash, you diva women n business n power took power over... What a lifestyle skill, my dear. Tell me, do all the men usually commit suicide before he figures it out? It's simpler that way, isn't it? I know what that feeling of confusion and you creating the chaos does to a person. It drives a person to a sensation of powerlessness and a loss with getting support from family. If that wasn't bad enough, everywhere resources should have been were gone. We're humiliated. We can't find answers, in the state you spun us into. It was impossible to see, or for anyone to believe what was occurring to us. How could you not knows was what everyone we tried to tell suggested to us. Like what, did we all turn to dumb and stupid men only after meeting you? We had no clue what was going on and no one cared to listen, or believed us. When they think they know everything, they had missed so much more. You figured that suckers not dead, yet. The money won't be your money if the owner buys another home. That's why you left commission on the table and didn't bother to ask if I had a place to live, or wanted help looking for a home? That would have been easy commission for you. Selling and purchasing a home is the business you claim to be in. Nevertheless, it was all his money. That's my money do you get that? When you hear the suckers' dead, you're in your glory. The Diva's Bitches n Business n Power cannot waste their precious time. If there is no return on their investment, which was what, just your time,"

James rolled out of his mouth.

"James, I took my time here with you today, and I've accomplished nothing. Needless to say, I will not make one red cent from your home," she admitted.

"Two weeks to richness, by, Diva Bitches n Business n Power. That is my book title thanks to you and Maria. The next book, "Diva Bitches in Business n Powers crash course" on, "Women, No Average Wealthy Man Can Beat, by the BNBNP, I'm using just the initials now. After that one, I can write, "How to get cash fast?" Then I will follow with, "Close the deal, with no details," James sputtered before sitting himself down in the chair.

"James, whatever you're boiling over about, is beyond me. I cannot follow you at all. Just leave here, please," Sandra begged. "I'm not leaving, I'm on a roll. I'll take that water Sandra, I'm calming myself back down," James said.

Sandra left her office, got the water and came back and handed it to him, "Here James, are you ready to go," she asked. He twisted off the cap and took a long drink then started up again.

"The process you bypass, along with time protocols. You follow the rules, late. Late nevertheless, but you can say you did. This drives us men crazy, with mental confusion. It takes us a bit to realize, we have not seen you in a while. When we try to call we cannot leave a message, or you just don't answer. You hit the ignore button on your cell, you know so well," James rambled on but he had to take a break and took another long drink of his water.

"Okay James, if you don't leave I'm calling the police, this rant of yours has gone on far too long." Sandra declared.

"You're too busy, burning holes in our pockets while stealing our life's hard work. It is how fast you work. You Diva bitches n business n power can slide in and out. Let's have a race who can rob the most men blind in the shortest amount of time. Its smooth just ask me, one of the Diva's Bitches n Business, n Power victims. We go on our own accord, while spun on drugs, or whatever it is you women used. We did not realize we were part of these Women in Business and Bitches in Power Heist. We were just pawns. That's how smooth and professional these Divas are, and they will never will be caught. Do not worry Sandra, when I arrived, I made sure to press video. I never realized I'd have any use for video cams, on cell phones. Now, I own all the book rights. The story is that of my life," cried James.

"Don't come up to me, to yell in my face," demanded Sandra.

He took a breather, dropped a card down on the desk, "Call this lawyer, he owns the largest law firm in town. Moreover, he has been my lawyer for most of most adult life. I can afford to pay for a very long time. The money you missed never was disclosed. Your little trip to the country, almost took my life. Thank god, for my kids and my dead wife, who knew more about law, then I ever did. The moment I press send, it goes live everywhere and, someone else can share. That way, your life can be devastated, in a way that mine was. How does it feel to have someone upsetting you, and your healthy? What does it feel like asking a person to leave, because you've had all you can take? Just imagine me sick, incapable of getting up from a couch, that was its own ride. Then you can think of a great woman, a mother who had no choice, no way to get off the ride that took her life, it was cancer. And Tanya was my wife, and my life. You people are heartless, and criminal to even think of pulling off this shit," James expressed wiping away tears.

"Please leave, James," she begged. "That's right Sandra you don't feel as free to say whatever is on your mind now, as you did when I first came in. It's been on record our entire time," he walked out turned around, "I bet you can pay people to crash computers systems, and, have them sign non-disclosure contracts, or any form of legal agreements to have it all go your way," James muttered, exiting the office doors.

James went to the coffee shop and spoke to his Lawyer. His lawyer was on a chat with him the entire time he went into her office. He placed things on the screen he wanted James to mention while he was talking to Sandra. James read what he could read off. James zipped his video and sent it to a website his lawyer suggested. His lawyer downloaded from there. The Lawyer called the office and spoke to Sandra and her broker already. But, he called her again and noted, "It was a complicated matter and he had been the family Lawyer for almost thirty years and wanted to have a copy of the Power of Attorney," which Sandra didn't have.

James Lawyer had explained, "The judge is expecting me to provide him with solid documentation on how this sale occurred, without everyone's awareness. So, please let me deal with everything, from here on in. Just go home and get some rest."

James was still not listening to anyone. Money and

feeling used and abused, overwhelmed him, "I can't go home, yet. Not until, I find this Maria. What else she's done to me?" he vented….

Eight

Brandy was startled when she woke. It took a few moments to realize where she was. The bedroom was a ray of sunshine as it beamed into the room. She cuddled herself inside her blankets and looked around the room. She heard her brother fussing in the kitchen.

She finally eased out of the bed and went into the bathroom, opened up a drawer and found a stash of new toothbrushes, opened one and brushed her teeth. She took the hairbrush from the shelf, removed her ponytail, and brushed her hair as she went into the shower. When she finished she fussed through Dave's drawers, found a sweat suit, and put it on. While she mumbled, "John Paul will be furious when he finds out his key didn't work." Then she realized he never brought any of his personal belongings to her place. The only thing glued to him, was his briefcase, and that left when he did. He had no reason to come back.' She became sad thinking about it and wiped away a few tears.

She walked into the kitchen, "Good morning Dave," she said with a smile. "Good morning sunshine, hope you slept well," Dave said cheerfully. "What are you making?" Brandy asked as she took a banana out of a dish, peeled it open and walked over to the stove. Her head popped over his shoulder as she looked into the pans.

"Brunch is on the menu, Eggs, Bacon, Sausage, Ham, Pancakes, Home Fries, and Toast," Dave shared. His hands were busy flipping eggs, sautéing onions, green and red, peppers, green onions, was all she could see, before he looked over his shoulder tossed his specula around her face as he said, "Now, now, young lady, out of my kitchen while I'm cooking."

Brandy went back and stood by the island eating her banana, and noticed his attire. His short blondish brown hair was under a beige mesh hair net. He wore vinyl gloves as he cook. His cotton beige dress shorts peeked out a slit in the back of his cooking apron. He turned around to empty his pan and this sky blue shirt shined underneath his apron. She immediately read the red lettering on the apron, 'I love cooking,' circled around a picture of him. She laughed, "I see you love to cook Dave and the apron is so cute on you," she expressed with a budding smile.

"Dave, why did you go through all the trouble? There is too much food. You had to be running around all morning to stores, while we slept. I can tell you're working out. The muscles are a lot bigger on your arms," she yawned as she said it. Dave insisted as he poured his sister a coffee. "Now, just let me cook. Go on….get out of my kitchen you. Thank you for noticing my arms, he responded as he flexed," and scurried her into the living room.

Brandy could not remember the last time she received so much attention. Sitting in her brother's chair, she felt like a queen. It adapted to the contours of her body and she sank right in. She took a blanket from the back of the chair, and draped it around her. She looked around the room, crystal vases with flowers were scattered throughout. One had, Red roses, with Yellow roses. Another held pale pink roses, aside pink lilies, with lots of greens in both.

At the table sat a purple smoky crystal vase. She got up walked over and smelled inside. A display of lovely lavender roses, pink Lilies, purple gilly flowers with purple matsumoto asters and Queen Anne lace were mixed with lush greens. It accented the table with the rich violet tablecloth. The place setting had an array of violet colored plates. Two Smokey colored crystal glasses sat to the left and right, beside its mate was a fruit and salad plate. The silverware was folded inside a light mauve napkin with pink lace wrapped around, and finished off with a green ribbon. Lavender Tea candles lit added more of the scent to the room and offered a calming mood.

Dave sang along with the music as he cooked. Her head bobbed along with the beat with him. The odd time she'd bellowed out a chorus, and together they sang it louder.

She could see he genuinely enjoyed cooking. For now, she decided to enjoy her cup of coffee and let the smell of Dave's cooking penetrate her senses.

Out came Conrad out of his room, "Morning family, how did we sleep last night? I'm not going to get kicked out before we share breakfast, am I?"

"No… no… of course not Conrad. Sorry for interrupting your evening last night," apologized Brandy.

"I guess we all have moments of despair, and I'm sorry if I wasn't pleasant, we were enjoying a fine bottle of wine before your arrival," apologized Conrad. "Good morning Conrad, please sit down for breakfast, and pick a smoothie you'd like," requested Dave.

Breakfast was wonderful, "I cannot believe how hungry I was. I ate everything on my plate, and took more. I believe 'love' was added as an ingredient that made it all the more delicious and special. And Dave, you pulled out all the fixings," gratefully acknowledged Brandy.

On the island, Dave had separate dishes placed with sliced tomatoes, diced onions, cut up pieces of ham, cucumbers, deviled eggs, watermelon, and several types of cheeses, thinly sliced. Another dish had different pickles.

His Smokey glass mauve crystal fruit platter held apples, oranges, green, and red grapes, along with bananas, which he added to decorate the table. "I felt like I was at a very fancy restaurant for brunch. Thank you Dave," shared Brandy, and gave him a kiss on his cheek.

As they all ate, Brandy and Dave chatted incessantly about nothing in particular, enjoying the odd story from their childhood. They all laughed and giggled as if they were teenagers. Brandy briefly forgot about her problems and lived for the moment. She did not want it to end. When Brandy was finished her last bite of food, Dave suddenly changed his lighthearted banter to a more serious tone.

"Now sis," Dave said sternly. "We have to talk about what happened, do you think he`ll come back?" Brandy knew this question had to come. "Aww Dave, I just want to forget about it." Brandy pleaded hoping to end the discussion. "You can't just forget about this Brandy?" Dave added with a disgusted look in his face.

Brandy was not used to seeing her brother with such a serious tone. It was nice to know he cared. Brandy knew he was disappointed that she interrupted his evening. "I'm sorry for barging in late last night, I wasn't thinking clear, obviously."

"That's okay Brandy we all have moments of upset, and confusion." Dave calmly assured her.

"Yeah, I just wished I had realized sooner this man was a pig, and wasn't into me, and was using me. I can't even call it that. I do hope I don't see him ever again that way I can forget all about him. It's so sad, he talks lovingly and then acted abusively," quietly mumbled Brandy. "Let it go, Sis. Move on. You will in a few days or weeks. It will be when you realize, he was a waste of your time. He's not worth a thought, and you're here with me and alive, and that is all that's matters to me." Dave added with a sigh and a sense of peace. "You just being here for me is enough for me… Davey," Brandy said with a smile as she hugged her brother. "Now I must be getting home," she announced.

"If you say so sis." Dave was more skeptical about John Paul then she seemed to be, "Do you think he'll come back?" Dave asked as he and Conrad walked Brandy to the door, "Doesn't matter, my door won't open for him again," she answered walking out the door. "Okay, bye, hon, see you soon," Dave said as he watched his sister going to the elevator."

After Brandy left, Dave put the dishes in the dishwasher, went to make his bed, and opted to change the sheets and tossed those into the laundry while Conrad showered. Dave was a very methodical person, needing to have everything clean and spotless. Yet, he never minded the work. Once he finished he sat down, and sipped his tea. When Conrad got dressed he came into the living room. Dave started to apologize for the night before. Conrad was snotty at first, not wanting to give Dave the time of day.

"Yeah... sure you're sorry Dave. You wanted me out of here so you had your sister came over. You didn't even offer me the guest room, I had to demand it. Did you plan that before I got there? I couldn't believe you expected me to drive all the way home, when I was drinking. That is a no- no in my books. I would have gone across the street and booked a hotel, if you kicked me out. I did bring an overnight bag, as you suggested. But, how soon we forget...isn't that right...Tell me Dave, were you cutting our time short?" disapprovingly Conrad remarked.

"If I didn't want you here, I wouldn't have had invited you now would I have Conrad? It was a family issue, that wasn't planned. I'm truly sorry, I didn't think at the time about you drinking and driving. Her arrival confused me, and from now on, you will always stay overnight when you drink here or if we are out having a drink somewhere," Dave added with a sense of privacy and guilt. "Well Dave, are you going to tell me what was so darn important that she had you in a frenzy. You're the most level headed person I know?" Conrad stated, with a hint of sarcasm.

Dave was annoyed with the direct question. "It's stuff about my sister Conrad," Dave nervously answered. He was uncomfortable divulging personal information about his sister to Conrad, despite his affection for him.

"Are you serious about us or not?" Conrad questioned defiantly. "Or am I just a fling, someone to spend time with Dave, Is that how it is? Tell me Dave are you serious about your feelings for me? I felt you cared. If this is going to go anywhere, I need you to start sharing with me too. I tell you everything, and you have only mentioned your sister was studying to be a Nurse. We haven't visited anyone in your family and you've been everywhere to meet mine."

Dave was still apprehensive about opening up, but he felt like a rat in a corner. Dave knew if he wanted to continue his relationship with Conrad he had to start opening up to him. "If I tell you, will you keep it private between us?" Dave conceded.

"Look Dave, I am here for the long haul. Or at least I want to be, and that means either you trust me enough to start building this relationship which includes sharing with me everything that we can share, or we stop it now," expressed Conrad. "I understand," said Dave, as he shook his head in acceptance.

Dave sat and tried to relax as he inhaled a few deep breaths, "You are right. I want to see if we can make this work too," he defined.

Conrad crossed his legs, placed one hand over the other on his knees, and leant into Dave's face, "I'm all ears Davey," Conrad added, waiting for Dave to spill his guts to him. "I think my sister moved in a dude that's into rough sex, drinking and drugs of some sorts. He was already screwing a friend of his and was still into having sex with my sister. That is how it looks to her."

Conrad facial muscles scrunched as he listened and spurted out, "Dave... oh my god, really? I am so sorry for your sister. That's disgusting....ewe..." Conrad instantly felt remorse at prying into Dave's personal affairs. "I'm sorry for acting like such an ass last night. I knew it was none of my business, and not knowing the situation, I acted like a spoiled brat. I was only thinking about me. I had no clue that her arrival at your home was so serious at the time." "How were you to know?" assured Dave "What happen," Conrad probed.

"I can't believe, I'm even saying this. My sister was in her place and the man she let come and go with a key, came into the bathroom while she was bathing..." Conrad interjected, with his hand up to Dave's face, "You don't need to tell me, everything. I overheard a lot she mentioned last night. I just didn't want to say I did."

Dave's eyes opened wide, "Thanks for not coming out, I don't think she would have told me anything, if she knew you were listening. To me it sounded like he was trying to make love to her and then got a bit rough, or some type of miscommunication occurred. It was what she said, he said, and did, that concerns me," Dave said as he struggled in his state of confusion.

"She doesn't know for sure if he was just pissed off when he stated he was sleeping with some other woman or if he did. However, she did make the mistake of having intercourse with him so fast, after just meeting him. And she knows nothing at all about this man. It's all so bizarre. I was transfixed on every word at the time," Conrad shared with a wide smile. Almost like he was thriving off the gossip and that's all it was to him. Yet, Dave didn't see it like that at the time. He was too focused on what he was thinking and didn't pay attention to Conrad's actions.

Dave reached for his tea, and said, "The strange thing is she called me early in the evening to drop by her work, but it slipped my mind. " I couldn't stop thinking about you, and called you to come over."

Conrad shook his head, sucked in his lips, and expressed, "I wondered why you called so late, but wanted to see you, so I thought, better not to bring it up. It did seem kind of odd to me, she arrived at your place about two thirty in the morning?" confirmed Conrad. "Yes she did… really strange… and that's not like her at all," Dave paused as he spoke.

"Did you hear Brandy mention, she fell asleep at work, and locked the doors? When she woke up, she came right here. She's going to lose her job." Dave added with a sense of disappointment. "Unbelievable, no I missed that," Conrad stated as he propped himself closer to him, to catch every word.

"No, no, there's more," Dave interjected, "Just let me finish then you can judge for yourself how strange it sounded." "Alright, Dave, please go on," agreed Conrad

"She lost weight and looks spun on drugs. She has never done drugs, or smoked cigarettes. He pressed her for information about her family. She does not know if he gave his real name, nor did she think to get his last name. She has no idea where he works, or any of his family business. He refused to talk about it. And she believes this was him being private, about his personal business. He must have money, because he dresses like a rich man. Model type but in a clean cut way. So, clean in fact she said that he has his nails done to perfection. That sort of straight male," Dave said as he recalled details his sister shared.

"Dave, not everyone divulges their private lives, look at us. Do not judge him on his appearance, look to the details. Not mentioning his work, has no rational in my mind, after all he did take a key for her place. And his family, perhaps he isn't close, it doesn't mean he is hiding something there," Conrad suggested.

"She complained some older man came to her work asking for some women her man suggested he was sleeping with. This is the only woman, Brandy has ever complained about, because when she met Brandy she laughed at her for waitressing to make money to pay her rent and buy food. Brandy is taking her course to become a nurse and needed to feel pride, and to know she could make it on her own. I'm off topic here, but it annoyed me to hell when she mentioned it to me. Anyways back on topic. This old man asked about the woman. He had pills and said he didn't know where they came from. He had the shakes, smelled like booze and Brandy told him to see his doctor. When he would not leave her work or go to the hospital, he passed out at a table at her work. She had to wake him in the morning to leave before she finished her shift. "

"The mystery is solved Dave, I know exactly what it is. It's all about sex and drugs and heaven knows what else. Your sister is sooo…sooo lucky she got him out now," Conrad faced cringed with what he said. "No, don't think like that," Dave snapped.

"I'm sorry for being so direct Dave, but people like that just don't care who they drug or drop, or have sex with and will do anything for money. He was asking about you, what did she say?" Conrad probed while he waited attentively for a response.

Dave sighed, his face was drawn and his voice went sad, "I'm sure she shared everything. I owned Condos, work in programming, dabbled with the Stock Market, and made my first millions at twenty-two in software development. I am just rambling what I'd imagine she told him. Brandy acts on impulses and does whatever she figures is right for her at the time. Not always in a bad way. It's just that, she used to quit jobs, and ran off travelling somewhere warm to escape the winter, and came back months later. She hasn't done that since she started school, as a promise to me and herself. Yet, I have to wonder if her impulses went towards men now?" he questioned.

Conrad had a sense of regret in his voice. "I don't understand why she would have shared anything with him. She's not like you at all. We still haven't been intimate, and it's getting on a year and I haven't met anyone besides her now in your family. But, you did tell me about them." Dave got annoyed with Conrad's bitching about what he feels he missed, "Do you have to bring this up now?" he asked.

"I don't mean to be a bitch Dave, but to me your sister is not too with it. She sounds impulsive, rushing him and kissing at the door. She slept with him, gave him a key after what a week she said. Did you give her money, or does she have any?" Conrad expressed, confidently. "No I don't give her money, and she never asks," snapped Dave. "I don't know what to say. Maybe when he realized she had nothing to offer, he left. Guys like that look for women they can use, or people with money," assertively shared Conrad. "That's what I want to figure out," angrily shared Dave.

"You don't know my sister. She is not one who mixes socially, outside of church, or school. She's had the same good friends from grade school. She is a good girl, who is just naïve. She thinks like my mother at times, but not as religious with the idea of marriage and no sex. I paid for her Nursing course, which I hope she didn't divulge. She mentioned she told him that we don't talk. Working where she works, and living where she lives, he wouldn't have realized she could ask me for money if she wanted it," shouted Dave. "Calm down, how long had it been that she went without sleep, before she arrived?" asked Conrad.

"I don't know. Why? What the hell does that have to do with anything?" Dave asked baffled by the question.

Conrad felt a need to be direct, and with more force. He sat up straight, crossed his leg, and placed his right hand on Dave's knee, "When people go for days without sleeping Davey, sometimes they get mixed up. She changed the locks, I actually heard a lot, not all obviously. She sounded fucked up, confused, and rambled on all over the place." He crossed his legs, the other way, took his hand placed it on Dave's leg, "Or I had too much wine and couldn't follow along. Eventually, I had to throw up. My head was spinning so much that when I tried to sleep the room was spinning with me. That was enough to make anyone get sick." He paused, took his right hand to his hair, and fluffed it, "Oh, and I see she gave you her new keys, so how about this…we can go take a visit to her place? This is your sister and she should be taken to the Hospital to make sure she's clear as far as drugs go… ."

"I tried to persuade her to go to the Hospital or the Police but she wouldn't go… I think she's too embarrassed. Perhaps he tried to get her to make love any way he wanted it and became abusive when she threatened to call the cops." Dave explained, pointing his finger in the air, with every point he stressed to build his own conclusion.

"What type of guy would do that to a lady," Conrad asked. "An animal." Dave answered. "Only an animal would do that," Dave repeated. "Where is she now?" Conrad asked, "She left to go home, you heard her," sadly answered Dave.

"Geez, his name sounds gayer them mine," Conrad laughed to ease the tension and took a selfie with Dave.

Dave gave a mild chuckle, and then continued, "She looked fantastic two months ago at our parent's anniversary party. She didn't know him then." "You're digging. And I wasn't invited to that either and there's more of a reason to go. Conrad said with astonishment and a tad bit of bitterness. "I know it sounds stupid," said Dave. "But I can't shake the feeling I have, and yeah, sorry, I didn't invite you to that either," apologized Dave.

"So what's next? Let's go now to her place," suggested Conrad. "I don't know? Maybe you're right. If you have nothing to do today, I can clear my schedule too. I'd enjoy the company. Welcome to the family." Dave uttered going into the guest room to finish tidying up.

"Well, I've heard the same kind of story from some of my friends. They met men they instantly wanted them on drugs, expected open relationships, and needed more money to support their drug habit, or high-level living.

"Dave gasped, "How can you tell if you were drugged Conrad?" " A lot of times you may not know and I know that for sure," positively answered Conrad.

"How?" questioned Dave. "A couple of friends, asked me to go to a party. We went, everyone was happy, friendly, and the house was massive. Food and drinks were free. We swam, music, was great. We went into the saunas, and hot tubs, and were having a blast. Really, it was fun. We celebrated most of the night outside at the place… No one had purses, jeans, or slacks on and no one carried any personal bags."

Conrad stopped to take a drink of his orange smoothie, "Here's a napkin, Con," Dave said as he handed it to him. Conrad went on, "When we arrived, we had to be checked in, and got padded down. If you had pants on, you went in this little room and took them off. We had to wait for shorts to come to us. They took our pants. We couldn't have cameras of any type or personal bags, purses, or cell phones. You got a bag from them and they gave your credit cards to you. It wasn't expensive to attend, just five hundred per person. It was well organized."

"Why were you padded down? And you couldn't you have your cell, purses, or pants, but got your credit cards. Your shitting me right. It sounds stranger then strange. What sort of place was this?" asked Dave.

"I'll get there…. When you walked to the pool

area, it was set up with swimsuits, for men and women. At night t-shirts, shorts, sweat pants, and sweaters arrived for you to take anything you wanted," explained Conrad.

Dave was intrigued, "Wow, what a party. What was it all about? " "Let me get to it. Several bars were all around the property. People were playing volleyball, pool, basketball, and golf. They had something going on everywhere. Everything we did, besides swimming, the hot tubs and sauna's you paid a fee to play. It does sound like a great night doesn't it Dave."

"Yes it does, sounds like you had the time of your life, in that experience, but what I cannot understand is, why did they take all your stuff, and why pay to play?" Dave questioned.

"I figured it was for guns and drugs and to make everyone felt safe. The place was stunning. There were four what looked like solid structured gazebos with dark glass stained windows. We knocked to enter, and when they let us in, they locked the door behind us. We could not see in from outside. The structures were solid, really well built. Immediately they told you how much it was to play. If you agreed, they took you to an area to take money from your credit card. Standing there, we could see people were playing cards. They had tables for poker and black jack. Just like a real casino. I couldn't believe every gazebo had fireplaces burning and a bar in the back. We had to sit on the couch as we waited for a free table. While sitting there we had table service, for food and drinks. When a table was free, they came up to us took us to it. A security person handled the money in dollar increments in chips. I played a few games of poker. We had to have five grand to sit and play in the cheapest one. I went into the second one, and the cost was twenty grand to sit and play. I went for a peek in all of the gazebos. The largest was two hundred thousand to sit and play," divulged Conrad,

"Why were they playing poker for money, isn't that illegal Conrad?" Dave asked. "I'll get to that... When I was finished playing, they took my chips, walked me back out to the lobby area, and gave me an option for a refund slip back to my credit card, or a run with your chips to another table or another gazebo. There was no need to wonder inside the house when it took us hours to take in each experience, in just the one gazebo," shared Conrad.

"That sounds like a rich men's paradise, and something I would have loved to have enjoyed with you." Dave stated, in jealously. "Doesn't it Dave. Up to that point, it was fabulous. We didn't know each other at the time. It was a form of wonderment for me and something you had to experience for yourself to believe," shared Conrad.

Dave sat intrigued, sipping back his coffee, "Yes, it sounds fantastic." "Dave, let me tell you the rest." "Oh, sorry go on," Dave waved Conrad on with his hand, "Please continue."

"At some point later in the night Stacy and I wondered to the house. There were casino tables, and people everywhere. I'm not sure who owned the home. " "Who invited you?" asked Dave. " The gals from work did. Stacy and I stayed late. She and I walked around the inside of the home. When I found a free table and sat down, I realized the cash being played was far from any money I wanted to waste, for a try and left," expressed Conrad. He took a break for a drink.

'Isn't that illegal?" questioned Dave. Conrad hesitated to share all the details, and slowly carried on, "It was a split for some Charity. I got some looks, of wasting these people's time when I took a seat and left. Each room you went in, you had a security guard with you when it came to money. I got a refund put back on my credit card. We left the house and found another small house off the side of the property way up a hill. We wondered inside. Tons of people were surrounded around a table. Stacy and I shoved through people to peek a closer look. We heard people celebrating loudly while saying, 'it's your turn and now you're turn'," Conrad said and got up. Dave jumped in and asked, "What were they doing?" nosily asked Dave.

"I thought it was some kind of game they were playing and you could watch, unlike the other ones. Fuck… Dave, when I got close enough, I seen a shit load of drugs on the table. Lined up lines of coke and shots were handed out to the person that took the next line. We just wanted to leave. Stacy whispered in my ear, 'go towards the door and I'll follow right behind.' Large dudes who looked like bouncers or security were at the door. I wasn't totally drunk, but feeling good by this time, I figure. Stacy didn't drink any alcohol. I got to the door, and the dudes wouldn't let me leave. Two days later, Stacy asked me to think about what occurred," confided Conrad.

"What do you mean you couldn't leave?" Dave asked in midstream of Conrad's story, "Yes, I was too drunk to grasp that myself, but I was inside the house, seen too much I'd imagine." Dave got pissed, "That's radical that you cannot leave it wasn't your fault illegal shit was going on. That had nothing to do with charity," Disgusted by what he heard stated Dave.

"Let me finish Dave…. The bodyguards held me at the door. A few dudes came up started hugging me. Where are you going my dear gay friend? It's a long weekend party no one just leaves, you knew that when you entered. One dude laughed, not afraid of some coke are you? You're next. I said, not interested. That's all I remembered. I woke up, sprawled out naked in some bed, alone mind you," Conrad said, as he wiped sweat off his forehead.

Dave was shocked, "Holly fuck Conrad, what did you do, lines of coke and a shit load of shots? I didn't know you experimented with those things."

Conrad looked ashamed his eyes focused down, "See Dave that's why I don't talk about it, but…no… not normally. The dudes, who came up to me, one tossed some coke up my nose. Instantly I inhaled and I know this because of Stacy. They forced a shot in me after that. Then another line, it was my turn again, and another shot. That was most definitely not our seen and I mean this. I had no memory of anything once I hit the door. Everything was a free for all and I became that way. Thank god I lived through massive stupidity and carelessness, on my high," Conrad shared. Dave was simply stunned, "Oh my…. Conrad."

Conrad wanted to barrel on with his story, "It was me being accosted by security when I tried to leave who didn't bother to help me."

"What did you expect someone else's security to stop you from taking drugs?" snapped Dave in a parental way. "Dave just listen, Stacy tried to tell me what I did. I did not believe her. She fired up her tablet and showed me a video. I was totally wasted. I ran around naked, and joined in some picture taking with one of several photographers they hired. I caressed strange women's breasts, slapped dudes buts, went in a few hot tubs with dudes, and started making out with some."

"Conrad, are you telling the truth?" Dave asked to clarify. "Yes, I couldn't believe what I watched on this recording. It was me. I could hear Stacy saying, 'let's go and try this now.' She was trying to get control of me to get me away from everyone. I tried to play poker. They kicked me away. I played black jack and lost ten grand. I honestly could not tell you what all occurred to me that night or for most of the next day. We left just after I woke up, but I was in tears, looking at what she showed me. I asked her how did she get all this. Stacy told me I was drugged. She went right to the beginning of her recording to prove it to me. She had recorded everything on her cell, and it started with me trying to leave. That's where a dude, held me in his chest by my arms, while another spun me at the door, with coke, and no one seen her taping it. I had white powder on my face, just after they did."

"How the hell did she get that past security if they took your cells and stuff?" Inquisitively, questioned Dave.

"She heard about shit from friends who went prior and she planned to record it. She did not know about the drugs. However, she stuffed the top of her bathing suit with padded material and stuck everything inside the pads, underneath her breasts. She has large breasts. Inside one of the cans, she tossed her cell into her hand while holding a napkin with food constantly, and dropped it into the bag they gave us when we walked around. I didn't even notice. Thank god she took care of me that night. She was afraid herself. She even came to the Police station to report it and gave them a copy of what she took. I was naked running around acting like a nutcase, until Stacy got me into a room, and out of the way and that's how I woke up naked. " Ashamed Conrad added "Where did we met, at work, I've never gone to parties with crowds of people, I don't know. And that was just over a year ago," sighed Conrad.

"I have heard stories like that with drugs," Dave said. "But I didn't think they were true. And why didn't you tell me, before now?" disapprovingly asked Dave. "Why? I'm ashamed." Conrad admitted. "You're alive, so don't be it wasn't your fault. Let's go as soon as I get my shower." Dave rushed into his room. "Oh they are true alright," Conrad said as he followed Dave around until he went into the bathroom and closed the door.

"It is a sick... sick world out there at times Davey." Conrad added. "Oh my god," was all Dave said before jumping into the shower.

While Dave was getting dressed, Conrad followed around, "How far does she live from your place?" he asked. "About a twenty minutes by car." Dave answered. "Let's take my car. We don't know if Brandy gave him your address. You know Brandy did mention that the girl John Paul is having sex with just showed up at a place where she had never been," Conrad seemed a tad bit paranoid in his statement. "You may be on to something." Dave nervously answered.

"Okay," Dave answered in agreement. "I think I want her to move. I'm calling my Agent and getting her a Condo in my building."

Dave called his Real Estate Agent. It went to voice mail so he left a message, "Hi Frank, Dave here. I need a one or two bedroom as soon as possible in my Condo building paying cash. Preferably, a two bedroom that is vacant now. I want to close tomorrow if it all possible or the following day at the latest. The one on my floor, or just above it, fit my criteria. You know my expectations. We've been through several, but forward me some photos after you negotiate, and before calling me back so I can see what where dealing with. Same rules apply," he said in his message, then hung up.

"I should call her first to make sure she's there before we go." conciliated Dave. "I don't know, Davey, why would you call her if you want to surprise her." Conrad asked puzzled making an odd look with his lips curled up under his nose.

"Just to make sure she made it home, I guess," Dave justified with a what type of idiot do you think I am look. He had already pushed her number on speed dial. "Hello," Brandy said as she answered. "Oh…hi…. good Brandy, your home," Dave sputtered out, with a sigh of relief as he looked to Conrad. "I just wanted to make sure you arrived home alright." "Yes, I did. Thank you for everything." Brandy gratefully acknowledged.

"Is your boyfriend there?" Dave probed. Brandy raised her voice, "No!" He took his business bag and has no reason to return Dave and he is never welcomed back here again. I already told you this."

"Sis," said Dave almost apologetically. "I don't want to sound like a broken record, but you really should go to the Hospital to see if you were drugged.

You look like hell." Bothered and shamed Brandy announced, "I just had a long bath, a coffee and cleaned up. I'm sorry that I look like hell to you and everyone else. He's gone now and I'll be fine and back to myself in a little while."

Dave took a deep breath in and yelled, "I wish you'd just take a god damn blood test for drugs sis. With the stories I heard, I want you to know for sure if this man was taking advantage of you in that way."

"I'm sorry I look pathetic Dave, I said, no, he's gone, and you know, I don't take drugs. What will it do, but ruin my career if there are any illegal drugs in my system. Did you think of that? How can I prove, I didn't take anything myself? Leave it alone, that prick would ruin my career and me. Have a fucking heart Dave. What do you think would happen to my life if it's positive for drugs? I am going to be a nurse for heaven's sake," emotionally stated Brandy. "I understand Brandy, and you're right I didn't think of your career and what that may do to you." Dave agreed. Good, I need some rest. Let's talk later," Brandy suggested. Dave lifted his hand up to Conrad looked disappointed and replied, "Sure thing sis." They ended the call.

Nine

James celebrated his newfound wealth in a small but quaint restaurant establishment that he used to frequent on special occasions with his wife Tanya, when she was alive. The restaurant boosted warmth, and offered a relaxing elegant feeling as you walked into the interior entrance. The strategically placed gentle shimmering lights added to the effects that projected a romantic and gentle calmness. James enjoyed sitting away from the piano player, and having the sounds soothing him into relaxation as he listened to it in the background.

James was not there for romance. He wanted a fine meal in comfortable surroundings. The waiter came. He ordered prime rib and baked potato. His large Caesar salad and a 6-piece shrimp cocktail came first. It was not like James to splurge on extravagant meals in a fancy restaurant, but tonight he truly felt like he deserved no less. Two hours had already passed and he was in no hurry to finish. He savored every bite and chewed each piece slowly, as if it was the last meal he was going to eat. The expensive Merlot complimented his thick piece of beef and a large piece of garlic bread sat conspicuously beside his plate. Strangely enough, James was not worried about his surroundings and was oblivious to the small group of customers sitting at a table across from him. He moved his legs in beat with the piano music while he enjoyed his meal. He would smile as he recalled memories he shared with his wife, when they were there.

"Would monsieur care for some more wine?" asked the tall, lanky waiter. "Yes, please" James replied without giving it much thought at first.

When the waiter came over again, James was on his fourth glass of wine, and mentioned, "It was rare that I would drink more than two alcoholic beverages. Therefore, can you please make sure you call me a cab?" The waiter agreed.

As James sat and drank he thought,' even as a young man, he did not have much tolerance to alcohol. Invariably, he would be the responsible one ensuring all his friends arrived home safely.' Now, he was drinking a couple here and there. Even last night he had a couple more. Tonight the wine was going down smooth and he wasn't having any ill effects, at least not yet.

After another hour, some chocolate mousse for dessert, and another glass of wine, James finished his meal and was on his second bottle of wine. The check came. It read $129.79. James could not remember ever spending that amount on a meal for just himself. "But it was worth every penny," he told the waiter. Although never a big tipper, James felt important and left $200 on the table, and left the restaurant.

Outside it was dark except for a small streetlight across the street and the neon lights emanating from local businesses. James head started to feel the effects of the wine.

He headed east along the sidewalk. It was almost midnight and he planned to retrieve some more of his funds from an ATM, but with each step his vision became foggier and his steps more displaced and haphazard. James realized that for the first time in his life he was drunk and not inside his home.

James opened his eyes and hadn't realized he was on the floor inside the Bank lobby near the ATM machine. He was unable to respond to the Police officer standing over him. He fell back to sleep. "Is this him?" asked the officer.

"Yes, officer that's him," said the manager of the restaurant. The waiter was also there and both confirmed the identity.

"He was quiet, very friendly and was on his own while eating. He left me a large tip, and I wasn't sure if he meant it as a tip or not. I rushed out of the restaurant to give him his change and to call him a cab. I had seen him wandered in here by the time I got here he had passed out. I couldn't wake him," said Franco the waiter. "Did you not notice how much he was drinking?" scolded the Police officer.

"He was there for over three hours, and drank quite a few, but he seemed in control," answered Franco apologetically. The Police officer attempted to nudge James with his foot, "Sir! Sir! Wake up," the Police officer said in vain.

The Police officer bent down to shake James in an attempt to wake him up, his snoring was loud, "He's fine, just drunk," he shared.

"He was fine eating his meal and did convey that he had never allowed himself the simple task of enjoying the wine and not worrying about the outcome. He also said to me son, please keep an eye on me so that if I do get drunk please call me a cab. He left when I was in the back attending to other customer's food orders. When I walked back to his table, he had left and on the table, he left twenty-dollar bills totally $200.00... His bill was $ 129.79. I couldn't accept it as a tip without confirmation from him," Franco said as he lowered his head and remained silent. The manager nodded his head in disgust at Franco.

"Let me look in his pocket and see where he lives," said the police officer, "I can drive him home," he suggested.

The officer reached into James pockets one after another and continued to pull out what he found. James wallet was on a top inside pocket of his jacket. He looked at the medication bottles, and placed them down on the ground, along with loose coins. He opened his wallet James driver's license was clearly visible in the clear plastic wrap, and it contained his address.

"His name is James and he lives about twenty minutes out of town," stated the officer. He checked for a contact number in his wallet, and sure enough, there was one.

The contact name and number showed a name Danny, with a notation beside the name that it was his son. The officer picked up his cell phone and called the number. After two rings, a woman answered the call. "Hello," the woman on the other end answered. "Good evening Ms. this is Police officer Wallace from precinct 6895. I would like to speak with Danny." "Yes, hold on please." The lady dropped the phone on a table it sounded like. The officer could hear shouting. "Danny! Danny! There is a Police officer on the telephone for you."

"Hello? This is Danny, what seems to be the problem officer?" " Sir, this is not an emergency," the officer continued. "However, is your father James?" "Yes, it is, why? What's wrong?" Danny questioned in worried tone.

"Well sir," continued Officer Wallace. "Your father was out at the Gallant Restaurant tonight having an expensive meal alone and seemed to enjoy a bottle of wine a little too much. The waiter and manager followed him out of the establishment. The waiter rightly assumed your father may have overindulged himself with his drinks and was hoping to call him a cab. It appears your father seemed to be having some difficulty with standing and fell asleep in a Bank lobby. When they couldn't wake him, they called us. Can you pick him up?"

"You mean you called to tell me my father's is drunk and passed out, in public?" Danny said in disbelief. "I'm afraid so sir," answered Officer Wallace.

"Oh my god", whispered Danny, "I've never seen my father drunk in his life." "Well this time he decided to indulge and mentioned that to the waiter, he was afraid of it himself. Can you come pick him up? If you do, it will save me from having to humiliate him when he wakes up inside a jail cell at the station. And he doesn't deserve that for a quiet meal out," suggested the police officer. "Yes of course, officer." "How far are you from the Gallant

Restaurant?" inquired he officer.

Danny rushed around getting his coat on and grabbing his car keys, "It will take me about ten minutes can you wait?" It would be in everyone's best interest if you pick him up in a hurry, but don't speed," urged Officer Wallace.

Danny and his son Johnny pulled up in front of the Bank. The officer knew it was them looking through the open window from the passengers' side the officer asked, "Are you here for James?" "Yes," replied Danny, looking through his son's window. "Good, just park here, I'll help you get him into the car." Officer Wallace offered. Danny and his son jumped out of the car and followed the officer into the Bank. Once the officer opened the glass door, Danny spotted to the left a man rolled up in a fetal position and sound asleep in the lobby, snoring.

"Here's his change from the waiter. Perhaps, you can bring the waiter back a tip tomorrow when you confirm your father's intentions. He returned his change to me. No tip was taken," Officer Wallace expressed.

Danny and Johnny stood there, stunned, in disbelief. They had never seen James drunk before, and certainly never passed out in a lobby of a bank.

"Help me lift him up," the officer asked crunched down embracing his back, and instructed, "You get this side of him. I'll get the other side and your son can hold him up from behind."

Danny reached down to start lifting his father. Johnny went around to the back, still in shock and not able to utter a word. "You're okay, Dad? I'm going to get you home," Danny told his barely conscious Dad. "Your father is out of it," the officer said and added, "Be careful."

Once James rose to a standing position, he was able to help them along with his feet, albeit very slowly and was disorientated and unsure of his surroundings. "Son, what are you doing here?" James mumbled. "Everything's okay Dad, just walk to the car with me," Danny pleaded. "Johnny is that you too?" James said embarrassed. "Yes grandpa," Johnny uttered.

They led James into the car and sat him in the back seat, closing the door behind him. "That wasn't so bad," the officer said as he half-laughed. "Are you two going to be okay or would you like for me to meet you at his home to assist you?" office Wallace asked "No thanks," replied Danny. "We should be fine. Please give this change to the waiter. I'm sure my father left it as a tip," said Danny as he handed it back to him.

"I will," Officer Wallace said as he took it. "This is not like my father," explained Danny. "I can tell," nodded the officer. "That's why I am letting him go."

"I appreciate you looking for my contact number, I do realize you didn't have to," gratefully acknowledged Danny.

It was a silent drive home. Danny and Johnny were dumfounded on the evenings' events. James was sprawled in the back seat, vacillating between sleeping and semi-consciousness. As they approached the driveway for James' home, Danny noticed a for sale sign with 'SOLD' embezzled across it.

"What the hell is going on?" Danny said to his son. "Is Grandpa selling his home Dad?" Johnny asked. "I don't know son. This is the first I've heard of it and no one called me. Stay in the car," Danny said to his son.

Danny got out of the car and walked towards the house, and fumbled in the dark to find his father's key on his keyring. Once he found it, he placed one hand on the doorknob and the other strategically on the keyhole ready to input the key into the lock. He turned the doorknob and the door opened.

With the door opened slightly Danny did not enter right away. He was fearful that a burglar was inside. He hesitated wondering whether to enter or call the Police. "Hello. Hello," Danny shouted while waiting at the doorstep. "Is anyone in here?" Danny pushed the door open a little more. "Police have been called," Danny said loudly.

Danny reached inside the door flicked on the light switch. He gathered enough nerve to enter. The smell of the home was musty and emanated an overwhelming odor he had never smelled in that house before. Danny walked through the home to make sure no one else was inside. Dishes were stacked high in the sink. Dust was thick on the furniture. The floors were sticky and dirty. Danny was astonished. His parents' home was always in immaculate condition.

Danny walked to the car where he proceeded to help his son Johnny carry his drunken father into his house. Once inside the house, they gently placed James on his couch. James was asleep the instant his head hit the pillow. Danny took off his father's shoes and threw them down beside him on the worn out area rug. He took his coat off, and threw it over the coffee table.

It gave a loud thud as it banged against the wood.

"What the hell was that?" said a startled Danny. "I don't know. It sounds like something heavy was in Grandpa's coat," Johnny guessed.

Danny lifted his father's coat and ruffled through his pockets. On the inside of his coat, Danny found an extra slanted pocket. He reached inside, and pulled out what appeared to be a towel with something placed inside it. Danny placed the towel on the table beside the coat. He unraveled it as if he already figured out what was inside and there it was.

Danny looked at the object in disbelief, "Why on earth did my father have this?" Danny questioned. What started as Danny rescuing his father from a drunken evening now turned into something more sinister. Danny threw the towel over the object to conceal it from Johnny. It was too late. His son had seen it. "Was that a gun?" Johnny queried.

"Sorry you had to see that Johnny," Danny apologized. "Thank god the officer didn't find it. Grandpa would have been arrested, if they did." Danny stated strained. "And with the state my father is in now, he can't provide any answers to why."

"Maybe he was hunting dad," Johnny offered as an explanation.

"I don't know son, but, something isn't right. I don't know what's going on with my father? He has sold this house. He is drunk, and has a gun, it doesn't seem right. What the hell is going on?" Danny exploded in anger in his confusion, while disregarding the fact that his son was in earshot.

James remained asleep oblivious to the trauma he has caused his family. "Johnny, we're staying for the night and until grandpa wakes up. I'm not leaving until I've had some time to speak with him. I need to find out what's going on? I'm wondering when this place is supposed to be vacant for the new owners. He hasn't done a thing."

Danny glanced at his son and noticed how traumatized he was becoming and taped his shoulder as he said, "Relax, it's okay. I was just venting." Danny walked around the house checking out all the bedrooms, and went into the basement and seen a wallet on the floor. He opened it up and seen a driver's license picture of a man when he flipped it opened under the plastic cover. He read the man's name, and looked at his picture. He rambled to himself, "This in my father's house and the door was unlocked when we arrived." Danny worried the man was still around the property. He whispered, "No wonder my father has a gun, someone is breaking into his home." He ran himself back upstairs trembling and afraid.

He sat down beside his son, "Look I found a wallet in Grandpa's basement and the door was unlocked when we arrived. Someone might be breaking in and the alarm to the house wasn't set. Perhaps that's why grandpa had the gun, and sold his house," Danny rationalized to his son...

"Dad, what's going on, let's call the Police." Johnny requested. He whispered, "Not now son, we have to wait until Grandpa wakes up. Let me lock up I checked the house, no one is inside the house, but us." Danny walked around locking up. "How do you know Dad? Hold the gun Dad and let's call the Police." Johnny cried in exhaustion...

Danny tried to firm his composure, not wanting his son to know he's afraid, "Just hold on son, and try to relax. I'll sit here with the gun in my hand. The lights are on, and daylight will be here soon enough. The alarm is set. We'll wait for Grandpa to tell us what's going on. A service worker could have dropped his wallet. It could be a simple as that."

Johnny fell asleep in the chair. Danny sat there, starring off in space until he fell asleep

.

James woke up disorientated from the couch. The surroundings were familiar. He was in his home. But why was he here? He closed his eyes, "What happened?" he questioned. "Think. Think. What happened?" James head was throbbing. He had made a fist, and took the inner portion of his hand, with thumb, and index finger and pushed it against his head, pounding it off in his attempt to get his mind to think for him. "I'm not used to feeling this way. It was the wine, that's what it was." His fingers snapped when he remembered. "Now it's coming back to me. I had a lot of wine. But after the restaurant it's a blur. How did I get home?" James remained motionless. He was too scared to move until he remembered what he did last night, or didn't do. He was falling in and out of sleep. He knew he had to go to the bathroom that's why he was waking up, but he kept falling back to sleep.

He could hear footsteps and whispers emanating from the kitchen. James tried to make out the voices, but it was inaudible. He could then hear the footsteps getting louder…and closer.

"Is he awake yet Dad?" asked Johnny. "No, not yet son," Danny responded bitterly. James recognized the voices. It was his son and grandson. "My god, what are they doing here?" he whispered. James could feel the sweat drip down from his forehead, down his neck and onto the drenched pillow. His back was full of sweat. He was sticking to the leather couch. James realized he couldn't pretend to be asleep forever. He needed a few more minutes to gain his composure.

"Okay I had enough waiting," Danny fumed as he began shaking his Dad, "Wake up Dad, wake up."

James grumbled a few incoherent lines and then groggily opened his eyes. "Danny what are you doing here?" James asked without wanting to hear the response. "I should ask you the same question Dad. What's going on around here? What have you' been up to?" Danny shouted. "What do you mean son?" James pleaded with ignorance. "Oh for fuck sakes Dad, what's with the For Sale sign on the house? When were you going to tell us?" Danny stated in a confrontational tone.

"Let me have a coffee son and I will explain, and move, I have to use the bathroom," shouted James as he tried to get up from the couch. "Johnny!" Danny shouted to the kitchen. "Pour Grandpa a coffee with a little milk and make it strong." "Okay" he answered from the kitchen.

James pulled himself up from the couch, "It feels like I've been beaten up in a boxing ring. Every muscle on my body aches." He was getting no sympathy from his son. "Looks good on you," Danny squealed as James passed him to go to the bathroom.

James splashed some cold water on his face after he threw up. It was not enough to relieve the pain, but at least it woke him up somewhat. "How much do they know?" James said to himself.

James sat on the toilet, "I need more to think." James was at a loss as to what to say to his son. He could not think of a convincing lie to tell him, and the truth was even more bizarre and unbelievable. James decided he might as well suck it up and tell Danny everything. He could not play this cat-and-mouse game any longer. He realized he might end up in prison, or worse, lose the respect and love of his family.

James entered the living room where Danny and Johnny sat. They waited patiently for an explanation. "Here's your coffee Grandpa," Johnny said as he picked it up from the coffee table and handed it to him. "Thank you my boy." James took a long sip before he started.

"Okay guys, what brought you here and how did I get home? Let me say, I do remember going to the restaurant, and that's all I remember the meal was splendid and yes, I figured I drank too much wine, but it was going down like butter."

Danny had to fill him in, "Yes, you left a nice tip on your way out apparently needed more money, and headed into the lobby at the Bank and that was as far as you got. Seems you took a nice rest there. Thank god, the waiter followed you to give you your change, and wanted to call you a cab. When he couldn't wake you he called the Police. The Police called me. We, Johnny, and I were lucky enough to pick you up and got you home. And here we all are."

James was stalling for time, "Yeah, I figured something like that occurred." Danny waited to see if his father was going to volunteer any information. James took fast sips of his coffee, and looked at his son, "Thank you for coming to my rescue, and taking me home. It's so nice to see you two, it's been a while, and the conditions obviously don't make me proud," explained James.

"Yes, Dad it's nice to see you to. It has been awhile and it was more of a shock, not a bother. Wish it was under different circumstances." James sipped his coffee as Danny spoke.

Danny became annoyed with the silence his father was displaying, as though that was all that occurred with him, "Okay Dad why didn't you tell the girls or me about selling the house? You do know you cannot sell it without us. I cannot understand how the house even got sold without us. I went into shock when we arrived, and seen the sold sign on the lawn. By the way, you left the door unlocked, and didn't set the alarm. I thought my god, was he robbed? While I was searching for a possible robber, I looked in the basement and here, tell me what do you know about this men's wallet? I found it in the down there? If you feel like it you can even start by explaining why, you have a gun inside your coat, and its loaded? The man's name is Jeff that owns the wallet."

"I'm ashamed son and I have a headache." James said as he was holding his head. "That's called a hangover Dad. Now what's going on?" Danny asked as he suffered in turmoil..." James didn't bother to give him an answer and held his head down with his hands embracing his coffee cup... "I need some answers now, god damn it Dad," Danny demanded.

James began, "After your mother died "I was inconsolable. She was my life. Watching her pass of cancer and seeing her suffer was surreal to me. When she was gone, I was alone. It was hard to accept. I had gone into some mental state unexplainable, even to me. Everything I did and saw reminded me of your mother and the times we shared. The doctor tried me on Valium for a couple of weeks, after she passed. On those, I contemplated suicide many times. I would have succeeded if I wasn't such a coward." "You are not a coward Grandpa," Johnny piped in.

"Thank you my boy," James interrupted before Johnny could continue, "You're old enough to know that heartbreak is a powerful thing. My mind did not know how to adapt. On the other hand, maybe I just didn't want it to? I honestly don't know."

Tears began to fill in James eyes. His son and grandson had seen him cry, when Tanya passed. They felt uncomfortable and were unsure what to say or do. However, one thing was for sure, they were enthralled with the story and wanted to hear more.

James continued through his tears, "The doctor didn't want me to have anymore more pills. The pills did not help. He sent me to see a mental health care doctor. I could not grasp, what telling him about my loss would do. Back on some more drugs, I went. Running around I felt like a robot. I could not feel anything. My doctor suggested I join a gym. I had my fishing, but I couldn't do it. I did not see you kids, no fault of your own. You were busy with your lives. I joined a gym. I met two people who I believed were trainers. They helped me do the treadmill, and worked me out with lightweights for the first week I went. I enjoyed swimming and the sauna, and it helped. I started to feel muscle aches from the workouts. After the workout, I would head over to the restaurant and had a nice lunch, breaking up the day while passing the time. The rest of the day, was a loss, I slept on and off."

Danny felt bothered, and snapped back at his father, "What Dad, are you just going to fill me in on your entire life since mom passed? It was hard on all of us and still is. What occurred for you to sell the house? Can you tell me how you sold it, without us? Did the girls, agree? No one called me. And why are you carrying a loaded gun around?" Danny stated in boldness.

James was exasperated, "I'm trying to get to it, I'm not a spring chicken son. The mind takes time to think. Things are slower for me now, son. I can tell you this, at no time, did I ever considered selling our home." Danny was beyond any feelings of patients with his father. He paced around, the living room area and just blew up, "I'm just pissed off completely now Dad. A few simple words are all it takes. What do you mean you did not sell it? That is what a sold sign means. It's sold Dad. Are you going to tell me, you don't grasp this concept? You're not an idiot are you now?" James slammed his coffee cup down on the table, and said, "Don't ever speak like that to me again son."

He went to respond back to his father in anger, pointing his finger in his face, when suddenly his hand went to his head as he snapped the thickest, lowest part of his palm against his forehead. His reply delayed when he realized, he was being hard on his father. He took a big breath in through his nose, and leaned his hand down on his father's legs, just above his knees, "That was wrong of me Dad. Sorry... I realized you have never bought or sold a home. Our family home was a gift to us from mom's mother. Therefore, I can understand you may have some sort of confusion with the process. It has a sold sign on the lawn. That means at some point you had to agree to sell it. My concerns are simple, but how did that occur when you cannot sell it without us being in agreement with the sale and added to that process. Maybe you don't remember when mom passed all our names went on the title of the house. That is what mom wanted. The lawyer took care of it. You will find the paperwork for that in your filing cabinet, filed under house. We knew you didn't hear or grasp anything at the time. It wasn't a big deal, but the house under the instructions in moms will clearly states the house will go through the grandkids and is never to be sold. It will always be in our family. It's clearly written. And mom, locked up a ton of money to ensure what she wanted was protected when it came to this house."

James tried to talk through his tears, "The house isn't sold anymore. Her Lawyer stopped the sale, when someone tried to sell it on me. I didn't know about the sale either. I came home one day, after leaving for a couple of hours, and found the sign on the lawn, stating it was sold."

Danny could not believe what his father just stated, "How can someone other than us sell our house?" he bellowed out in his frustration.

James knew his son was not going to understand or display compassion, "Son can you please just sit down," he asked taking his hand against the couch cushion, motioning him to sit as he continued speaking, "And please wait for me to share what occurred along the way. I think only then will it make sense to you." Danny sat beside him and he rushed right into his story, "Cory and his wife Stephanie, the two people who helped me at the gym, offered me some vitamins," James expressed.

Danny stopped banging his feet off the floor with his legs crossed and stood up to move in front of him and sat down on the coffee table, and interrupted his father, "Dad there's so much you seem to be avoiding to tell a story, rather than just answering a few simple questions. Just answer my questions and trust that I am not an idiot. I can figure out what questions, I need to ask to get to the bottom of this without you stressing to figure out where to start your story from."

James dropped his tissue, Johnny handed him another, one, and he started talking again, "Son, let me talk. I'm not an idiot either. So, all your questions will be answered if you shut the hell up and let me think what the fuck, happened, along the way." He waved his hand, when he remembered, "Yes that's right. Okay, those people helping me at the gym Cory looked like body builder, not as large, cut, more defined I say. Both he and his wife Stephanie had golden blonde hair, blue eyes and dark tans. A healthy glow to them…God, they looked fresh, young and energetic with their skin all plumped up and had damn clear, happy fucking eyes. Anyways, I had explained how hard my wives' passing was on me, after they said my eyes, look bulky and had black circles underneath them. They noticed the color of the whites of my eyes, and sympathized with me over my loss. Cory gave me five or six little bags of vitamins, and I paid him fifty dollars for them. He said be careful, take one for a few days, and see how they made me feel. He worked at the place and got discounts, he mentioned."

"But Dad…" Danny tried to intervene but was cut off by his Dads need to explain, "It's okay Danny. I went back to the gym one day. The two were not around. I figured they shifted their shifts so I asked.

No one knew them and figured they were guest like me. Then I recalled they weren't from town. They were staying at a hotel doing some trade show for work when I looked at his business card," James explained.

Danny was beyond ticked off, "Pills Dad, where are they? Did you ask yourself why would you take drugs from a stranger? They go anywhere to get people on drugs today and have for years, it's a money grab."

James was upset, "I wasn't finished, saying what I wanted to say. They're either in the kitchen or the bathroom. I know they are somewhere around here."

He scratched his head, and carried his ramble on, "I had gone to the restaurant one day after the gym, and this new waitress came over and talked to me. I told her, you have a twin at the gym. She laughed, we talked I invited her to the gym and she came. One day I was trying to do what the man did for me. I did not check the weight of the weights. It was okay for me to lift them up. I told her lie down and I will help you bench press. She stretched her arms up, and I lifted the weights up from the bar and she went to grab the bar. It was too heavy for her and down went the weights, hard on her chest and stomach area. I tried to lift them up and slipped myself, injuring my back. That made them land back down on her," James shared holding his head reliving what occurred.

Danny eased a look on his face as to say, I don't think you can lift that much weight so he asked, "Oh gees Dad. How much weight was on the bar?" he questioned with a laugh. "It was about one hundred pounds in or there a bouts. We went by ambulance to the Hospital. I left the hospital and went to see my doctor, after he called me back and said he was free. I had already waited five hours, and hadn't seen a doctor. She stayed in the hospital for a few days, and came up here about a week later. Both of us had prescriptions. My doctor gave me a mild pain pill, and she had stronger ones apparently. But at the time, I was not aware what the doctor had ordered for me. It was either pain or not paying attention. It doesn't matter now, I don't have an excuse. My physician told me, I had a mild pain pill, just the other day," James revealed. Then got up and went for more coffee.

Johnny began to squirm in his seat. He was not sure if he wanted to hear what his grandfather was about to say. His father sensed his uneasiness.

"Johnny, there's no need for you to stay," Danny said in the hopes of giving him a way out of the conversation. "Why don't you go to bed? You had a long and rough night, son," Danny added.

Despite Johnny's' reservations on listening, he also knew it was important to stay and listen. He was almost eighteen. He could not just walk away and think nothing had happened. "No Dad. I want to stay. I have to stay. It's okay," Johnny answered in a confident tone. "Good son," Danny said proudly. "Thanks Dad, continue," Johnny said to his father.

James took another sip of his coffee. His hands trembled, a small amount of coffee slid down the right side of his mouth. He wiped it off with his sleeve and continued. "Her name was Maria. She was a lot younger than I was, but she was mature and full of life. Whether you approve or not, she kept me alive and so did the two people at the gym."

Danny and Johnny listened. Yet, James could tell by their facial expressions they were shocked and disappointed. But he continued, "At first, we, Maria and I, went to the gym to the movies or out to lunch. We were just friends, and I never thought of her as replacing your mom, but for the first time in a long time, I felt alive. Is that so wrong? I had company. Isolation is a confused state, my kids."

"Dad, I want to know more about the house?" Danny said with a puzzled look on his face. "I'll get there son. Give me time," begged James waving his palms down in the air. "But first, I need something for my head. Every time I move, it feels like my brain is moving all around inside my head. A headache pill might do the trick," James said and went to get up.

"I'll get one for you grandpa. "I'll look for the pills the person sold you too," Johnny offered.

James sat with his hands in face. He knew the more he told the story, the more disgraced he would appear to his family.

"We were having a great time." James said as his voice cracked, "Except for a few odd glances from people who thought I was with my daughter, our relationship or friendship was wonderful." Johnny handed his grandfather two pills and said, "Dad, I cannot find the pills Grandpa said were in bags, in the kitchen or bathroom," "It's okay son, we'll find them later," acknowledged Danny.

As much as Johnny wanted the courage to continue to listen, he could not. It was unbearable for him to think that his grandfather, his idol, the man that could do no wrong, was having an illicit relationship with a younger woman. He left the room with tears in his eyes, making sure his wet eyes were not visible to his father and grandfather. He made no verbal gesture that he was leaving and went out to the patio.

"Let him go Dad," Danny said as he noticed his father was about to follow him. "I was making her a dinner one night, spaghetti with meat sauce and you know that is the only decent meal I made that wasn't on a barbeque. It was the first time, I had seen her since the accident," James shared.

Danny nodded in agreement, but deep inside there was also a resentment brewing, "That is considered your tradition for our family Dad. You prided on making that meal for mom, on Mother's Day, and all of us when we've visited."

"Maria loved the meal too," James said with a glowing pride. "So do all of us Dad," Danny squeezed in.

"The night, Maria and I ate, we drank red wine with it," he thought to correct his story, when he noticed the astonished look on his son's face. "Or I should say I had a few glasses of wine and Maria drank the rest. It was after we ate when I poured us a glass of wine. We celebrated our health, after our injuries. We cheered with our pill bottles. They took a fall, and I now believe when we were picking them up, we mixed them up, and her pills and my pills, went into each other's bottle."

It was at that moment that James realized Maria was probably drunk that night, and on her painkillers. However, this part he kept from Danny. He did not want to add speculation. "That was the first time we were intimate and she pleasured me with her hand," James said somewhat embarrassed. James sipped some more coffee. He needed the jolt, and the quick break, to be able to continue.

"Once that occurred, our relationship changed.

She eased out, it was us together forever. She sounded like a schoolgirl, not a woman twenty-five or so. There was a change in her. I am not sure if her painkillers were screwing with her head. I wasn't the same either, but I didn't realize it at the time," James shared taking deep breathes as he went along.

Johnny had listened and figured there was more to the relationship with the woman, and when he didn't go on about her, he returned to the room. "Grandpa, I want to hear the rest of the story, okay?" "Of course Johnny you mean a lot to me," James confessed.

Danny and Johnny sat facing James. They knew the story was not going to be a happy conclusion but they were now in a trance-like state, waiting for the next chapter in their patriarch's life.

"I thought the good times would last forever. We saw each other every so often. Now I can say, money, money, money, money, was what she was after. Like a whore, or a prostitute in some way, just no willing to put out or give up of herself in that way. Not two people sharing passion or making love. Not even a cuddle, but it wasn't like I seen it at the time. I hadn't been single from a young age. Your mother and I grew up together, and she was my first and only love. And I can proudly state, she still is. Maria and I never did have sex and we kissed just that one night, only. I swear on your mother's deathbed. Somehow she talked me into cashing one of my investments in and opening up an account in both our names, and for whatever reason son, I did, but the outcome didn't occur like I thought it was going to, in my mind," James shared and stopped to take a drink.

Danny felt his father, was not all there, "Dad, if I asked you a simple question, can you answer it?"

James smiled, "Son, yes, I will, go ahead ask." Danny eased closer to his father, "Okay good Dad, how can anyone just get you to sign away the one investment you had in your name?" James did not take time to think, "I told her I had it. We went to the bank. I think I was high or mesmerized by her," James shared with a half-smile.

"I think it was more than that Dad, something doesn't sound right." Danny said, as he poured more coffee and zipped his hand to his mouth to Johnny.

"I didn't understand at the time. Later she coerced me into making an offer on a Condo deal in the city. I wrote out a check for one hundred thousand and offered to low. It was not accepted. It felt odd to me and I was nervous at the time. It was just my name on the offer. The reason was to stop her from moving to Columbia. Before this, she offered me to visit her family for a month or so," James offered as an explanation, but was struggling to make sense out of what he was saying.

"Here's a fresh coffee Grandpa," Johnny said, as he poured in more coffee to his cup."

"Thank you, Johnny. I do know she left working at the restaurant the moment she met me son. I realized she is one of those women who waited to be picked up, spoon-fed, so she could be treated like a princess, and I was the pansy who fell for it. But, at the time I felt like this was love of some sort's son. I was talked right into anything and then came her needing a new car," James slammed back coffee, and kept the cup to his mouth. Afraid of what his son might say when he caught himself giving too much information. He was after all, in the company of his grandson.

"Sorry guys. I can tell this makes you

uncomfortable," James said apologetic. "Dad, you're an adult. You had needs. Hard to believe you were not getting anything in return, and you do know what I mean. But please continue... you have my full attention please go on," Danny, said surprisingly with his hand gesturing for him to continue. James looked over at Johnny. Johnny was rocking back and forth in the rocking chair, "It's okay grandpa, continue," Johnny whispered.

"I didn't get any needs filled sexually son. It was once and when I was like this." He stretched himself out on his couch, and tried to recreate the time. "I was like this, and she sat down right there on the floor. It was just the one time that she touched me guys. It was a joke..." He stopped talking they refused to speak to him. "Don't look at me in disgust. My dink has been in retirement for years. She asked me what it was like for a man at my age and I told her it retired and I laughed about it. There never was any sex, or hand job son... come on... I'm a faithful man. Oh, let me get your heads out of the gutter here. At my age it takes a little more than some young girl to get me going. I would have needed a drug that offered me a stiff night, she told me. That might have strengthened, and lifted it from his deathbed down there. It's only useful for pissing now a days and that's lacking the flow half the time," James screamed what he said at the end.

James reached for his coffee, stood up and gave a big stretch. They looked at him disgrace and couldn't be bothered talking to him. He sat back down, and continued, "I'm not a complete fool, I have watched those shows on Real Estate. I thought I was somewhat educated, when I made an offer. When I came home alone, after I made the offer on the condominium, I thought what I am doing. We never had a mortgage. Your mother and I never bought a home. Yeah, you are correct mom's home belonged to her family and they gave it to us. "

"Dad, you knew better," argued Danny.

James mood went somber, "She called me one day, I found another Condo and it's vacant. Offers today only and it cuts off in an hour. It was valued at three hundred and forty thousand, and she wanted to make an offer right away and on her own. Highest bidder gets it. I said, no. I never heard another word about it. Considering the Agent knew I was the only person signing on the first offer, I assumed they would not do an offer without me. I hadn't been able to get a hold of Maria and hadn't seen her for a while after this. When this real estate idea came up our agreement was to be with her family having access to seized properties. They sold them cheap. We were going to flip them for profit, and it never did happen. The prices she picked were all market value prices, nothing was cheap," shared James with a disappointed look on his face.

"Oh my god Dad, what were you pussy whipped, fucking drunk, or stoned." Danny slammed his hand down on the dining room table. His deep brown eyes, rolled around in his angered state. His lips pierced together. His forehead muscles tensed leaving lines that beamed across and held its place for the longest time. James noticed his son's tension, and was disgraced at his son's comment, "I don't have an answer to my mental state son. Moreover, you raging mad, is not helping this situation here. Do you want to know what occurred to me or not?" James wanted to know and asked.

He wasn't happy to give in, but answered, "I'll try to hold back Dad go on. But, I'm not going to deny this is really bothering me."

"Okay son, calm down. I inquired at her Bank where the funds went. I asked for a copy of the account transactions and I learnt my name was not on any accounts at her bank. It wasn't a joint account like I thought it was. What I was agreeing to at her Bank was to place my certified check into her account. How they got me to believe it was in a joint account is beyond me. The cops removed me from her bank when I refused to leave. I could not do anything about it. I gave my money away with a simple signature at my Bank, son. What sort of recourse do I have? None, my Bank Manager said, he explained everything to me at the time. It was awkward with her tagging along he said. Yet, he wanted to make sure I knew what I was doing. I was fucked up, I was like, Oh yeah, yeah,"James waved his hand in the air, "Of course, I know what I'm doing. I went back and spoke to him," James said as he shared in his humiliation.

Danny defiantly noted, "It's impossible to believe Dad, when you're talking so clear now. What you weren't capable of comprehension then?"

James was insulted by his son's remarks, "She took me for a ride son and it wasn't in her new car, and that was only once to take my money at her bank and I paid for it all."

"Yeah, I wondered if that's what you meant earlier, and then came the new car. I thought I was listening to a fucking television game show, for Pete sakes Dad," commented Danny.

"Yes, I'm ashamed to say it wasn't a fucking television show. I did it and after this all took place it took a few days for me to get a hold of her and when I did. I went to meet her at another Condo. When I arrived, there was a different male real estate agent with her. Inside, it had a few appliances not a stitch of furniture. I demanded to know what was going on. She confidently stated she needed another fifteen thousand to furnish it. Three Hundred Thousand, in a pinch of stupidity, disappeared... I demanded to see the paperwork indicating I owned the Condo, or for her to return my money. She cried, and cried and gave me a lawyer to call. This lawyer assumed I gave the money as a gift. I screamed no fucking way this happened. He told me, he had statements from two Bank managers which indicated, I signed away my money to her," James added still in disbelief.

Danny looked to have a case of the lice, the way he was scratching his head, constantly and then looked to his fingers to see what he rolled off his scalp and rolled it in between his fingers, as he said, "Why in the hell would you do that. It was your money. It has to be traceable. Legally speaking, there might some long drawn out court case to get it back. Sometimes you have to pick your battles and this might be a good one. It could be a sticky situation and I really don't know how the law works for shit like this. Jesus Christ Dad, just call your lawyer. I don't know how to deal with this shit," he freaked.

James was even more annoyed, when he figured he was losing his attention. "I went back to the last Condo where I met her at and she didn't live there. No one was sharing any information with me. I called my lawyer he is looking into everything son. So there was no need to pick the shit out of your scalp. You might end up with some fucking scalp disease getting stressed out like you did just there."

Danny breathed some sort of sigh of wind out his mouth, as he shared in a form of momentary release, then burst out, "Oh good Dad, glad you got on that. I thought it was odd when you said, the sale stopped. It's like you have moments of real stupidity to you, and then moments of clarity. What happened to you with this woman?"

James sullen in his own naivety, "For Christ sake son, I don't know. I had passion again. At times, she made it feel like an adventure. I wasn't thinking straight obviously, and I think I was on some sort of drugs, that lapsed my own damn reasoning. Is that answer good enough for you?"

"I want straight answers, okay Dad. Can you at least manage to roll some of those at me? But, let me say this first. Why on god's green earth did you have a gun in tow, when you were dining by yourself? This is sick, me having to bring this subject up with you… It's really pissing me off the more I think about it and how lucky for you that Police Officer didn't search you thoroughly. He found my number after going through your coat, in your wallet." He pinched his fingers together as he said, "So the cops' hands were that close to the gun."

James was shocked, "Are you saying they searched me, when I was sleeping? They can't do that?"

Danny could not believe his father's response, "Well, if the lone officer didn't search you, at the bank, how do you think you would have felt waking up inside a jail cell, and having that part of your day today? You were drunk in a public place, plus carrying a loaded gun around without your permit is against the law. If the cop did his job, and didn't have a heart we would not be sitting here right now. He searched for your wallet and lucky you, didn't search you thoroughly."

This story was taking its toll on Danny and Johnny. Their faces cringed with each new testimonial from James. Nevertheless, they could not let it end there. They had to know the whole story.

Danny padded his father's back then rubbed it in a circular motion, "Are you okay Dad? Do you understand what could have happened to you?" Danny stated with concern and without malice. "I'll be alright, son." James said with a forced smile. "I feel, so bad for you guys."

James said, "My headache is beginning to subside. Regardless of how distasteful and uncomfortable my ramblings are to you. Your family and I was able to release the demons from my mind, son. I was going crazy with mental confusion all by myself."

Danny wanted more coffee, "Go on Dad, I'm refilling, do you need one?"

"No son. I didn't put the house for sale and, never did agree to any transactions with it. This Real Estate woman came by the house. Maria answered the door and let her in. She tried to wake me up to talk to her, but I was sick and refused. She was like a fucking kid who thinks just because someone knocks at the door, you answer it let any asshole in. I honestly didn't remember it and when I finally realized something sounded familiar, it felt like a dream, and in my mind, I barely recall saying, no, no, no, not interested. So it was only a few words spoken by me when the women tried to pressure me to sell or list to see what I could get for it. I couldn't even lift my body up from the couch to look at the bitch. That was the only time the topic came about. "

Danny asked, "Is that the Agent that sold it?"

James stood up walked towards the front door, "Yes, she was the one who did. I came home a few days ago, after Maria's bank manager booted me out of the place with the cops. I felt like a fucking fool...when they did. I drove home and seen the sign on my fucking lawn. I figured the sign was on the wrong address. Don the dingbat assistance to the criminal real estate agent, gloated it was my home that sold and he knew for sure. He was the asshole that put the goddamn sign on the fucking lawn. At first, I didn't believe him, and then I lost it when it sank in. it was like a lightbulb went on, inside my head and another shut off, when I realized this was fucking happening to me," James shared.

James paused and walked up a couple of stairs and pointed up them, and through tears he shared, "I went upstairs to my room, sat on my bed, and placed the gun inside my mouth, and was going to kill myself son. That's how the gun came about. It's not a dream, it happened to me."

Danny rushed to his father, "You did what Dad?" "Son, it was a shit load of chaos and bizarre things occurring. I couldn't make sense out of any of it. I felt less of a human being, crazy or nuts however, you want to paint the picture of me for doing what I did. It occurred. And before it did, everyone I spoke with believed they lived in the law of perfection, along with the wonderland of credibility and here I was the rat in the corner, asking questions and these people piled shit so high it backed me in. I couldn't see a way out at first. Everyone I spoke to said," he pointed to his chest, with his fingers as he went on, "It was my fault, all me son. It felt surreal. I don't even know how it all came about. I still don't know. Somehow, I was able to stop myself from pulling the trigger on the gun, because I'm still here. It had to be your mother, in some way who halted me, because this here son." He pointed to his head, "It wasn't here, or I wasn't there. I remember, I went to the city to find Maria. If my truck isn't towed it still sits parked at city parking garage. I must have parked it there by force of habit. Perhaps, I ran off adrenalin and a mixture of pills son and I'm sure the alcohol didn't help. I must have blacked out, at some point. I can't recall putting the gun in my coat. I only remember my mind telling me to find Maria, get answers, my money, and our home back for your mother." Danny hugged James and led him back to the couch to sit him down. Johnny handed his grandfather his coffee when he did.

James carried on, "Along the way, I called the lawyer, spilled my guts to him and he took me out of that dark corner. I started to feel human again and wasn't crazy alone. I stopped talking my medication, and that helped too. Yet when the lawyer said he stopped the sale of the house, go home. I couldn't. The house wasn't mine anymore. That's how I felt. Just hearing it was, wasn't good enough for me son. The when, the how, the why, and the thought of who could think to do such a heartless thing, lingered, right here," he expressed forcing his fist to his head, banging it off a few times. "In my mind it told me go find Maria and even the score with that crazy bitch," James stopped talking, dropped his head against the back of his couch. His eyes closed. He took a moment to redeem himself.

Danny unmasked his concern too, as his head rested against the back of the couch. He talked through closed eyes, "I understand Dad. When I drove up and seen the sign last night, I felt empty. No one called me, and I'm a grown man, with a home of my own, but, I wasn't expecting to see our family home leaving without me knowing. That alone destroyed me. It played with my fucking head. I considered my family took it upon themselves not to include me in the decision to let it go and somehow devalued moms wishes and bypassed the will."

He twisted his head, looked at his father, and said, "Like what the fuck was up with my family, I thought? The only thing keeping me sane was waiting to speak with you. I had to keep it together I had a gun loaded, I ran around trying to figure out where to hide it. I had my drunken father passed out on the couch and a strange man's wallet in my possession." He closed his eyes again, and gave a heavy sigh.

"I get it son, I too was anxious when I woke up here. It had nothing to do with a hangover. This is the first time it felt like a home, since your mother passed." He lifted his head away from the couch, and sat up. "Danny, Johnny, it's …like," James sobbed as he attempted to speak. "It's okay Dad, take your time, I know it's hard." Danny said to comfort him. Johnny cried as he listened.

James reached for his coffee cup. "I'll get it for you." Johnny offered as he handed his grandfather his cup. Danny stood up.

James thought to say, "It took you two to get me back home again after a drunken night of stupidity."

Danny could not internalize the emotional

confusion his father felt at the time. He imagined the gun he was looking at inside his father's mouth as his eyes panned from the gun to his father. His legs weaken, "I could have loss you by suicide Dad. Thank god, you didn't kill yourself," Danny stated while he grabbed the gun, "So am I son." James expressed with his head resting on his hand as his elbow leaned against the armrest of his couch.

"I want all the guns and all bullets in this house," demanded Danny.

"Did you give this woman power of attorney over you?" Danny probed. "No son, you kids are. It's in my will," confirmed James.

"Perhaps, she figured, you were some old man with no family so, she took advantage, not realizing us kids own the home too. That stopped her there. We weren't around, so she figured she had free range," Danny believed. James was distraught, "Take the gun, I don't need it anymore, son."

As Danny was removing the bullet he asked "Are you sure your lawyer stopped the sale?"

James was mentally exhausted, holding his head, sweat pouring down his face, "You don't believe me son? I only know what he told me. All the details, I do not have. I figure Maria must have thought she had signing authority for everything and getting the money from this house into her Bank account was going to be a cakewalk. The Real Estate Agent is new. They had buyers looking for a house in our area, and we don't' have much turn around up here. That's why she came to the country hoping to entice someone to sell, she said. I'm not sure I believe a word out of her mouth either."

Danny asked, "When were or are the new owners

to take possession Dad?" "I don't know son, I just don't know," James replied.

"Here Dad, can you tell me this wallet, I found last night after I establish the doors to the house were unlocked when we arrived. I thought you'd been robbed and while checking the house, I found the wallet in the basement," Danny explained.

James mauled backwards in time, on that terrible day he left with the gun, "Let me think, I don't believe I locked the doors when I left. As far as the wallet, I have no clue. Perhaps, another one of her men," James sputtered out.

Danny ruffled out one of the business cards from inside the wallet and called the number from his cell, "Hello," came from the other end. "Hi, I'm looking for Jeff." "This is Jeff," answered the mail voice. "Did you lose your wallet?" questioned Danny.

Jeff quickly said, "Yes, I did and cancelled all my cards. Did you find it? Who am I speaking too?"

Sarcastically he stated, "I'm Danny, and what were you doing at 1748956 side road 55? That is where I found your wallet in the basement." Trying to gather his thoughts Jeff realized where that address was, "I purchased the property, and I'm not sure how I lost it down there. Perhaps when I bent down looking at the furnace, it could have dropped out of my pants pocket. You people are nuts, and hired a lawyer to stop the sale. What a fucking mess your god damn family involved my family in." Danny realized its real, "I'm sorry it's a complicated matter," he could only think to respond.

Jeff was still enraged, "I have three small kids, just transferred back here for work and I wanted to raise our kids close to home and around family. What a welcome home we got. I don't have time to waste on this shit," yelled Jeff.

"Sorry Jeff my Dad and my family didn't agree to the sale of our home. Some women and Real Estate Agent were not ethical. It looks like it, at this point to me," Danny squeezed in.

Pissed off with all the inconvenience, Jeff yelled," I did not need this headache. As soon as we heard we had to seek legal avenues to push the sale through with no guarantees, we went out to look for another home. Thank god, we found one. This time I was not faxing shit from out of town. We were not happy with whatever the issues were on your end. I haven't decided if I'm going to proceed with legal action against you. I didn't value my mother being served with a court order cancelling the sale. And what you people only know when to call, after you figure out what's god damn well best for you. Like the wallet. Why didn't you, people call me the day you found it?"

Danny felt a moment of relief and breathed heavily, away from the cell but went back to say, "I have three kids and I couldn't imagine having to go through what you did. I am having a hard time understanding how anyone was able to secure a sale on a home, I am an owner of and no one talked to me. I just found out. I am truly sorry for the upset this has caused you and your family. I just found your wallet a few hours ago. Thanks for being understanding. I'll have your wallet back to you, by courier, but will need an address, if you're in the city now. The address on your license is for another country." "You can send it to my attorney," Jeff shared.

They hung up the call. Danny turned to his father,

"You're so lucky this man had small kids and wasn't into fighting you, and us for the house. His wallet must have fallen when he looked at the furnace. He found a new home. He is not sure if he will proceed with legal action and he has good reason to. I know I would if someone fucked me up like we did his family. He purchased our house while out of town. How did you not see him inside your home when he looked at the furnace?" Danny asked.

James looked around and was confused, "No one came to look at the furnace or the house when I was here son."

Danny probed, "Does this woman have a key?" James snapped, "Hell no. Maybe I left the door unlocked and they came inside," James suggested.

Danny picked up the cell, and yelled at his father, "Why aren't you setting the alarm, it's rough out there today." He pushed redial, "Hi Jeff how did you get into my father's home when they didn't have a key? And when did you come here?"

Jeff was annoyed, "Why are you calling me with your questions? I'm not the one with the answers." Danny's face turned cold with anger and went beat red, "I think you can answer what day you came here, you had to realize you lost your wallet soon afterwards."

Jeff sarcastically answered, "It was late at night, almost a week ago. I met the Agent at the house, and I assume he had the key. He and I were using a flashlight trying to see the property outback but we couldn't get passed the steel black gates. We didn't get far and headed back to the front of the house. When your Dad I imagine it was came home, we heard the front door slam. My Agent went to tell him we were there, and I left. I had seen a truck, in the driveway. You're father does have a pick-up truck doesn't he?"

"Danny quietly answered, "Yes. Go on." Jeff continued, "To answer your question on the wallet. I just flew in that night. I was exhausted and didn't realize I had lost my wallet there. I thought I lost it at an Airport." Danny figured his father gave a key and knew about it, "Okay, thanks Jeff." They hung up.

Danny's stomach rolled in internal confusion, he grabbed it, "You had to give out a key he came with his Agent, he said."

James smiled and cleared his throat, "I have my home. My accounts are secure. It's a good day, despite the minor three hundred thousand Maria took and the little extra's she got and spent, but we're all okay and let's be grateful for that. I do not remember giving anyone a key. I need to change my locks and recode the alarm."

Danny was very angry with his father comment, and started shaking his fist, "Sure Dad, you missed criminal charges for drunk and disorderly, and toting a loaded gun around. Poor lonely Maria had some nice pocket change from you while my son and I picked up my drunken father. The family home looks trashed, sold, but not sold now. I guess we can leave now, but before I go, how about we get you some medical help at the Hospital. Perhaps, you have lost your marbles Dad. Your problems are still not over."

James was agitated, "Yeah, that's not all that happened to me and I'm willing to drop it there"

"What else could have possibly gone wrong in your life, besides all that drama you created all by yourself? Come on Dad, enough is enough. You went looking to cause issues," Danny fumed at him.

"Oh really. So, you think I did this all to myself, like the rest of the assholes I had to deal with eh. I'm sure I caused this issue too. Just take a look at these pills, before you beat me to death here with your pissed off words." He handed his son his pill bottle.

"What's this, are you sick?" Danny sneered as he aggressively took the pills from his father's hand.

"No! Just look at the pill bottle, and tell me if you notice anything odd and then look at the pills."

Danny eyed the bottle, dumped some pills in his hand, "Okay you have a few different pills here." "Look at the pill bottle again." James stated under pressure. "Nothing Dad, I don't know what I'm looking for. Is this a game now to you?" Danny asked.

James laughed, "Ha… ha….so fucking funny. A game, is that what you think. You wouldn't have realized it either. The name, look at my name. The pills are different, you're right. We mixed our pills up I explained this to you already."

Danny looked again, "The name is James, but it's not our last name. What are the pills for?"

James smiled, "A mental illness issue, and god knows what else. The doctor didn't know either."

Danny tried to compose himself, "Oh, my, god, Dad you have a mental illness? Is that the answer? No wonder you did not realize you were robbed, ripped off, while buying drugs from strangers and what did you intentionally go to the doctor to help plead for your case and figured insanity would work? And I bet you told him, I'm suffering from an acute episode of stupidity once I got a hand job from this young hot sexy twenty five year old woman. When we had some wine, my dick did all the thinking for me. So I figured

I'd start using a false name and get pills under that now too?"

James laughed for the first time in a while, "Thanks for the love son. No, I did not, but I will keep that in my back pocket, just in case, insanity works. Even more baffling to me was the fact that I took the pills. I imagine stupidity wins there. I had honestly thought, I had visited the doctors, and he prescribed me this medication." Danny slammed down the pills, "Dad, are you fucking deranged? This is the icing on a cake. Where did you get these pills?"

James stood up, "Sit down son, please just sit down. I went to pick up my prescription at the drug store, for a mild pain pill, and they gave me these instead. I didn't know what the doctor had prescribed for me, at the time, and if he told me, I forgot. It was not my fault. I didn't read the last name. I guess it was a mix up, with the names and no one called to let me know. I just started taking them. I was getting weaker and more confused by the day and then when we mixed up our pills drinking, which did not help the situation. I had the old medication he prescribed for me after mom past. They were on the table. I hadn't taken them all and those little fucking line up lids, I can never close. Those pills made me depressed and weak. The next day, like I said, I was so sick on the couch with stomach pains, sweats, and massive diarrhea and stopped eating. The agent came that day. I didn't take any pills for a couple of days, and started to get well. Yet, I didn't attribute that to the pills at the time."

Danny was stunned. His dark brown hair, he pulled at so much, it stuck together, "Dad, I can clearly see this person's name is not yours. I can believe that the mix up was possible. But I cannot understand why no one called. I guess the person wasn't aware there was a mix up either, but how dangerous. "

James laughed, "Son… just wait…. On my mental breakdown, which I truly believe it was. I went back to the restaurant to see if I could find Maria. She wasn't there but I sat at a table. I was just getting ready to take one of my pills, and I dropped them. I thought I lined up the lid and didn't. My hand hit the table going up and knocked it out of my hand. Some kind-hearted server helped me pick them up and she noticed the pills were different and knew they were for a mental health care issue. She is going to be a nurse. Luck had me that day son. I stopped taking them immediately. Had they not dropped, I never would have gone to the library to read up on them. Nor would I have gone to the doctors. He was trying to commit me for evaluation son and I had already taken at least four pills the day before."

Danny became furious with his father, "When was this how many days ago?" James even more transfixed on what he wanted to say, "Let me finish. Days, son, I don't know, I couldn't even take a guess."

"Dad you knew enough to go to the doctors to call your lawyer, and to go for dinner," Danny wondered through confusion.

James became frustrated, "I cannot recall every single step as it occurred, son. It was after I stopped taking the pills and then got people to help me and still I was confused."

"Dad, I don't know what those drugs are for or what you mixed up with Maria. I don't know what you bought from some man. I feel like I am listening to a deranged movie idea that got rejected. However, the house sale and the cancellation of the sale and the confirmation from the alleged purchaser, with his name and wallet in my hands, have my son and me still here. Attempting to blow your own brains out just kills me. Thank god, my son is not sitting here listening to everything that came out of your mouth. Dad stop saying it was not me, someone else did it. You're acting like a kid who doesn't want to take responsibility for his own actions."

James held his head with his hands, "Son, you summarized everything I said, in a few sentences, but I had to go through a confession to you. Whatever those drugs are or what they do, I had no recollection at the time of where I got them. The body builder offered vitamins. I was also on pills to calm down my nerves. That feeling changed, once I got the drugs from the pharmacy. Then the combination we made when we spilled them and I ingested, was a powerful combination that distorted my reality. Dr. Flannery kept the painkillers he found inside the bottles that must have belonged to Maria, for her pain. But, at the time, I believed she was drugging me to get more money from me and the longer she kept me fucked up, the easier things were for her."

Danny was madder than hell, "You took drugs at your age without checking with your doctor? We never missed a week on the telephone Dad, before mom passed away. That was you Dad always touching base with all of us. I could not get a hold of you last week. We went out of town, and just got back in late last night. We were unpacking the car, when the cop called. Make sure you put all our contact numbers in your wallet. ”

James hesitated in shame, “I’m retracing my steps, here with you. Everything is clearer. All the drugs are purged now from my pathetic system. I had to been stoned in some way, and coming down, wasn’t nice. My heart raced. My thoughts were unclear. I had to tell myself this is normal. I was paranoid, and sweated profusely. I became highly depressed in a moment and then it turned to rage, and I trembled. I’m ashamed to even say, I drank without realizing how much alcohol, I was drinking. I felt a bit more settled in the morning. The moment I took the pills, I felt off balance. Weird, I cannot explain it. I wasn’t there when I cashed out my investment son. Not enough to ensure my money was protected or my home. It was Maria who took me for a ride.”

“Dad I hate to say this, but perhaps dementia, or Alzheimer’s is setting in. With what you’ve been, experiencing sounds like the early signs of the disease to me, because you hadn’t had the mix up of pills, when you took drugs off some stranger, did you?”

“Danny, I remember things, but at times, I get confused, and forget simple things. It happens to everyone,” James added in disappointment then slammed down his coffee, crossed and uncrossed his legs, “I don’t want to talk.” He went to the bathroom.

Danny sat on the arm of the chair when his son walked into the room after he had showered. “I have to consider the possibility of Alzheimer’s, and with the stress of losing grandma, it might of masked us from noticing that Grandpa wasn’t well at that time son.”

James came back to the room, “Dad, you weren’t responsible for the pills, from the pharmacy. If you didn't know about the house, you weren't responsible for the lady who tried to sell it. She never called us. The moment they went to close the title would have alerted the lawyers and automatically delayed closing. The sales agreement wasn't legal without all parities signing. You may have been lonely and sad, but your mental state was already in question. We should have come by. At least we could have called and, dropped by. It's only been what.... four months since mom passed away, and look at all the oddness that occurred."

James wanted to continue his pathetic rant, and share in his misery, "I answered the front door one day. This guy came swinging a bat while screaming at me to fuck off and leave his girl alone." Danny was startled, "His girlfriend, what Maria had a boyfriend?"

James got up and got excited, "This guy was like a mad man son. He certainly would have killed me if he got the chance. I had nowhere to go. I was pinned on the porch. All I could do was hope he would get tired and leave but the bat kept swinging. Then one of the legs broke off the table. Then another swing of the bat cracked the table in two. I turned around trying to get back into the house and had no luck. I walked towards the damage table, held two-pieces, one in each hand, and started swinging back at him. But the shitty old table was no match for this wild man and his steel bat."

"What are you saying Dad?" Danny tried to talk, but his father kept going on.

"While he was swinging, he fell flat on his face on the ground. I couldn't believe it and it startled me. I stood there holding broken pieces of table in my hands wondering what happened to him. Then I saw it, there was a large rock in Maria's hand, she was standing over him. I stood motionless not knowing what to do. The guy made a few whimpering noises and then I believed he was dead. I couldn't believe it. There was a dead man on my property," James vented rushing through his story without stopping.

"Oh my god, Dad," Danny reacted, "Don't tell me, you shot him."

James clasped his hands over his face, "I almost wished the man with the bat would have won the fight. At least I wouldn't have had to go through this agonizing confession." "It wasn't your fault Grandpa," quipped Johnny.

James was surprised at Johnny's comment. But he was also relieved. "Thank you Johnny, and no I didn't shoot him." James replied with a forced smile. "Grandpa, you were defending yourself. Anyways, you didn't kill the guy. That girl did," Johnny said in confidence.

James raised his eyebrows with what his grandson had said. Not because Johnny was defending his actions, but because he blurted "that girl" to describe a woman that he thought, he was in love with, until recently. "That girl's name was Maria," James said with a sense of guilt and anger. "I don't care who she was. She wasn't my Grandmother. I know that," Johnny shot back. "What did you do next Dad?" Danny asked.

"Maria convinced me that the Police wouldn't believe our story that it was self-defense and that she was the one who hit him with the rock when I had table pieces in my hand." James was standing as he continued and had his arms flaying back and forth as if to give credence to his story. Danny screamed,

"What did you do Dad."

James revealed, "At first I said, we can get an old fishing tarp wrap him up in it. We can then scrub any blood with bleach and we can put his bloody clothes in the fire pit and burn them. I also suggested we can burn his wallet with his I.D." "Where is his body Dad?" Danny inquired.

James went on, "Then I told her, we can dumped him in the middle of the lake and make sure he was weighted down. There would be no way that son of a bitch will be floating to the top anytime soon."

Johnny sat bewildered, slumped in the chair. This was excessive and too much information to take in all at once, he blurted out, "How can someone I looked up to all my life be tangled up in murder?" Johnny knew it was self-defense at the start, but once his grandfather started suggesting things to do he had to know did he actually did it?

Danny was not sure what really occurred, "Did you help dispose of a body too? Why wouldn't you have just dumped his body in the big fire pit in the back, and let the son of a bitch burn to death? So what did you? Did she really hit him on the head with the rock? Is the man dead Dad? I need to know, now."

James flaying his arms around still, not concentrating on his son's last question, "I was assaulted with his bat. Not at first he was just threatening me and smashed the table as a threat, and broke it. He came here, see, see my leg, he hit me right here. If she hit him, I don't know. He wasn't dead, he rolled around and got up and ran away. I got to whack him with the wooden table when I whipped it at him as he ran away. He was a big man, over six feet tall, dark hair, light brown eyes, nicely dressed. I slammed the door, locked it and yelled, you and your fucking boyfriend get the fuck out of here. There was blood, my blood... let's go see son."

James, Danny and Johnny walked to the door. Neither had exited the house after coming in when it was dark the night before. Danny feared this man was dead and a shit load of blood was on his father's porch. They opened the door. The table had been tossed away from the porch, and was broken. A small drop of blood was on the ground. James lifted up his pant leg again. "See he hit me. I don't believe she hit him and as you can see, if she did his head was right there, and there is no blood, and like I said, he got up right after I said the way to dispose of him. I think they were trying to freak me out or something. But I cut my hand with the wood." James held out his hand and displayed a cut that is healing on his palm.

Danny turned to his son, Johnny, "Go find something to do. Look for those pills." Johnny snapped at his father, "Why do I have to leave now. " Danny scolded Johnny with a tone change in his voice, "Don't question me son." In a huff, Johnny left slamming the wooden screen behind him.

"Dad," Danny said, "Don't fuck with me, did you kill and dispose of some man's body and did she hit him, and did you clean up the blood like you said? And that little scratch running up your leg looks like it came from wood, not a steel bat. You would have had a broken leg and ended up inside a Hospital, if a bat hit you with any force, on any part of your body. See the damage with the table imagine that being your leg, or your head. You have a little scab that's all and probably, from yourself."

James started laughing, "Son, trust me, no one died and there was no body disposed of. She had mentioned she was serious with a man for years and told me they were High School sweethearts, which of course I ignored, but listened to when we met. In my state, I forgot her saying this. I think he was jealous, and while he was here —all he did was swing and scream something about me bothering her and giving her drinks and pills. They showed up right after I was demanding my money. I haven't heard from her since, and I tried calling her cell, but her voice message, states it's full, so I cannot leave a message. The next day I went out, kicked the table over there, and left it. I was so fucking pissed off, and wondered why was she bringing a man around my fucking home and with a bat?"

As they stood, outside Danny looked around, then walked up to his father, "For Christ sake Dad there's no more is there? I cannot take anymore. Please don't tell me you killed Maria to? Who are you? Everything else you lived is real. Don't fucking lie to me now."

"Calm down, Danny," said James. "If you calm down I can continue. Please Danny, come inside the house, sit back down, and listen. This isn't easy, it's ripping me apart, I was going to shoot myself." Danny choked back tears, "But you didn't Dad, you're here. Its only money and you have your home, your family, and your life."

"Son, I understand, this doesn't sound good," James said anxiously. "Oh, no" snapped Danny, "Did you kill them? That's all I want to know now Dad?" Danny pleaded.

James kicked some shoes around by the door, "Damn you son, who the hell do you think, I am? I went looking for her don't you remember me saying this? Then I learnt about the drugs. If the two idiots were dead son, think logically. I wouldn't have packed up my gun and went looking for her, nor would I have tried to kill myself?" " You didn't say she was dead Dad you said, her boyfriend. Did you kill him? Or, did she? Is that why you tried to shoot yourself?" Danny demanded an answer. "No, son, I didn't kill him, nor did she. When they were here, they left alive," James assured him.

James let his body drop down on the couch, "No son, whatever con they were playing out. Her trying to get me to believe I killed him or she did, was messed up and totally deranged. That's what bothers, me, we didn't have to worry about this shit when Mom was alive. It just feels like a bad dream, a nightmare actually. There's no more story. That's all that occurred to me since your mother passed away. Didn't I get punished enough?" James asked. "By the way, how's everything with you and the girls?" James spluttered out.

Danny's face softened, "I cannot believe you're trying to change the subject and this happened. If you got into the house in one piece and they left, you're one lucky bastard." "Yes, son I do say so myself, I was a lucky bastard. It's just as strange to me," James agreed.

"Dad, I'm hungry and completely emotionally drained from this entire ordeal. I've missed work. The wife had been calling, I sent a text, the last before you woke up, and silenced the phone to give you my full attention. The first thing we have to do is go through this house with a fine toothcomb to make sure there are no drugs or something else that we don't know about lingering around. Then find out what drugs you were taking. We can hire someone to clean this place up. Talk about you moving with one of your kids. You need some medical tests. One to see if you have Alzheimer's, because to me, it sounds like you treated Maria like mom and didn't understand what you were doing. We have to sit down with your lawyer and tell him everything face to face. But for now, I have to get something to eat and so does my son. Please don't tell me there's more. Please tell me this is all you have to say," Danny thought to ask.

"Okay son," James quietly answered with his hands folded on his lap and his head down, like he was a 6-year-old boy scolded by his parents. His son was now the responsible adult. Their roles reversed. "And then," Danny continued, "I will help you find this Maria."

James went into a state of protection jumped up and tossed his hand at his son, "No son, you shouldn't get involved." "I'm already involved Dad," Danny suggested.

Johnny came down from upstairs, "I found the pills. They were in Grandpa's room, on Grandma's dresser. Inside each bag is a bottle that lists the ingredients, and how many to take a day. All of them are white. The man's name is Cory Franklin. Here is his business card. He left one in each bag. One of the bottles indicates they're for men over 50 and the other is some form of zinc. They're vitamins the label reads."

Danny felt internal settling as he sighed, "Dad, consider yourself lucky, if these people at the gym weren't ripping you off. I still want to confirm that's what they are. I'm taking these with me and the pill bottles you have there." James reached out to grab them from his son, "What if I need them for evidence son?" James instantly questioned.

"It's like you hear fuck all Dad. I don't want you to take them." Danny put his face up to his father's, "Who are you going to give them to…. as evidence? You could have purchased illegal drugs. Do you even know Maria's last name?" James thought for a moment, "Yeah Sanchez. That's it."

Danny was too weak to focus anymore, he waved to his son, "I've had all I can take. I feel like I'm on a roller coaster going round and around waiting for it to stop. Its stopping now, I've got to get off Dad. Johnny, let's get some breakfast or lunch, just food whatever works for you. Do you want anything Dad?"

James crossed his legs, and then his hands in front of his chest, gave a side look as he said "Whatever you pick up, is fine for me." Danny walked back over to his father, pointed his finger in his face, "You listen here, and I don't want any excuses. Don't you for one minute think if someone knocks on the door, you're going to answer it. I don't want you to open that fucking door to anyone," he expressed as he moved his finger towards the door, then back in his father. "This is my key for this house and that door. When I leave, I'm going to lock the door, and I'll unlock the door when we get back and don't set the alarm. Can you understand this?" Danny asked.

James body coward, "Yes, son, I'm listening. I promise I won't." Danny asked, "You won't what Dad?" James tossed his head down, "I won't answer the door to anyone." He said then lifted up his head, and continued, "But do you want me to help you with the food when you come in?" "No Dad, look at me, this means no, we're big men and can carry three meals, on our own," answered Danny.

Johnny wanted to go into the restaurant instead of going through the drive thru. He needed to use the restroom. "Not a bad idea, I haven't gone myself in a bit." Danny said in the car. After they finished in the bathroom, they stood in line deciding what to order.

Johnny was taller than his father, but was thinner. His brown hair sported crew cut styled haircut, letting his long dark black eyelashes draw a person's attention to his light green eyes. You couldn't help but notice them. A few young girls glanced over at him. His father teased him," Look at those girls gawking at you." Johnny smiled, and responded, "Thank god, I had a shower, my hair was a mess." His Dad laughed and whispered, "Yeah, there so much there, you didn't even need to use shampoo."

Danny looked up on the television screen before them and let his son flirt. There was a picture of a man the Police were talking about, but he couldn't hear. A dark haired young man, good looking and Danny thought…. "Oh my fucking god, don't tell me my father did kill this man." "Dad, Dad, I ordered for all of us but you have to pay." Johnny refocused his mind to his son. "Here's twenty." Johnny tapped his father, "Look the bills more." Danny paid the bill, "Son, go fill up the drinks, and I'll wait for the food."

Danny placed the food at the kitchen table. No sign of James but Danny heard the sound of the water running. Johnny asked, "Is Grandpa in the shower?" "Sounds like it son, go knock on the door and tell him we're back."

Danny took his food sat down on the couch and turned on the television. Johnny asked, "Dad, aren't you going to sit here and eat with me?" Danny paused for a moment before answering, "No son, just stay there and relax. Grandpa will be out soon to join you. I need some peace."

James was walking down the hall as a flash came on the television with the picture Danny had seen at the restaurant. Danny ran up, grabbed his father, pulled him towards the television, and said, "Look does that man look like the man that was here?"

Danny held James head, "I don't know it was dark out but that man looks a little older and dirty looking. This man was clean, shorter styled hair and was dressed up in a suit, Modellish looking man son, and my head hurts. Let go, please," expressed James.

Danny released his grip on his Dads head and sat down, "How fucking odd that the same sort of man you initially described is missing. You sure you didn't fucking imagine this man was here when you were high on drugs, and were watching TV?" Danny sarcastically stated.

James felt annoyed, "Yeah, and then after I watched television, I went out broke and kicked my fucking table, for no fucking reason at all. And I told you that don't look like the man. No one was hurt but me. Why would I lie about this son? Believe me, why can't you just believe me?"

Danny took a sip of his pop, "Just go eat with Johnny before your meal goes cold Dad." James stood there, "No, I'm not hungry anymore." Danny was beyond upset. He went up and whispered in his father's ear, "Just go sit down with my son and make it a happy moment, at least for him. I'm still not buying your entire story just yet. I don't want to hear a word about anything you went through until I ask you a question. Don't talk to me at all,' snapped Danny. James walked over to the table, sat down, and started to eat with his grandson.

Danny turned up the volume on the television and searched for the news. It came on again. He listened for the first time. Adam Scallo a carpenter who went missing over a month ago was found dead. Adam had been called out to the area of 874563 for a service call. There was no such address. His vehicle was located in a ditch not far from where his body was found. Police are still investigating anyone with information. Danny turned the television off. It wasn't near his father's home and he wasn't sure why or who would call a man for a service call when there was no real address.

"This world is getting more fucked up." He muttered.

He picked up his cell phone and called the Police. "I'm inquiring about a man you found dead." Right away he was transferred to a sergeant. "This is detective Hallotacta." "Hi my name is Danny. My father had some adult male with brown hair come to his home with a bat. Apparently, this woman named Maria was saying she killed him with a rock to his head. My father thought it was a joke that this man was dead. He told me the man got up and ran away and then my father slammed the door when he came back into his home. That's was the last time he heard from her or seen her even. He doesn't know the man. It was dark out. My father believes the man had brown hair, and was well dressed. To him model looking. I noticed in the news where it reported this man went to a false address. Apparently, this woman took three hundred thousand from my father. Then listed his private residence for sale and sold it. He had gotten some drugs from some man at the gym to take which he took. Then he mixed those with medication that he got from the Drug Store, that didn't belong to him. I'm not sure if any of this is connected, I just found out today and I'm exhausted. But it was the false address that got me."

The detected asked, "How long ago did this attack occur?" Danny said, "Hold on. Dad when was it this man was here at your house with the bat?" James said, "A couple of weeks ago perhaps. I don't remember." Danny nodded his head in amazement that his father couldn't, answer a simple question, with clarity, "I cannot confirm the date they were here, but my father is under the impression that it was a couple of weeks ago. I see it was about a month ago this man went missing. I don't know if this is connected. I hate to think someone is rolling people for drugs and money," Danny said baffled. Detective Hallotacta said, "I'll send a car out to get more details."

When the Police arrived, James had no idea his son called them. Danny stood outside the door and explained what his father said, about burning his identification, dropping the body into the lake, and cleaning up the property with bleach. The police and Danny walked into the house. James was floored when the police questioned him, "It was what I could do, not what I did." James bellowed out in tears, "My son's a rat. I'm the victim here, look at my leg, and my hand, and my poor table was destroyed. I was destroyed. Look at me. I didn't do it. Trust me, and that man looks nothing like this man did. The man who was here was Modellish looking, tall, over six feet," James rambled out all riled up.

They got Maria's telephone number from James. Looked at the pills he got from the Pharmacy and the man from the gym. Looked at the wallet, and couldn't believe what occurred. Four cop cars came, and several SUV"'s. They separated everyone James felt he had to prove himself. They followed him outside.

After he explained what occurred, James grabbed a piece of wood from the table and told everyone to stay back. It happened like this. He was displaying how the man went berserk. He re-enacted the man with the bat. He went swaying his arms pretending to hold a bat and went towards the door being him and then went back to being the man with the bat. He placed himself down on the ground. He said, "I cannot do the fall. I don't want to hurt myself. Perhaps, he smashed his stomach that's why he was whining at the time. Maybe he lost his balance. He is the only one who knows for sure what happened. The rock wasn't that big, three inches at best," he shared.

As James stayed there, Johnny came out of the house with an officer. He called to Johnny, "Stand over by my feet. See she stood way back there, by his feet with the rock and then he did this." James rolled himself over a few times, got up and ran towards the driveway, then ran back screaming, "He's alive, I say, he's alive."

Just in case he wasn't alive the Police wanted to see the garage and the boat. It had layers of dirt, odd tools, and a ton of other stuff on top of the tarp, which covered the boat. There was no way the boat or the cover had been moved in years. They walked out to the fire pit, looked inside and all around, not an ash. They took samples of the blood on the porch.

Sergeant Clark said, "I called the woman Maria. I don't believe your father killed anyone. It was Maria's ex-boyfriend with the bat. He is alive. Your father can charge him. I have his name."

"Thank god," Danny commented with heavy breathes coming from his nose, as he had his mouth closed. The officer went on, "I called the Real Estate Agent, got the buyers Agents name and number from her. He was the dark haired Modellish looking man you were first yelling at when he knocked on the door. He wanted to let you know they were there. Some man came up with the bat and ran in front of a woman he said. Maria, confirmed it was her. The Agent figured it was a family issue and left. The mix up with the pills occurred with two males named James Johnston. Do you have a nephew named James Johnston?" He asked James. "Yes, I do, he was at the drug store when I was there," James agreed. "At the counter, didn't he say, make sure you cross your t's and dot your I's?" the officer asked. "I don't remember, but we know he has some sort of mental health care issue," James confirmed. "

"It looks like that caused the mix up at the pharmacy. Your nephew dropped coffee on his last name, where the letter T was. Another officer looked, it was impossible at a quick glance for anyone to see the t, was missing unless you looked close in between the letters. The pharmacist asked you James, if you were to get two prescriptions. You stated. Yes, and said, you had told the doctor that you might be going away. So, he must have ordered two. It was on camera and at that pharmacy they also have voice recording. This confusion permitted James to receive his nephew's prescription by mistake. His name is James, Jamie Johnston, isn't it? His middle name was not on the prescription. It seems both James had seen the same mental health care doctor, which was on file in the computer data system at the pharmacy. They just added Johnson and asked for James, and Mr. Johnston, you got those prescriptions. That is why, your father prescription bottle had the name Johnson, not Johnston," Sergeant Clark confirmed.

Danny jumped in, "Yes it is, and he was named after his great grandfather. It is my father's brother's son. He got into drugs, at a young age and wasn't able to attend school, but they kept whatever they were going through private."

"How did you find out all this so soon?" Danny probed. Detective Hallotacta shook his head and said, "Your fathers doctor, already called the pharmacy and the police after your father visited him and ran out. He left messages on all your machines, and no one called him back, that was when he called us. Your father's answering services on the house phone and cell are full. Your nephew called your father to let him know, what occurred, but no one answered. We checked the messages on all your machines after we got a search warrant. Apparently, your sisters were out of town for two weeks. We got a hold of them late last night. They're arriving today. They told us your family returned home from your home in Mexico yesterday, because your wife had a business meeting to attend to today. We went to your house at seven this morning, no one answered and your wives been tied up in meetings all day. We finally tracked her down. Rather than head back out here this morning we went to your home. We finally called your security company. They noted they had some oriental man, on camera. We got a search warrant to view that material and we were going through it when we considered the possibility that your family had been kidnapped. Then we got the call something about a murder might have occurred here at this address. That's why there are so many cops are here.

We weren't able to leave a message on any of your machines at home, so we got a search warrant to, search all your telephone records. That's how we spoke to your sisters yesterday. The doctor wanted to get your father evaluated at the hospital the day he was there and signed the papers for us to pick him up. We've been at his home several times a day, but no one answered. Maria mentioned she had been prescribed the same pain pills your father's physician took out of the bottle in his office. The police have them. Apparently, your father and her had been drinking when they spilled their medication which caused additional confusion." With an astonished look realizing there was an investigation going on, "Oh, my god, you cops don't play around. I only heard all this today. Why I didn't think to look at the boat or fire pit, before calling you, is beyond me. Nevertheless, we never would have learnt so much and gotten closure with the pills. I can only say sorry my family wasted your time. As for my Dad, do you want to charge him?" James sullen in his son's actions, "Don't...even think to talk to me.... no I don't. I've been through enough, god damn it."

Sergeant Clark said, "It has nothing to do with the death of the person you seen on the news. As far as your house, it's in the court system we've been informed by your lawyer and both agents. It's out of our hands, right now." The Police left.

Danny hugged his father, and Johnny. All he could think to say was, "I'm so sorry Dad. Just so sorry we weren't here for you. We should have come by and called and I'm so happy they never found the gun."

James quietly asked, "Can we watch a movie together, before you leave, I don't want to be alone right now."

Danny gave a big grin, "I'm going to be here for a week, or so, let's go pick up some clothes for my son and I, along with a few movies and let's see if your truck's still where you believe you parked it." "For the movies, let's make it a comedy. I cannot take anymore suspense, mystery or drama, and I don't want to see a romance," James suggested…

James truck wasn't at the garage, it had been towed. Johnny drove it back to James.

Ten

Conrad and Dave arrived at Brandy's Apartment building. Conrad was all-paranoid, "Let's be careful, and sit here in the car for a while. I got my trusty cam right here. Look for well-dressed man with dark hair and see if he's stalking her or watching her or us." Davy confusedly asked, "Why?" "Davy if its drugs and money. You do not understand how these people work. Several people could be involved." "Conrad my sister has no money and doesn't take drugs on her own." Dave announced pissed off.

Dave's cell rang, "Hello...okay.... yes... how much...umm... yeah... you talked him down.... The lowest you can get. Just a minute let me see..." Dave did an electronic signature, it is on its way, and we close tomorrow...? Thanks Frank."

Conrad asks, "You got a Condo for her that fast?" "Dave was reading the paperwork," Yes, the two bedrooms down the hall from mine. You remember that one Conrad?"

Conrad's was styling his short brownish ginger hair with the visor, "I didn't like the dark kitchen cupboards, and it's a little smaller then what I want.

Oh, but it did have real hardwood throughout, not that engineered flooring. The stainless steel appliances and the full laundry room was a nice touch along with each bedroom having full bathrooms, and double sinks. What did you pay? Wait do not tell me. I do not want to know. I am still waiting for the offer to come back for the one on the floor below with the full balcony and in ground pool."

Dave looked at Conrad confused, "How is it my offer was accepted and we close tomorrow and you're still waiting to hear back? Let me have some hair gel Conrad," Conrad handed Dave his gel and took out a bottle of water from his bag while Dave fixed his hair in his visor.

"The sellers have not moved once from their listed price and Frank and I have done five offers. I've went up over forty thousand from my original one. Now, twenty five hundred dollars is what separates us after he presents it today. Dave spun his head around to look at him, "Well, Conrad that's just too bad you're thinking of losing the one you want over twenty five hundred at this point. And you've signed offers five times on the same property?"

Conrad swiveled his body around and looked to Dave, "Five times, isn't that bad?" Dave hand went to his mouth, holding back laughter, "You have to be joking." "No, Dave. Why are you laughing at me?"

"You're lucky they didn't refuse to see another offer from you. How bad do you want it?"

Conrad's face crinkled up, his muscles tensed all over his face. "You get upset and feel stress with the topic, don't you Conrad?" Dave questioned. "It's all new to me and will be my first home. I am not sure how it all works to be honest. Frank tried to explain things, and when he does, it feels like my emotions take over. My mind goes blank. It's a scary time actually making an offer to buy a home and every time it doesn't get accepted, it's just one more heartache that blows me apart inside," Conrad shared.

Dave smirked as he padded Conrad on his shoulder, "That's okay, you're learning. You think money and a new life and hesitate. If one place is causing all the stress, you have to wonder if it's really worth it. I have four rentals in my building, and I never waste time on price," Dave told him.

"What do you mean Dave?" asked Conrad. "I offered twenty five hundred less than their asking price, first offer, if it's priced right. It usually works. You have to know if their entertaining multiple offers. Do not go messing around with price unless, Frank tells you it's listed to high. He knows the market conditions, history, and all the details he can print out for you. It has to feel like a home to you and something you are willing to part money for, to get it. A small price of twenty five hundred will not make much difference in your mortgage payments. You are always in charge of what you are willing to spend. You can walk away, or even put in conditions to make sure, the home isn't hiding anything that might be costly later on to you. I'm sure Frank has told you this," conveyed Dave.

"That makes perfect sense Dave. I'm paying cash." Conrad affirmed. "See it's not hard, when you decide. I just have to tell Brandy and move her out of that dirty lonely place. Frank already called movers for tomorrow. It's not that stressful," Dave assured Conrad.

Conrad curled up listening to Dave talk, "What a

loving brother you are. Big kiss from me to you," as Conrad kissed Dave on his cheek. "I'm calling Frank?" Conrad confirmed.

Dave barged in, "Wait Conrad find out if Frank presented the offer you have now. If not, what is twenty five hundred dollars for what you want? If you feel you've gone up enough, tell Frank to say this is your final offer and stop abusing yourself over one place." Conrad educated him and smiled.

Conrad called Frank, "Have you presented my offer yet?" Frank was sitting on a patio at coffee shop, "Not yet. Waiting for tonight, the owners aren't around until then." Conrad mumbled out, "Frank should I give them what they're asking?" Frank was going over paperwork, and stopped to focus on his call, "What? Are you suggesting for me, not go in with this offer and offer their full price?" he questioned.

Conrad's body leaned in to Dave while he was on the cell so Dave could hear, "Hold on Frank." "Dave what do I do, he hasn't presented it yet?" Conrad asked.

"Put him on speaker. Hi, Frank Dave here too." "Hi Dave," said Frank. Dave went on, "I understand you've done five offers, and they haven't moved. If they won't accept twenty five less, just walk." Conrad screamed, "No don't walk, I love it, I don't want to lose it."

Dave laughed, "Frank you up to do two more offers for Conrad, just to see what will happen, but if you say you'll walk they may not accept your next offer when you are willing to do full price. By the way, have you asked if any other agents presented offers? Are other agents still going in with clients?

They could be waiting for multiple offers to get a higher price, so full price may not seal this deal. How many corner units are available right now?" asked Dave.

"Their agent isn't sharing any information. It's like I'm dealing with a brick wall and there are no similar units for sale right now, and they know it," added Frank.

Conrad was in a bundle of nerves and started biting his nails, "Oh gosh, I can see myself cooking in the kitchen, and I love the bathroom. If I get it, my commute will finally end. Frank, change my offer to full price and if they don't accept it too bad for them, I'm done." He said, wiping his hands together, and then spread them apart, as if that will force the problem to disappear. "I'm not playing money games. If they want more than they listed it for then I will wait for something better to come my way. It's like cars, they always say this is the best, and once its sold nothing else will do. Crazy sales people, eh, always wanting us to believe their shit," Conrad stated firmly his limit.

Dave and Frank started laughing, "Are you sure Conrad, I don't want you all messed up, going in with a higher price which will be their exact asking price. If you need time to think, just call me back," assured Frank.

Conrad was sluggish in his seat, "The decision is killing me inside, but let's do it, Frank." "We've been to the Condo at least ten times. If they accept it Conrad, dinner and wine is on me," said Frank laughing. Conrad eased back and cracked a smile, "Yes, I'm sure. It's what I want. Please let me know as soon as you can Frank," Conrad said. They hung up.

Dave was going over his new real estate deal and looked up to see Conrad gazing out the window. Dave looked across the way to see what Conrad was so intrigued with. After the call, he went silent.

Conrad noticed a good-looking brown hair man had walked out of the Restaurant looking as though he was about to cross the street. Yet, he stood there. He was exceptionally well dressed. What are you looking at?" Dave asked.

"Look Davey, look, do you think that's him? He has been standing there for a few minutes, "Conrad pointed, "In front of the restaurant, that guy." Conrad stressed. Dave inquisitively looked, "Nice looking man, well dressed but how would I know?" Conrad thinking, "Watch this."

Conrad jetted out of the car and ran across the street bumping right into the man, with his head turned to the side, and then touched his arms to display he lost his balance, "Excuse me, sorry, I was in a hurry," apologized Conrad. "Watch where you're going," noted the man. "Can I offer you a coffee for my ignorance? It's the least I could do," asked Conrad. "I don't think so buddy, I'm not interested in men, and your approach was the worse, yet. I think you came running out of that red sports car there, didn't you?" said the man.

Conrad became nervous, "Oh, huh…um…..yes, I did, only to grab us coffee. And for inconveniencing you, I don't mind buying you one. I should have introduced myself." Conrad held out his hand, "I'm Conrad, what's your name?" "Look buddy….go get your coffee and have a good day," the man said and walked away.

Conrad carried his tray with coffee and rushed across the street and jumped into the car, and slid his body down in the seat, as he handed it out to Dave, "Oh my god how fucking embarrassing. He knew I literally meant to bump into him, and thought I was picking him up. He noted, he wasn't gay. I offered to buy him a coffee. I gave him my name and he did not give me his. How stupid was I? I'm so humiliated. He knew what car I came out of. He's standing in front of Brandy's building now," Conrad expressed, hiding the side of his face with his hand.

Dave's mouth dropped open as he listened, "You should have mentioned what you wanted to do. I would have said, don't do it. How could he not see what car you came out of, he was looking right at you. I needed a coffee anyways. Just sit here and look like busy. Read some paperwork, or look at the pictures," added Dave.

Dave showed Conrad the offer for the Condo and read some of details wasting time. The man stood in front of the building. Dave was fed up, "I'm tired of sitting in the car, and it's nearing ten minutes. Let's go see Brandy and tell her the good news. The guy is not leaving. Put some change in the meter and bring the parking sticker back and place it on the dash," said Dave.

Dave knocked on Brandy's door. There was no answer. Conrad moved around impatiently, "See Dave, you didn't believe me when I told you that something could happen. Just unlock her door with your key." Dave fiddled with the lock, opened the door, and called to Brandy. She did not answer. "She may have gone out." Dave suggested. He and Conrad walked through the Apartment and seen the door to her bedroom closed. They knocked on the door. "Open it up Dave, don't wait, damn it I'll do it," snapped Conrad. Brandy was barely breathing, in her bed. "Call 911," yelled Conrad.

Dave nervously dialed 911 on his cell phone. "I need an ambulance to 9875 Valley street unit 902." A voice of reason was on the other end tried to calm him down, "I don't know… I don't know, something is wrong," is all Dave answered standing over Brandy. Conrad grabbed the cell. "Possible overdose, but I cannot say for certain she did this herself when just this morning, she was adamant she didn't want drugs in her system to ruin her career as a Nurse. I cannot believe I said that, sorry Dave," stated Conrad.

He carried on, "She was afraid her boyfriend was drugging her. I'm a family friend, and her brother is in shock of some sorts. I found some pills beside her on her bed. Yes, she is breathing lightly but not awake. I'm watching her. We can carry her down to the front lobby to meet the ambulance. I don't want to waste any time. I know we aren't supposed to move her but we don't want to risk her life." Conrad answered while he stayed on the phone to follow the instructions given.

A knock came to the door Conrad ran to open it and led them to the bedroom. Dave noted, "My god you ambulance drivers arrived fast. It's nice having you one block away." They moved them out of the way, did what they had to do. Dave noticed an oxygen mask and broke down in tears. They rolled her out to the hallway on the stretcher, took the pills, and offered one of them a ride. Conrad was hugging Dave, "You go in the ambulance with her Dave. I will drive my car and meet you there," suggested Conrad. Dave was fumbling to lock the door. Conrad pushed Dave out of the way, "Give it to me," he said, as he locked the door and handed the key to Dave at the elevator.

They took Brandy away from him and into a room at the Hospital. Dave had to do routine procedures answering her medical details. Conrad's arms outstretched ready to hug Dave, as Dave stood up. "My god Conrad, don't come up from behind me, you scared the shit right out of me," snapped Dave.

Conrad quietly said, "Sorry Dave, I wanted to let you know I was here. The man was still standing in front of her building when we left. Did you see him?" Dave leaned into him and whispered in his ear, "Damn, it Conrad, if that's him, now he knows you and your car, and your fucking name and me. I glanced at him as we went out."

They were there for hours before told Brandy was going to be fine. They left…

Dave was doing up his seat belt, "Conrad do you think we should go back to her Apartment tonight? Frank does have the movers coming tomorrow for ten am. She does not have much to move, more her keepsakes. Her furniture is old and can go to dump, I will order new. She deserves it."

Conrad was tired, "Yes, let's get something to eat and stay there tonight. I can take the couch. We can order new furniture online and have the movers pick it up at the warehouse. What does she need a couch, chair and a few tables and two bedroom suites? We can split the cost. I noticed she doesn't own a television set. I'll buy her one and later we can go out and get her some Knick knacks." Conrad offered.

"Conrad it's kind of you, but you don't have to. I am exhausted and need some food," quietly expressed Dave.

They stopped at a drive thru and arrived at Brandy's building. Conrad gazed around the place, "My god the man's gone. I guess he got tired of pretending dressed in a designer suit, he was security for the building."

Dave could not bring himself to sleep in Brandy's bed, both he and Conrad passed out on the couch. It was the first time they slept together. There was a light knock on the door.

Conrad was the first to wake to the point of thinking he heard something. Another small tap, he starting shaking Dave's arm, "Wake up, wake up, Dave, I think someone is at the door. I'm going to see."

Conrad peeked through the peephole, looked at his watch. He ran back to Dave, "Its only eight thirty, a man is at the door, just one. It's too early for the movers isn't it?" Dave was groggy, "Don't open it ask who it is." Another tap at the door occurred.

Conrad ran back to the door, "Who is it?" "We're the movers," answered the voice behind the door. Dave wobbled down the hallway, "It's the movers Dave," Conrad whispered.

Dave asked, "What company do you work for and who hired you?" "Frank hired us and wanted us here as early as possible. I think he told you ten, but we got finished early," answered the man.

Dave was still waiting for the name of the Company, "What's the name of your Company?" "Oh yes, I forgot we have a code Frank sent to me for the Company name. Let me check my email, hold on," the man said. Conrad and Dave stood there afraid to open the door for one man. Conrad asked Dave, "How can one man move all this stuff?' "Dave said, "I have to get my cell I don't know the code either. Ask him how many movers he has."

Conrad yelled through the door, "While you're looking for that code, can you tell me how many movers you have with you?' "It's just me here now, and the rest of the crew will be here in about a half hour. I figured I'd come up with some boxes and start packing while I waited for them," confirmed the man.

Dave pointed to his cell, "I got it ask him if he found his." Conrad placed his face to the door, "Did you find that code yet?" The voice answered, "Yes… it's Frank Company Business Condo, for Brandy through Dave. Then Frank 60050215 is that correct?" the man asked.

Dave agreed to Conrad, "Tell him okay, and open the door let him in."

Conrad opened the door, "Welcome, I'm Conrad and this is Dave and who are you?" "I'm Robert, Frank's brother in law. I was just going to leave. I was knocking for about fifteen minutes. I must say, I've never met anyone who used codes to move household furniture. New thing for me, safety, I imagine. I was just going to get a coffee and use the bathroom," expressed Robert. Dave and Conrad smiled. "You can use the bathroom here," said Dave, as he led him down the hall "It's in here."

Dave noticed Brandy had a coffee percolator, coffee, and milk in the fridge. "I'll make us a pot of coffee."

As Dave was spooning, the coffee into the dispenser he noticed white powered mixed with brown coffee grinds. He walked over to Conrad and Robert, "Look I've never seen white stuff inside my coffee grounds before. Have you ever seen something like this?" he asked.

Conrad stiffed in disgust "No, never, not at all. Is it old or bad?" Robert looked, "Oh my. What is that white stuff?"

Dave smoothly said, "I just don't know, but there will be no coffee from here, for us. But there's a Restaurant across the Street, I'll treat, what do you want?"

Conrad sat straight up, "I'll have a large regular coffee with a bagel and cream cheese. What do you want Robert?" Robert smiled, "I'll have the same." Dave left…

Conrad noticed Robert did not have any boxes with him. "Where are the boxes you brought with you?" Conrad asked. Robert spoke the first four words one at a time, pausing in between each word, "They….are…..in…. my…. truck." He went back to speaking normally, "I wanted to make sure someone was here before I carried them up. If I had to come back at ten, I can't leave them in the hallway. Then you people mentioned making coffee, so I didn't run down to get them yet. Trust me they're down there, inside the truck. You guys okay? Frank was in a hurry to get this booked late yesterday, for early today."

Conrad hesitated to answer, "Yes, we're fine, and Dave is the only one who knows why this late move. I just stayed here last night with him. I can help you carry up some boxes, if you like while we wait for our coffee." Robert put his hands on his legs and stood up, "Sure, if you don't mind we can go now." Conrad eased himself off the couch, "Sure lets go."

They stood in the hallway as Conrad closed the door he remembered, "I can't go with you. I don't have a key to lock the door. I cannot leave and leave the door unlocked. Sorry, I do not know what I was thinking. I have not had my coffee. Perhaps, that is why my mind is not working well. You can go now or wait until Dave comes back. I'll go down with you when he does," added Conrad. Robert figured, "I'm in the hall already, I'll bring them up."

Dave got back with the coffee, and placed it down. "I'm so embarrassed. I asked Robert where the boxes were. He responded with, 'why would he carry them up when he wasn't sure anyone was here.' It made sense. I offered to help him. We walked out to the hallway and how humiliating when I had to tell him, sorry, I can't go with you because I don't have a key. Like, it totally made me feel like a fucking idiot, kicking him out of the apartment to do some work. Thanks Dave," blamed Conrad.

Conrad and Dave were finished eating and Robert still wasn't back. Dave questioned, "What happened with Robert. Did he just leave because of what you said? It's been about twenty minutes since I got back. His coffee is cold.

Conrad walked to the door and opened it. A pile of boxes not made, leaned against the wall, but no Robert. He walked back and told Dave, "He must be making a few trips a ton of boxes not made are leaning against the wall in the hall. Maybe his crew arrived?"

Dave had a full day ahead of him and asked Conrad, "Can I borrow your car? I have to go to the Lawyers and the Bank. You can get a ride to the Condo with Robert. Frank will be waiting there for all of you."

Conrad annoyingly projected, "Why, why, can't I go with you? Robert is capable of packing up and driving to the Condo himself. That's how all movers work Dave." Dave was completely overwhelmed, "Fine, fine!"

Robert and his crew dragged all the boxes inside the Apartment. Robert ordered them to drop them against a wall inside the doorway. Robert was now in a rush, "Dave, what's going what's trash?" he asked.

Dave gave Robert the details, handed him the key, "Do not give the keys to anyone, or let anyone in. If I miss you, please hand the key back to Frank at the Condo. If your drivers can pick up these orders at this furniture stores and set the stuff up, I will pay extra. Leave your bill with Frank. We're leaving to ensure the closing of the Condo went well."

Dave and Conrad went on their way. While Conrad drove, Dave was calling the Hospital to check on his sister. She was awake, on and off, but still not well enough to talk.

Frank ordered Pizza for the movers. Conrad and Dave finished Dave's business transactions and headed back to the Condo.

The new furniture for Brandy was all set up when they arrived. Roberts Company had just finished. Robert thanked them for the Pizza and let his crew leave. Then handed Dave the Condo key and Brandy's key, and reassured him no one came by the Apartment, other than the super who put the elevator on service. Then checked the suite to ensure no damage occurred before they left.

Dave looked around, "By the way where is Frank, Robert?" Robert stood five feet six and had a little weight on his stomach, and big arms. Robert eased Dave over to the door, "He had to confirm the elevator was finished on service here, we're done." Dave seemed incapable of rational, "Oh yes, standard procedures. That is why I hired him. Thanks Robert where's your bill?" "Frank already took care of it," he answered.

After Robert and his crew left, Dave and Conrad went to their own places. Dave wanted a shower and to get to the Hospital to see Brandy alone. Conrad did not put up a fuss to go, he was exhausted.

Dave walked into Brandy's room. She was alert and confused as to how she ended up there and was stunned to hear drugs, came back in her blood work. She was baffled with how they got there. Dave demanded, "No lies, sis I want to know everything." Brandy tried to recall what occurred, "I made a pot of coffee, went to my room, and got one of my books to study out of the side table as I lifted it out there was a clear bag, with something inside. I found pills in capsule form. I took a couple out to look at and I honestly do not know what they were. I had a few cups of coffee while reading and then cleaned up the kitchen. I felt dizzy and unwell. Didn't take any of the pills, but recall going to my room and that's all I remember," she shared.

Dave recalled the coffee. "Fuck Brandy that coffee was either rotten or dropped with some sort of white powder. We were there this morning. I went to make us a pot of coffee, and it was loaded with white shit. What white powder did you have around?" he probed.

"You think some cockroach powder fell inside? The super scattered that around the Apartment after I noticed a shit load of cockroaches in the middle of the night in the bathroom and kitchen. That is the only white powder I seen. I was making us a pot of coffee when he placed it around the cupboards. He and I shared a cup," acknowledged Brandy.

"That explains it but they said drugs. Have they mentioned poison?" questioned Dave.

"I'm not sure what they found," Brandy answered embarrassed "I don't know what to say Dave. No Doctor has spoken with me and I have never taken drugs. I made coffee a couple of times since the super put it around the place. It had a rotten taste, but yesterday, I did not notice. I looked at the light brown coffee grinds mixed with white and thought it came like that. Those drugs in the table must belong to John Paul. Did you get them?" she asked.

Dave stood up from the chair, leaned into talk to Brandy, "It would have taken anyone two seconds to toss a few specs of poison into your coffee. The super could have had it rub off his arm when he placed it down. John Paul could have emptied a few capsules in the can as well. However, it would take a shit load of capsules to make that much white powder mixture in that coffee. I grabbed the can and will get it tested, and let the Doctor know about it," firmly stated Conrad.

Brandy was too weak to think and respond, "Yes, Dave it could have easily occurred. I didn't think of it. I was busy, and stopped paying attention. "Dave figured it was time to tell Brandy what he did, "As far as your Apartment you've been moved into my Condo building, same floor I'm on. We did this today. Everything is set up. I'll do some grocery shopping for you, when you're coming home. And from now on Brandy, let's communicate about things you don't think are relevant."

Brandy was falling back to sleep it was after eight when Dave arrived. He gave her a kiss on her head and said, "Get some sleep, I'll see you tomorrow. Visiting hours are over."

The Hospital had retained the pills they found with Brandy but Dave wanted to make sure they checked her for poison and thought he could leave the can there, but they refused to accept it. They agreed to mention poison to the doctor.

Dave called the mover Robert, "Tell me when your men were packing up did any of them find pills in bags or any form of drugs in my sister's Apartment?" Robert instantly replied, "Yes, there was some found and they left them with Frank. It was odd, really. When I left her Apartment, it was empty. Apparently, they found a bag, call Frank."

Dave looked surprised, "Robert, why does Frank have it?' "Oh my lead hand went up after the super was complaining he needed to see Brandy's Apartment to make sure we didn't cause any damage after he took the elevator off service. When my man, went back up to the apartment he found a bag inside her bedroom and took it. I think it's the supers. He was outback talking to some white fat tattooed dude by the garbage bins. I noticed he had taken a bag from the dude. When I closed the truck door he was standing right behind me. I handed him the key.

"I told my lead hand to go up and get the key from him. I thought it was odd, considering I had done a walk through twice and the apartment was empty, before I gave him the key. I was gone when my man came down. He tossed the bag in the front of his truck, and forgot about it until he went to leave. I had been upstairs with you and, he seen Frank, so he gave it to him. Just in case it was Brandy's, what else was he to do?"

Dave called Frank in haste, "Frank, its Dave." "Frank started laughing, "Yes, I know Dave your number comes up with your name on my cell." Dave laughed, "I can't believe it, now I'm starting to act like my sister. She does that all the time to me. Robert mentioned his worker gave you some bag with drugs they found at Brandy's old place. It's not like she did drugs, but some dude she was seeing is into some crazy shit and they must have been his. That's why there was a rush to move her out. You still have them?"

Frank was startled and immediately started yelling, "I didn't look in the fucking bag. What the fuck am I holding on to here? Is it illegal drugs?" Dave tried not to freak Frank out, "Frank… calm down, I don't know what they are. Just hold on, I'm coming over. Meet me outside your house in twenty minutes.

Dave drove to Frank's. He had been looking out the window. When he arrived Frank ran out the house with a knapsack and handed it to Dave through his car window.

"What the hell, it's a kid's knapsack?" oddly stated Dave.

Frank looked through his window and freaked out, "I had this full fucking bag of drugs in my home with my wife and kids. I didn't know your sister was into dealing illegal drugs for Christ sakes Dave." "She isn't Frank," Dave confirmed in confusion.

"Thanks Frank, this dude my sister met is unbalanced in some way. I'm taking this to the Police.

I've had all I can take."

Frank firmly growled, "Don't tell them I held them for you. Just don't involve me or Robert into any of this odd and illegal shit we have families."

Dave drove himself to the Police station sat down with a couple of officers and told him everything he knew, but didn't say Robert or Frank knew about the drugs. He let them know his sister was in the Hospital for an overdose, but he believed it was because of cockroach poison the building super put down. He briefly noted, "Some drugs were found in her blood work, but his sister didn't do drugs." He gave them the coffee container and left.

Dave felt like a criminal he had to show his identification, and signed stuff. He didn't think about going to see a Lawyer before he rushed it and said what he did. The Police offered him the opportunity to call one. He had nothing to hide and feared for his sisters' life. He wanted someone else to help him sort out the strain and confusion.

The Police went to the Hospital and spoke to Brandy all she had was his first name, no last name, for John Paul. "How stupid and ashamed I feel," she said stressed.

She felt something was not right, when they were continuously asking her about the pills she had with her when the ambulance arrived, "I don't know where they came from. And the man I gave a key to wore suits, and had a brief case, not a kid's knapsack." She paused, before continuing on, "I met him where I work, and never got any personal details from him."

The Police probed Brandy about the alleged abuse by him that her brother had mentioned. She denied that occurred, "I was shocked and disturbed by what occurred, more his attitude and actions," and she shared what did.

For the drugs in her apartment found with her, "I've never seen them before, and I can't confirm the bag they found was in fact inside the Apartment, because I wasn't there."

She did confirm seeing white stuff in her coffee can, and mentioned the super's son had put cockroach poison around. She shared he was slow or delayed in some way, but did not know what health issues and felt lucky that Dave came to her rescue and believed, it was all just an accident. And firmly mentioned she had never taken any form of street drugs.

On the officers way out they stopped at the nurses' station, and one of the officers mentioned, "I can't believe she was poisoned by cockroach powder."

They got the name of the super from her, and went to see him.

Eleven

The volunteer entered with a wheelchair for Brandy. "That's okay, I don't need it," Brandy said embarrassingly. "Now… now Brandy, Enjoy the ride. I'll take her out if you don't mind," asked Dave. The volunteer usually would have objected, but her heavy workload required her services elsewhere and she welcomed the chance to download the job to someone else.

When the three arrived at their car in the parking lot, Dave positioned himself into the back seat with Brandy. Conrad had volunteered to drive.

The three drove off in silence, unsure what to say. The men did not want to trigger a negative reaction in Brandy. Brandy starred out the window upwards to the sky, tears noticeably sliding down her cheeks. Conrad looked in his rear-view mirror, as he drove, unsure of what he could say to make her feel better to add some form of normalcy, "We should pick something up for dinner tonight. I am sure no one is in the mood to cook," he thought to say.

"Great idea," Dave agreed. But let's go straight home, we can order in." Dave had given directions to

Conrad to avoid the traffic and he entered it into his GPS.

Conrad slowed the car down as a red light was about to happen up ahead. He stopped and noticed an SUV was edging its way up, beside them in the other lane A motorcycle then pulled up in between both vehicles. Conrad recognized him. "That's the guy, in the SUV beside us. Look the man from the building."

They had nowhere to go. The SUV spun ahead when the light changed. A car ahead idled to make a right hand turn when pedestrians walked across the street with light. Conrad noticed the man on the motorcycle didn't move and hadn't edged ahead of his car to get into his lane. He just sat there beside them. Then he reached into his coat and looked to be pulling out a gun. Conrad shouted, "Get down everyone, he's got a gun."

Conrad leant his body towards the passenger's seat, slammed the car into reverse to get more room, and hit a car behind him. He put the car in drive, hit the gas, and spun the wheel towards the man on the bike, hoping to knock him off as bullets flew into the car, and knocked out some of the windows. Well Conrad leaned towards the passenger seat he slammed the car in park, and placed his body across the passenger seat, holding the button on the side of the seat to go back to position his body underneath the dash.

Conrad felt a surge of pain as bullets hit his shoulder. It seemed like the shooting would never stop. The motorcycle drove off without checking inside the car to see what carnage he unleashed.

Conrad was in severe pain as he put his hand on

his shoulder to stop the bleeding. Tears streamed down his face. It was not from the pain. There laid Dave's sister, riddled with bullets, blood was everywhere. Dave was sprawled in the back seat, bullet holes somewhere and had heavy blood spots all over his shirt. No one spoke. He feared his man was dead along with his sister. Conrad knew instantly that someone did not want Brandy to testify against John Paul.

Conrad laid there full of blood and tears, waiting for an ambulance and Police to take him away, or to die beside his loved ones.

Conrad could hear the sirens of ambulances getting louder as it sped towards him. He could hear muffled sounds of people outside the car. It was difficult to understand what they were saying as Conrad went in and out of consciousness. Conrad struggled to fight the urge to sleep. He knew that if he allowed himself to go unconscious he might never wake up again. He kept one hand on his bloodied shoulder and with his other hand, squeezed the hand of his friend Dave. Conrad did not want to die, but he also struggled in his mind on why he may have his life spared?

Conrad could now hear the car door, was jammed. He tried to make out the figure that forced the door open but his eyes blurred with blood, tears, and pain. However, he believed the man was in uniform. "Don't move sir," the voice yelled from outside the car.

The man was soon in the car and Conrad could feel the man all around him. It was now clear to Conrad that this was a Police officer.

"Ok guys the car is clear," the Police officer said to

the paramedics. "There are no guns."

The paramedics took over from the Police and began treating Conrad. A male paramedic on the driver side ran his hands over Conrad's body checking for bullet holes and other injuries. A female paramedic on the passengers' side checked the vital signs of Brandy and Dave. Their conditions were unknown to him.

She then began to assist her colleague in tending to Conrad. Another two paramedics showed up with a stretcher beside the bullet-holed vehicle. Conrad could feel himself lifted gently onto the stretcher.

"Am I going to die," Conrad said with a weak whisper. "We'll take care of you sir. Just try to not to move or talk, right at the moment," replied the female paramedic. Conrad could hear the sirens blaring as the ambulance sped off towards the Hospital.

He was not able to feign sleep any longer. Conrad gave in and closed his eyes, hoping that this was not the last time he would do so.

The surgery is over," the surgeon stated matter-of-factly. "Conrad will survive. He was lucky." Dave and Brandy were still in surgery. Brandy had bullets in her arm and back and Dave had taken a bullet in his upper stomach area, arm and shoulder.

The detectives arranged for Police to guard Conrad, Dave and Brandy at the Hospital. This shooting was a hit and they knew whoever was responsible would want to ensure they were dead and would not hesitate to finish the job. Dave was smart to go to the Police with the drugs. The police did not realize it was that serious at the time.

Conrad was a little more aware on his fourth day, "Good morning Mr. Kerman. I'm Detective Sheridan and this is my partner Detective Dunmore. We'd like to ask you a few questions if you're up to it." "Okay," responded Conrad, almost incoherently. "Did you see who shot you?" continued Sheridan. "I did," Conrad whispered. "And...?" coaxed Sheridan.

"He was on a motorcycle," Conrad continued in obvious pain as he spoke. "But he was wearing a helmet so I couldn't see his face." "Is there anyone you could think of that would want to try and kill you or your friends?" asked Detective Dunmore

"I'm gay. There are many homophobes out there. Nevertheless, it's not my friends, or my enemies. It had something do with some good-looking model type man this woman was seeing. My boyfriend already went to the Police. They even questioned the woman Brandy at the Hospital when she was overdosed on poison and some sort of drugs. He tried to kill her... I know this....I told Dave, when its drugs, sex and money you cannot be too careful."

"Anyone in particular?" Sheridan asked as he scribbled notes in his notebook.

Nervously Conrad rambled, "All I know is this man went by the name of John Paul. He was in the SUV right beside us when we left the Hospital. He moved up slowly heading to the light before having to stop. I had seen him, and told Dave, but John Paul, didn't shoot. The shooter was some dude in a motorcycle. Oh yeah the motorcycle pulled up in between us and then the moment the SUV pulled away out came the gun, bullets everywhere. I have a cam in my car."

Detective Sheridan probed, "Your cam was destroyed. Had you ever seen the man before?" Conrad sputtered confused, "Who John Paul, or the shooter?' The man in the suit I bumped into getting a coffee and seen him in front of Brandy's building the morning she left her brothers home. That's when we went to her Apartment soon afterwards and she was barely breathing. I only seen this man that day, and again beside us when we left the Hospital. The shooter, I don't know who he is. How are my friends? Are they alive?"

Defective Sheridan, whispered, "Your friends are unaware but stable, and alive at this time."

Conrad felt he was repeating everything, "Can we talk later," he pleaded. "I'm tired."

Conrad closed his eyes, held his hand to his head, and sobbed. The detectives had decided it was enough for him and left

Detective Dunmore and his partner arrived the next day and brought a sketch artist. "Would you be able to describe this John Paul character?" Detective Sheridan asked. "I suppose so," answered Conrad. "But I am a bit foggy right now."

They got a close identification as they could in Conrad's condition. Detective Dunmore asked, "What type of motorcycle was it?" They showed Conrad pictures of motorcycles.

Conrad was overwhelmed, "I'm not into bikes more into clothes and furniture. It happened so fast. I didn't take notice," he pleaded.

Detective Sheridan inquired, "What made you take the back roads?" "I'm from up North. Dave suggested it was easier to get into the garage for his Condo and less traffic on that road," he confessed.

Detective Dunmore realized Conrad could not identify the shooter on the bike. Detective Sheridan expressed his concern with Conrad, "Do you remember the man you ratted out that coked you? Conrad in a confused state answered, "Yes, I do. Why?"

"We busted him on coke related charges, he drives a motorcycle, and you're scheduled to be a witness along with the woman who provided a video tape. Can you say now that the shooter looked like that man?" Conrad behavior went wacky. He started moving his body all around in the bed and mumbled. "Are you okay, there?" asked Sheridan. He disapprovingly said "I didn't know he was charged. Are you people... just trying to get me and my friends killed?"

Detective Sheridan gave a head twist, and chin flip while he said, "That was the paperwork you signed at the station. He was charged with other criminal offenses but wasn't detained by the court system. Is it possible it was him who had the gun?"

"I couldn't say. It was a man and he was wearing a helmet, along with dark glasses. I didn't have full view of his face," he admitted.

Detective Sheridan went on, "We got a partial plate, from several witnesses, and the man in the SUV, is one of several witnesses who provided us with the details. That man in the suit is a Real Estate Agent, and we believe it's the same man you had the skit artist draw."

Conrad could not fight sleep any longer. His eyes overcame his longing for justice. He drifted off to sleep.

"Well partner, let's get back to the station. This guy will be no use to us for a while," said Detective Dunmore.

The police left guarding the hospital when the

shooter confessed, after they arrested him and had obtained video of him from the surrounding area.

Conrad was told Brandy and Dave were out of ICU and went to their rooms. They were sedated, and sleeping, so he didn't have a chance to speak to them before he was released from the hospital. He was the first, to leave.

James seen the news heard the name Brandy and kept calling the hospital but they refused to disclose if a Brandy was there. He went to her work, and heard she quit. A server confirmed it was Brandy on the news. He went to see her.

She was shocked when he walked into her room. All Brandy wanted to know was why he did not like Maria. He sullen in the idea, of what he thought, "I believed she took me for a ride when it came to money. It was the drugs you picked up, which caused additional confusion. It was not all her fault, she tried to help me after I lost my wife, and I had taken her in the wrong way," James confessed.

Brandy struggled with her speech, "The drugs you dropped were different." James wanted to clear her concerns, "It was the drugs you seen which initially got mixed up at the pharmacy. Those were mental health care medication. You were right, but they were not mine. When Maria visited my home we toppled over old medication bottles which I had not closed the lids on when she visited my home. We just picked the pills not realizing they were different and tossed them into the two bottles you seen. She tossed the old bottles into the trash, not realizing they also fell and had pills inside. Brandy it was luck for me to drop them with you there. I never did take another pill after that. Had you not interfered, I hate to think what could have happened to me. I was a mess," James shared.

"I was worried about you James. Thanks for the visit, but I have to rest now," she told him. James placed an envelope beside her, "I left a card with my numbers and a little money is inside. I moved in with my son and things are better in my life, because of you. Thank you again…Brandy," he left.

John Paul went to the Hospital. James was inside the room with Brandy so he went for coffee. When the nurses asked who he was, he said, "I'm her boyfriend." They limited visitors to family. James told them, he was a grandfather, which he is, but didn't say he was hers. John Paul pulled a chair close to her bed, held her hands in his and rubbed her hands, and cried.

The Nurse came in to take her blood work. Brandy started to wake up. She looked to see John Paul, in a fit of nervousness, "Get out," she muttered. Her response, hurt, "I understand you hate me. The police have questioned me and wanted to charge me but they didn't," he explained.

"You're an animal and a pig. I don't deserve that from anyone." She fell asleep. He stayed by herself until the Nurses told him to leave. John Paul went back the next day, and the next. He let her yell at him before she went back to sleep. Each day, she'd look up and say, "You're still here, I told you to leave."

While she slept, he held her hand, rubbed her back, washed her face and hands, and brushed her hair. He bought a toothbrush and toothpaste for her. When she told him to leave, he asked, "Can I help you brush your teeth?" With one arm cradled, she valued the aid. He helped wash her hair with the Nurse and put Brandy into a new nightgown he bought. 'She felt clean," she commented. She was too weak to fight.

He had gone for a couple of weeks, met her parents, and went into visit Dave with them. Together, they ate and talked over coffee at the hospital. It was tough on them. He told her parents he was just a friend and gave his full name, but didn't disclose what occurred between them.

Dave struggled with his injuries and was sedated a bit longer then Brandy.

John Paul brought some hair ties for her hair and placed them on her side table, kissed her on her forehead. She was conversing with the Nurse, so he sat down and waited for them to finish. Brandy turned to him and said, "Why are you here? I hate you for what you did to me." She turned her head away holding back tears.

Through tears he expressed, "Brandy words will are the only way I know to express my regret for what I did that day, and to apologize for the hurt that I caused you. I can never take back what occurred. In the deepest part of my soul, I feel awful for what occurred. Sorry is not enough. There is no excuse. What I did was wrong. This is not an explanation as to why I did what I did. It's how I internalized me when I was waiting for you to tell me that you had an ex-boyfriend who still had a key and came in for a booty call."

"A what," she fumed. "What do you think I am, a fucking whore?"

"No, not at all... Shit... That wasn't what I was thinking, but rather than having an adult conversation with you, I beat around the bush with the topic. That is what I did wrong. I tried to asked you 'who the man was coming in and out of your place all hours of the night,' in hopes of getting you to come straight out with it to me. I wanted you to be honest with me. Not me probing you and that was wrong of me. I became a tad bit jealous, and insecure with the thought, you had been secretly making love to someone else, besides me," shared John Paul.

Brandy was too sick to fight, "John Paul, I think you're looking for excuses. I told you I dated one young man from High School for three years. If you didn't drink so much, you'd have the maturity to recall conversations and have adult ones that talk on topic and have decency and respect attached to them. How you came out with a booty call, was just another punk who plays mind games with people's heads and holds no value for love, with the people they're having sex with. You talked on an issue in a sleek way that would only led me to believe you were talking about you at the time, which was your mind game. It came across as you were almost bragging that you can come and go anytime you felt like it at my place."

John Paul pondered his own stupidity, as he sat beside her and rested his arm on the armrest, so he could hide his face anytime he wanted. "Okay, here it is straight up. I had no idea at the time a man was breaking into your home, using his key to get into your Apartment. That morning I left, and you had kissed me, I was at your place prior that night and had been sleeping but around four in the morning a man unlocked the door and came inside your apartment."

"Stop, I heard enough." Brandy yelled. "Please Brandy listen. This man turned the light on in your bedroom. I was hiding naked inside your bedroom closet. The man went into your kitchen, stayed there for a while, and came back into your bedroom. I then seen his face and realized it was not your brother. Don't you remember you showed me pictures of your family on your cell phone?"

Brandy tried to follow him," What are you saying someone was in my Apartment and you didn't tell me because you figured I wasn't truthful, and may have been having sex with him? It's always sex to you."

John Paul jumped in, "Yes, I'll admit, I was childish?"

Brandy cried through the confusion, "I cannot take anymore, Please, just stop with your mind spins. You said you had sex with Maria too. There is your sex topic again. Although she admitted to knowing a John Paul, she did not outright state it was you. What are the odds, it wasn't? That alone towards me was selfish and took away my right to live in a relationship with safety for my own goddamn health. I don't expect a man to be unfaithful while still in the relationship with me. You want to have sex with others, at least have the balls to face it, be honest, and leave the person. We all deserve choices in life and not on your terms. Dealing straight up, and not being self-serving, is a common decency assholes like you don't grasp. Add, smashing my phone, grabbing me and barging into my private space in an inhumane way, just added to your childish, fucked up lowlife attitude ways."

John Paul stood back in state of protection, "Brandy, I admit, it was wrong of me to smash the phone and enter your private space. That was not me, but it became me. I do not know Maria. I have never met her. You displayed a selfie on your cell of her, you, and others at work. I said what I did in spite. I told the police what occurred and gave them a description of the man who came into your apartment. That matched your super's son description. That punk believed he was entitled to enter any unit at any hour of the day and night, without notice. He knew your schedule and came in your place anytime he wanted. He was charged finally by the police," expressed John Paul.

"What are you talking about John Paul if that is your real name? Charged? I'm not following you," she said.

"Brandy the Police arrested your super's son. He was mixing pills in your apartment that he sold. What he used, and how he did stuff, I don't know. What I do know is while there, he smoked his pot. He deliberately dropped some drug shit into your sugar. I wasn't able to find out all the details. But, I learnt that." Brandy could only surmise he was lying. "Whatever," she said to cut him off from speaking to her.

"Honest this is true. I used the sugar when he left your place, when I made a tea. He tossed cockroach poison into the box of tea bags, and shook it off. That's, why they looked white and pasty. I got tested and a small amount of cockroach poison was in my results, along with traces of some sort of drugs. I haven't went back to find out all the details, because I've been coming here after work," he shared.

Brandy didn't believe a word out of his mouth, "You heard I was poisoned and now you want to use it as an excuse and say it happened to you too. If you were so sick, why didn't you end up inside a hospital, as I did? Stop, no more, just leave…. Please, leave, ” she expressed with her head turned to the side, and her hand covering her face.

“Perhaps, I’m larger and had more of the drugs from the sugar then poison. I did use three spoonfuls of sugar, after he left that morning I made a pot of coffee. Then when you came home, you made a pot of tea, I used more, and seen you use the sugar too. All I know is his father hired a locksmith, because you changed the locks and his key did not work in your lock anymore. His son left a knapsack inside your apartment, after the people moved you out. He thought he could come up later that night and do his thing. When he and his father entered your old apartment, the bag was gone. The police found my business card in your study book at your new place, and then found me. Some dudes barged into the super’s apartment with a gun and held it to his son’s head in the hallway, and slammed the door closed while screaming something about drugs his father stated at the police station. He mentioned he stayed in his bedroom and called the police. I was at the police station being questioned when the police brought him in along with the dudes with the gun. At the time, they figured the super’s son was a victim. Then the movers showed up and confirmed what they knew about some knapsack. We all got detained there. The police thought it belonged to me. The kid spilled his guts after his father freaked out on him. That’s, all I know,” voiced John Paul.

Brandy was overwhelmed with what she heard, “Who shot us.’ “Conrad was drugged and that man wanted to kill him for taking him down,” answered John Paul.

Brandy broke down in heavy tears and curled herself up in her blankets and was covering the bottom half of her face with them, while she listened, "My god damn life and my brother's life... almost lost over this. This does not justify your treatment that day towards me. You have serious issues with anger and abuse over communication, rage to what instill fear? To control not respect, I will never take treatment like you displayed from anyone. Please just leave. I've suffered enough," she vented through her tears not turning to look at him.

John Paul stood up when to walk to the door turned back, looked at her, choked back tears as he expressed, "I understand. It wasn't respectful. I'm ashamed that I actually thought you were into rough sex or role-playing when you kissed me at the door like you did. It confused me. I'm just an old fashioned type of man, and I tried to read you. What a stupid way to think, read people. If I had of talked to you as a person, all of it would have been avoided. I've learnt a valuable lesson, now, but at the time, I was stunned this man came in like he did. It pissed me off afterwards when I came to hate myself, when I didn't jump out naked and confront him at the time. I admit my treatment towards you was inhumane, as you mentioned it was. And you're so right, you did not deserve any of it. I'm sorry," he said and walked out of the room.

He was walking down the hallway, when he heard a woman asking the Nurse for Brandy. John Paul asked, "Are you looking for Brandy? " Yes." She answered. "Here I'll take you to her." John Paul asked, "Can I ask who you are?" "I'm Maria, and this is John." "Would you give me a moment to see if she's up for company?" he requested.

John Paul stood at the door, "Hi Brandy two people are here to see you." "I thought I told you to leave?" she grabbled in annoyance. John Paul edged himself in the room, "Yes, don't worry I'm leaving but a couple were asking for you at the desk. Are you up to seeing them?" "What are you the fucking visitor's Police now?" she shouted.

John Paul waved them towards the room, "Okay, okay Brandy, calm down, it's just Maria and John. I thought you'd like to know," he said with a smile and a smirk.

Maria rushed to Brandy's bed. 'I'm so sorry honey, I heard what happened. I tried to visit you earlier, but only family were permitted. I called every day, but couldn't get any details. I'm so happy you're still alive."

"Maria…. what are you doing here? We don't even know each other and have never had one decent conversation," Brandy expressed knocking her head against the pillow.

Maria refused to leave, "I'm not a cold hearted bitch like you think I am. My family owns the restaurant you worked at. They did not want you to lose hours, and were keeping that shift going for you because you needed the hours to make money while you were attending school. They were waiting for you to say cut it out at midnight. That is why I laughed at you for still working those hours, when we first met. This is my John Paul and this is Brandy. His first name is John, and his middle name is Paul. When I'm in a good mood, I call him, John Paul, or JP. Is this your John Paul?"

John reached his hand out to John Paul. "Hi, this is funny isn't it? Two John Paul's, she calls me that to piss me off, call me John, please."

Brandy smirked, and waved her hand, "What are the fucking odds of that. John Paul gloated about having sex with Maria. I have to wonder if there is another Maria, too. It's funny how those two seem to show up around the same time. You must be really close to that John Paul," she said sarcastically.

John Paul went up to Brandy, "Come on Brandy, I was already pissed off at myself and tried to piss you off when I said what I said. Gees…Maria…. she showed me a picture of you on her cell phone and mentioned your name. I cannot believe I'm standing here having to justify what I said."

Maria had to jump in, "See Brandy, I wasn't far off. I was right on the money there. That's what I told her when she told me you said you were fucking me and apparently, I loved the way you fuck."

John Paul was embarrassed, "Oh my god, Brandy, I cannot believe you told her this. Rather than talk to me, you rambled to people I don't know. And I didn't say all that. Maybe I did, and tried to take it back. But, here she is giving me shit for not asking her about some dude running around her Apartment. But that wasn't her fault she didn't know about him."

Maria laughed, "She said, she wouldn't have given you a key had she known you and I were having sex. I thought my John Paul wanted to let me know he went with her, and used the pet name I have for him, for me to realize he cheated so our relationship was finally over to him. I told him, if you ever cheat, don't come back. I figured he used her to break the news to me. I call him John Paul, no one else does. My John and I have known each other since middle school. A few months ago, he left me. I called him every day, and he refused to pick up. We got together, a bit ago, but it wasn't the same."

John wasn't going to stand back without protecting himself, "Hold on Maria. You didn't accept my proposal. Your reason was, we've have been together from the age of 15 and you needed to live a little. So after she had some freedom she said, we can talk about it again. How did you think I felt? I was humiliated. I planned everything to surprise her. I got her a two carat diamond ring went and seen her father. He gave his blessing, along with her mother. Then, I called both sides of our family to come to an expensive restaurant. Hired musicians to serenade her then I got down on one knee, and she laughed when I was down on them. Her response was, not now. I have to say no."

Brandy was not going to let Maria get off so easily, "Did she tell you about James?" she asked. Maria went to talk and then paused, "Oh Brandy, I didn't know James then. But, do you know what happened with James?"

Brandy was too tired to explain what James said, so she responded, "Not really he was here, but didn't say much." "I'll tell you what I know. He was at the gym one day, when I was there. Then he was at the restaurant. I went up to his table and introduced myself. He mentioned he had lost his wife. He was depressed and lonely. I felt sorry for him and John wasn't talking to me, so, I offered to spend some time with James at the gym since I go there every day, but changed my schedule around to accommodate his. He thought it would be nice to have company and I figured why not. I realized a little too late that he thought differently of me, and my intentions."

"He didn't look like a man that went to a gym to me," Brandy snarled.

"He did, long and story short of it all. At the gym, he had been working out with weights and said come here, and I'll help you bench press. I had just finished a spin class, stretched out on the bench, looked up, and he said, grab the bar. The weight was over a hundred pounds. I didn't know it at the time. He let go. I could not hold that weight myself, and it smashed down on my breasts, He attempted to pick it up, and he fell. Down again it went on my stomach and he fell again. Someone else rushed in, grabbed it off me and mentioned you can sue him for that. Why don't you? I ended up in the Hospital and on painkillers. He went to the hospital too but left," expressed Maria before John Paul interrupted, "How painful. I got a visual of that and it gave me the chills. Sorry, Please go on," he stressed when he realized he had interrupted.

"About a week later, James called me crying for company and was sorry for what occurred at the gym. I was in so much pain when he called begging me to go visit him but I went to his house anyways. He made dinner and we had some wine. I had taken a couple of my painkillers earlier in the day, and the last one I took was just before I left for his house. I was heading to bed at the time and had already taken too much, but didn't realize it at the time," shared Maria.

Brandy slurred out, "You know he came to the restaurant and dropped his pills, they were all different and he smelled like alcohol and he asked for you saying he was a friend, but stated that he wished, he never met you."

Maria was ashamed at herself, but despite how she felt it was nothing to what Brandy was living through. She continued, "I'm ashamed to say, we both were drinking wine and then beer that night. He wanted us to take our pills together, and with the wine. I did not think about how many I previously taken. I was emptying a pill into my hand when his hand came hard against my pill bottle, when he cheered it. I went flying over his coffee table, down went my bottle of pills and his and the wine. Pills were everywhere. We crawled around picking them up. I obviously couldn't tell the difference, between his and mine. His lightbulbs had blown in his living room. The only a light aiding us came from the kitchen. Neither of us smoked, and he didn't know where his flashlights were at the time. Now I downloaded an app for my cell that has a flashlight."

Brandy understood now, "I understand that's why he had all the different pills inside two of his bottle and he was upset when I tormented him about the drugs and drinking, when he came to the restaurant."

Maria jumped into her flow, "He bought me a car, and gave me three hundred thousand dollars, and I bought a Condo. I had only gone to the movies in the afternoon with him once. He took me the same day into a new car dealership. I had borrowed my parent's car to see him and had to wait to visit him when they weren't using it. He didn't like this arrangement and expected me to have a car of my own. So he bought one and told me to drive it. So, I did. John wasn't taking my calls, or returning my messages. Then his voice mail was full, from all my messages. I figured I'll go visit my family in Columbia for a couple of months and get over him. I offered James to come. So, he could see there was still more to his life. That never happened. He took me into his bank, cashed in one of his investments. He wanted to try flipping houses. My cousin, does have a contract with the banks and does do renovations, and offered to give us heads up on properties that perhaps we could flip. James complained, about me living with my parents. He figured I should live on my own place. With his check he came to my bank and told the bank manager, put this into her account. He thought it was an automatic joint account, with both are names. But, I didn't know this, nor did my bank manager understand what his expectations were at the time. What we missed was when he heard her mention the word joint, he figured it she wasn't a dumb woman and could figure out with that kind of money people just don't go handing it away. He walked out of the bank assuming he had a new account in both our names, but never mentioned it to me.. I told him about a condominium deal. He did an offer, with just his name, and offered one hundred thousand dollars less than the asking price. He didn't get it. I called him again on another one, and he had no interest. Then I showed him a Condo and it was for me. He came and I didn't realize he figured his money was only for him, so I spent it all. I bought the condo. It was a complete mess. I was on his mental health care pills he got by mistake, plus my painkillers and whatever the pills were that he had in his old bottles that toppled over. It was a strange high and when I crashed, I was exhausted. At the time, I figured it was the pain from the accident beating me down, every day. ”

"How dangerous for the both of you," John Paul stated.

"That wasn't all that occurred. He didn't remember signing to sell his house or giving me a key to give to the Real Estate Agent. Those days are still a blur to me. Wasted from the night before, and for weeks afterwards, we both were. These drugs spun us both. I had no idea that he thought I loved him or that he believed I stole his money. He may have the beginning signs of Alzheimer's, and is going for tests, now," Maria shared.

"How did you find out he thought you loved him," Brandy asked. "A cop called me stating he knew I could tell him who had the bat at James house. Then said, he was charging both of us. James had already called, screaming about the money that he gave me. I gave him my lawyers' number. He called my lawyer who got letters from James bank manager and mine stating James clearly stated to them, he gave me the money to me. I learnt a lot but through upset and pain, but it wasn't as painful as what yours is today, or what you lived through," expressed Maria.

Maria had to stop talking. She was explaining through tears. "It's okay Maria take your time." John told her in support.

"I sold the Condo and got a certified check. John and I then went to James to apologize for the broken table, which John broke after he went crazy on James at his home screaming that he was giving me booze and drugs. James wanted to know if I hit John with a rock, and I did. John actually fell down and I thought I killed him. I was so stoned. James did not want his money back and said keep it, along with his family. At the same time, he explained his kids were to sign any agreement with his house. So the sale was no good. That saved him from moving at the time. Now, he lives with his son, but James still owns his home. Then he told us his nephew seen James at the drug store. He thought it was funny playing around with the prescriptions they had, considering they had the same name, and he figured James would have realized what he did, if it worked. He blocked out a letter in their last name. He tried to call James to tell him, what he did. James hadn't been checking his voice mail messages, so he didn't learn about it sooner. Good news, John's grandmother runs a support group for people who lost their spouses to cancer. She lost her husband over ten years ago. James is now friends with John's grandmother. He has met a wonderful group of friends, and has support and love all around him," shared Maria.

Brandy smiled, "It all turned out well for you. But, I cannot get over you saying you have a gold mine between your legs, don't forget to use it or something, along those lines?" expressed Brandy as she stayed unemotional as she listened.

Maria chuckled, "Fuck, those drugs, spun me into some superior being, and played with my emotions. I went into tears one minute, a sexual goddess the next, and my rational was completely off. I must have meant, any dude, would pay you for sex. I'm sorry, Brandy. I think your very pretty, and the light colors in your nightgown really brings out your eyes. I cannot believe someone shot you. Its fucking crazy, really. I'm glad you survived. I wanted your mind to rest, knowing that I had never met your John Paul or had sex with him. It was unexpected to meet him now and the situation isn't a pleasant one at all."

"You didn't need to explain." Brandy answered.

Maria looked to John and gave him the head twist to leave. He waived his hand at her to stop, "I'm embarrassed. I don't expect you to accept my apology," Maria turned to say.

John Paul walked over to Brandy. He wanted to leave on good terms with her, "You never know what can happen in life and we screw up as human beings not thinking at times about the value in people. So many things go haywire which screws with our thinking and our behavior. We don't need drugs or booze to do fucked up things. And on a personal level we are responsible for how we treat another human being. Sometimes what we say or do will kick us in our own asses, while we kick others down," suggested John Paul. "Well stated," confirmed John.

"It was nice meeting you Brandy, John, and Maria. I did something to Brandy. I was abusive, not just with my mouth. I smashed her telephone and refused to treat her like her own person. What I did to Brandy was not as ending in the form of life itself. Nevertheless, it was ending in the form of love, care, human compassion, concern, respect and lacked in her having her right to feel safe, and in her own place. Perhaps she questioned her ability to trust, and that person was me. I was heartless in a way that's hard to express. I hate myself for what I did. After I sat here for weeks, hating me, and wanting to take back what I did. I could not take back what this person did that got her here. His decision could have taken her life and two other people. One wrong move and god knows how many people he could have killed. We had choices and we made ones that hurt her. I do not ever want to get in a headspace like I went into that day. I'm going now, take care," John Paul said then kissed her forehead, and continued, "Brandy, all I can say is, I'm sorry. I've said everything I had to say to you. When I went with you, it was because I cared. What I did lacked in care. I know sorry is not enough. I will always remember you and the times we shared," he left...

Twelve

John Paul bought a few dresses for Brandy, and had them couriered to the Hospital. When they arrived, there was no card to say who sent them.

John Paul's mother had a stroke and he rushed to be by her side. He had been in the Hospital visiting his mother for a few days and wondered if Brandy was still there. He went to the room where she was but someone else was in the bed. He went to her brother's room and he was not there.

John Paul was leaving when a Nurse recognized him, and said, "Hi John Paul, I haven't seen you in weeks." John Paul was happy to see her and asked, "Can you tell me if Conrad went home?" "Oh yes, he made it. I see the strain in your eyes. He left a few days ago, and Brandy left last week. I asked Brandy what happened to you. She seemed to be looking for you to come back and said, I guess he was fed up with me saying, don't come back and so, he didn't. I remembered the way she said it and the tears in her eyes, as you have now. I hope you two can figure yourselves out. Life is really too short to squabble over petty stuff," she thought to mention.

John Paul gave her a hug and said, "Thank you and I agree. I'm here now with my mother, she had a stroke." "Sorry to hear John Paul. It has been a hard month for you at the hospital, with Brandy, her brother, Conrad and now your mom," expressed Margo.

"It's been harder for everyone else, Margo. Thanks for letting me know they went home. Talk too you soon. Bye," he said.

John Paul, went to pick up his mother to bring her home from the Hospital, and parked the car close to an exit door in the hospital parking lot. As he was walking towards the front entrance of the Hospital, he noticed Brandy had exited the hospital and was walking in his direction with her head down, listening to her music with her earphones on. He was happy to see her. He clicked her shoulder, with his finger when she went to go by her. She stopped, looked around and took her earphones out. John Paul said, "Oh, my Brandy, it's lovely to see you. You look great." Brandy was startled, "Yes it's nice to see you too. I just came for a follow up appointment. You look stressed," she added. John Paul thought to say, "It was nice seeing you," and walked away.

As she continued walking she looked over her shoulder a few times, and seen him walk into the Hospital. She walked fast to catch up to him. He headed in the elevator. She ran in behind everyone.

"Hi, I figured I'd come and ask you what you're doing here?" John Paul was surprised, 'I'm picking my mom up to go home." "Oh, so you were visiting her when I was here, and came to see me too," suggested Brandy.

"Brandy no… my mother wasn't here when you were here. She had a stroke, after I seen you last. I was here a couple of days with my mom, and went to see you. I spoke to the Nurse and she mentioned you left along with your brother. No matter what I say, you'll always have a distrust of me," emotionally stated John Paul.

"I'm sorry to hear about your mother," Brandy said as they walked into his mother room. "Hi Mom, this is Brandy the lady I told you about," John Paul said. His mother wasn't able to respond. Brandy leaned down to speak to her in her wheel chair, "Hi John Paul's Mom, I'm Brandy and it's nice to meet you."

Brandy followed them to the car. John Paul offered her a ride home, but she had her own car. She got his mother's address and met him there. She helped him get things together for his mother, and had to leave. She wasn't up to full strength herself. "Okay John Paul, I have to go," she announced. He walked her to the door and she said, "You have my cell number, I don't have yours."

John Paul pulled out his wallet, and handed her a business card, "This has all my information on it. Perhaps, if you give me a call, we can go on a date." His eyes, and eyebrows lifted up and he gave a wink. Brandy said, "I'd kiss you but, I don't want you to think all I want is sex, if I did."

John Paul asked, "Can I have a kiss? I'd hate to force myself on you for one, and you think I'm abusing you or all I want is sex." They laughed, kissed, and hugged. Brandy said, "Seeing you with your mother and how you treated me in the Hospital, displayed to me, you're a kind hearted man, but you just have to learn to talk and stop drinking."

He said, "Yes, you're right. I was drinking for a few months there, and I hadn't done that before. I even had you drink with me. Perhaps, it wasn't proper but hey, I never would have met you and shared time with you if I didn't. I was going through exams for my industry, that's why all the late nights. It was really taking its toll on me."

Brandy's lips emerged on John Paul stopping him from talking. She took her hands undid his jean button, slid her hand down inside his underwear. He wasn't about to stop her.

He lifted up her dress, placed his hands inside her underwear. As they kissed, he lifted her up, and carried her upstairs to a bedroom, kicking the door closed. She lifted her dress up and off, undid her bra, and dropped her underwear to the floor.

She pulled his jeans to the ground, as he pulled his shirt off. She grabbed his head, and brought it towards her. He spun her around and entered her from behind. He could hear Brandy heave and sigh. No words were being exchanged, she didn't yell stop. He knew she wanted it.

He took it out, lifted her up, and placed her down on the bed. He proceeded to ease himself on top of her and entered her again. Her hands twilled in his hair, as he rolled her on her side. He lifted her leg up. While making love they kissed. All of a sudden, he spun her around placing her on stomach, and he entered her again. He pumped for a while, took it out, and spun her around placing her body on top of his, where she allowed his manhood to enter her. She gently moved her body, while he embraced her breasts with his hands. All of a sudden, he spun her around, tossed her back on her back, and once again, he entered her. Together they heaved and sighed, until they came. Brandy laid her head on his chest, and fell asleep.

Maria, John, Brandy and John Paul got together for dinner, and went bowling. Brandy got Dave to agree to meet John Paul.

Dave invited Conrad, Brandy, John Paul, Maria, and John to his Condo for a movie night. They ordered dinner in, and enjoyed some fine wine. They even played cards. John Paul slept over at Brandy's and in her bed. Maria and John took the guest room in her Condo.

Conrad did get his Condo in the building. They accepted the offer the same night. Frank surprised Conrad with a housewarming party. Everyone brought gifts.

They were waiting to attend Maria's, and John's wedding. Brandy is going to be the maid of honor, and John Paul, Dave, and Conrad are going to be groomsman. James is attending with John's grandmother.

Brandy invited her parents for dinner at her Condo and invited Dave, Conrad and John Paul to join them. Dave's parents already knew Dave was gay but were happy to meet Conrad, and found him loving and supportive. Brandy and Dave never spoke about having sex outside of wedlock to their parents. They never asked, so they never shared.

John Paul moved home with his mother to be by her side. Brandy and John Paul alternated their time together between both places. Brandy started working as a Nurse, at the Hospital she was in. After she took the trip, she had planned.

John Paul and she traveled together, for two weeks. Brandy had a hard time adjusting to the scars on her body from the gunshot wounds when it came to wearing a bikini, but she gave in and wore one after John Paul told her, "Why stop enjoying life when you were given another chance. Scars are nothing, your life is worth something, and I'm glad you're alive and here with me, to share in the pleasures living life gives us, now just wear one."

Maria poured herself a nice cold drink, turned up the music loud, opened the patio doors, and walked out on the deck. While dancing, she admired her new ocean view. She took a few sips of her drink, placed it down on the table and proceeded to pull up her hair, spinning it into a ball, and placed an elastic band around it. She took off her rob, leaving herself naked as she placed herself down on her lounge chair, and fell asleep.

She felt a cool drop on the middle of her back, and jumped. A hand pressed her back down and she knew, by the touch of his hand who it was. He rubbed cream into her legs, and massaged her feet. Once he was done, he came up from her lower back, and placed one hand on each side of her spine. He pressed his hands fully open and ran them up and down her back, until she fell asleep.

When she did he left, he poured a cold drink, and took a shower. When he was finished, he took the lounge chair beside her, until he finished his drink. He got up and whispered in her ear, "How long have you lived at this beach house, Maria?" She stayed still, "He whispered, I love you." She turned to him and said, "John Paul what are you doing here? Come on, baby, you know you want me too," he confidently stated.

His arms slid under her body as he rolled her into his arms. She wrapped her arms around his neck. He took her to the bedroom and placed her head down on the pillow. He tilted her legs open with his hand, and walked to the end of the bed. He moved his fingers softly up her legs, bending one leg at a time. He kissed her inner thigh and moved his face before her vagina. He proceeded to stimulate her clit, with his tongue, and placed his fingers inside. She grabbed at his head turning it with every movement she felt.

He eased up her body slowing kissing her pelvis, and moved to her stomach. As he moved towards her left breast, her nipple sucked into his mouth. He moved on to the right one, and sucked for few seconds than moved towards her face, where they kissed passionately. She gently touched his balls, embraced his penis in her hands, and pulled herself up, on top of him, guiding his penis inside her. John Paul`s eyes closed as he enjoyed every movement, of her body, with his.

He lifted himself up, embraced her back into his arms, turned her around and placed her back onto the bed. He moved up and down, up and down, taking time to share in a few kisses. The gasps of joy grew louder each time John Paul pumped inside of her. He knew it would not subside until he came inside her. A loud shriek was heard. They both came. The gasping was over.

THE END

About The Author

Dana Rey was born in Toronto, Ontario, Canada and The Gasping is her first Fiction novel. She is a mother, a new grandmother to a beautiful little girl, an aunt to some amazing kids.

She is someone who had no thought or ambition to write a book before reading a book that led anyone to believe they can write an eBook, and make massive money. She had no desire to read that book either, and wish she never did. Hence the line in the book, but here we are today. The book she read was called something like, 'Write an E-book in x number of days and publish it, without being a great writer, and make massive money,' that she somehow stumbled upon. That's is it above in a nutshell for the reason why she started writing this book The Gasping and then walked away from it.

History of the author's journey to writing....

THE GASPING was born over five years ago if you're in the New Year, today is Jan 1 2015 which this wasn't when she wrote this but is editing only this today. The book was given its title back then, 'The Gasping,' which was being written in email,

and left by both writers back around the year 2010., when life changing occurrences occurred. Deaths had occurred, yet *they* weren't the reasons for the departure from the writing of the book, or the reason to write.

The issues that enhanced not writing or writing were avoidable. This means, it would have only taken one person a split second to care, and they only cared when they were running women around like rag dolls and I imagine that meant they were still alive, but didn't care who else lived a decent, life, but them…

That is the premise of a truth, and became the structure somewhat for each fiction book out now for Dana.

Perhaps Dana will take those words she just thought of now as she wrote them, and bring them in as her next outline for another book and hopefully it will not take a year to get them straightened out or perhaps she will do the smart thing, write her life story, gain some justice, and take back what someone else stole in far too many ways….

Sometimes in life a person might believe at some point they were shafted, but who can they turn to they might wonder? So the original writings in the draft of The Gasping killed off all the characters, Brandy, Dave and Conrad… But, in writing we can bring them back to life, if we desire too, so she did. In real life, we aren't so lucky.

A story can be flipped around, but in reality each situation, has a reality to someone in real life. The truth in writing isn't always the bitter truth, is it?

Maybe in professional industries they strive for truths, and yet sometimes the truth is never known, but the idea of the truth in fiction writing can be closer to the truth or it can be altered to make a person wonder if it's real or fake. Either way, it takes those with an amazing talent in the skill of writing or storytelling to create that wonder.

Dana is not into storytelling or manifesting a story, especially for nothing. What a word manifest...

Along the way, the other author gave all rights to the written material between them to Dana Rey (AKA).

Dana didn't look at what was written again until, around January 2015. The material written for "The Gasping" only had a few scenes, and a few characters, but no plot to give a solid structure on the storyline. Neither of the writers had shared in the development of their story ideas. One idea came across, and the other took over from there. Dana split some scenes up, and developed two story ideas from the material already written. When she picked it back up to see what she could do with it, only because the other writer had developed some nice scenes and interesting characters.

"For You My Love which took the start from the original writings from "The Gasping" but got moved around in both books until it came to its place, and created not just a moment, but a moment of heart, and soul for her, before it found its place…

The Gasping she used the original characters, and drafted scenes around them and added additional characters and scenes into it. It was a long and slow process. Both books went out in public on amazon with about 40,000 words and changed with bad editing, and in pure honesty, she didn't have a clear understanding on the characters and held a true hate for the story line and didn't want to write it or write this at all....

She had to find a comfort level and to fall in love with the concept on the idea to build meaning inside the pages for her, and perhaps, someone else might share a laugh, gain a smile, or even shed a tear…

She had roughed out a draft For You My Love, but both books have grown to over 80,000 words at She has done a read through of The Gasping again just on her own and perhaps it's a guarantee she missed a lot in editing, but please don't worry wherever you purchased this book you can get 100 % of your money refunded, if you didn't enjoy it and wanted to experience what she did as a self-published amateur writer. Together we arrived here, so from the bottom of Dana's heart she wanted to take a moment to thank you for taking a chance on her book…

The Gasping and For You My Love are complete as far as the story line goes.….It will not change again unless a publishing deal came across, and made it worthy of human value which is almost impossible because it's not made for many but a few…

As of this date neither book has been professionally edited.

The ending might not be the end for characters in The Gasping, but Dana doesn't know yet, and is waiting for those characters, to take her somewhere with them, but not in the same way, if she does write again …

For her it was tough writing about death, shootings, and upset, and it did take a lot to keep her in that mind frame to keep going along with the story for the characters in both books and perhaps that's why it was a longer process for her which made it more difficult for her to see the errors in editing, she believes. She was too busy feeling the characters. It wasn't light, fluffy, or funny many times, and became emotionally draining and confusing to keep going where these characters were taking her, while she was fighting them off when they missed her idea of what she wanted them to be like, and they desired to tell who who they were.

She had some struggles when her desire was to remove the drugs completely which was the main storyline but after losing some close people to drug overdoses, the story stuck in memory of them, and for their siblings, mothers, fathers, family and friends who have suffered greatly along with everyone who loved them

Was it what I said, or didn't say, with clarity, was how she originally wanted to start the book and she still feels it was right for her. But she didn't write for her she wrote for James and it took weeks altering the new beginning to bring in Doug and to understand how we might relate to each other when our hearing or memory starts to fail. She isn't suggesting it's the same for everyone or even fact or close to it, but she took her concept on it and held off writing it until the end, because we might not see it or understand it.

More to the story, but in time and maybe, by then "The Gasping" will be on its way to the professional editing department somewhere, or off the market completely. Nevertheless, until then, we hope you enjoyed the story... and feel free to leave a review either way. From our hearts to yours, may you have family, love and friendships all around you.....

www.ingramcontent.com/pod-product-compliance
Lightning Source LLC
Chambersburg PA
CBHW021504110726
47899CB00001BA/292